W9-BBE-956

LAST
CHANCE
DANCE

Also by
LAKITA WILSON

(for younger readers)
Be Real, Macy Weaver

LAST CHANCE DANCE

LAKITA WILSON

Viking

VIKING

An imprint of Penguin Random House LLC, New York

First published in the United States of America by Viking,
an imprint of Penguin Random House LLC, 2023

Library of Congress Cataloging-in-Publication Data is available.

Printed in the United States of America

ISBN 9780593525616

10   9   8   7   6   5   4   3   2   1

BVG

Edited by Kelsey Murphy
Text set in Marion

For Leilani.

When it comes to a mother/daughter duo?

We are the perfect match.

Prologue

THE FIRST MAJOR chance I ever took on love paid off big-time. And that's surprising, because before high school, I never really had a solid example of what *lasting* love looked like. Sure, my parents were married for close to thirteen years. But by eighth grade, they were giving me and my younger sister, Riley, the *divorce* talk and splitting assets.

I was obsessed with reality TV dating shows in middle school, but it seemed like *that* love only lasted through the taping of the season. By the time the reunion episodes aired, the couples were always sitting on opposite sides of the host debating over who was at fault in the breakup.

Still. I wanted to believe in a forever kind of love. And I needed to experience it for myself to truly believe it could exist. Then fate stepped in.

Three days before freshman year, Mom and I were walking out of Target with all my newly purchased back-to-school supplies—at the same time, the most gorgeous boy I've ever seen is walking in. His brown skin resembles a freshly scrubbed penny, only a few shades darker than my own honey-brown skin. His thick, bushy eyebrows hover over the biggest brown eyes. His sideburns and full pink lips send me over the edge, and before I know it, I'm thinking: *This has to be fate.* Cute boys *never* shopped in this particular Target.

Now, there's two major rules when it comes to reality dating shows. The first rule? Speak up for what you want, or get cut in the first episode.

So I stop Mom from walking out of the double exit doors. "I think I forgot something," I tell her as the cute boy grabs a shopping cart.

Mom holds up two shopping bags and raises an eyebrow my way. "Whatever you don't have, you can order later from Amazon." She lets out a long, exaggerated sigh. "Besides, my feet are tired."

But I can't take no for an answer. The boy, who's wearing a crisp white polo shirt, slim fit jeans, and the freshest Js I've ever seen in my life, is turning the corner and disappearing from view.

"But, Mom, I need a graphing calculator in my hand to*day.* Bree heard from Eva, who heard from Ashli, that if we don't have everything by the first day of Pre-Calc, we're basically headed down a slippery slope of flunking out of school."

At this point, I'm sure Mom knows I'm full of it. But she's probably tired of standing there holding the heavy shopping bags, because she digs in her purse, hands me her debit card, and goes, "Make it fast, Leila. We have to be out of here in time to pick your sister up from summer camp."

I blow my mom a kiss and say, "Back in a second!" as I dash back into the store.

Because reality dating show rule number two? Never let go of a promising prospect too soon. Because they'll only show up on the reunion episode looking ten times better than the first time you laid eyes on them. And you'll wish you had taken the chance on them when you could.

I couldn't risk losing sight of this cutie only to have him show up in one of my freshman classes, already taken and looking one hundred times better, on the arm of some thirsty girl from an earlier class period.

So while Mom walked off to find the car, I beelined my way through the back-to-school shopping extravaganza. I ducked past the five-dollars-or-less sand trap, ignored the jewelry display case, and followed the giant yellow cardboard pencil cut-outs down the middle aisle, to the back of the store where all the school loot was on full display.

I know what you're thinking. *Leila, are you taking a chance on love? Or are you just a tad thirsty, chasing some dude you've never met through a store loaded down with security cameras?*

But look, Mom had Tinder and a well-manicured swiping finger to meet her latest dating conquests. If there were apps for teen girls who wanted to browse boy candy from the comfort of their couches, it would be predator city.

So—I saw an opportunity. And I took it.

I finally found him lurking in the office supplies aisle, biting his fingernails and comparing brands of Scotch tape.

"Double-sided *sounds* like a good idea, but it tends to stick to everything except your paper—just go for the regular stuff," I told him, trying hard not to sound all out of breath from the running I just did.

When the boy looked my way, the fluorescent megastore lighting bounced off the little flecks of gold in his light brown eyes and—*whew*—he was fine. Initially, I thought he was Black like me, because we shared the same brown skin. But up close, I noticed his hair didn't have a curl pattern and his shade of brown was closer to copper than mahogany. I wanted to ask him what his background was, but like—how do you ask something like that? Asking "What are you?" is just rude. Even fresh out of the eighth grade, I knew that. So I waited for more clues to fill me in.

"You in one of those Instagram fandoms, or something?" he asked. "You obsessed with all things tape?" Then he barely chuckled—like some sort of *tuh* sound mixed with a breath, like he was too cool to laugh at his own corny joke.

His smart mouth didn't throw me off. If anything, it made me go at him harder. Because if reality TV taught me anything, it was how to flirt like a boss.

"No fandoms over here. I just suckered you into doing me a favor."

There's no real way to look sexy leaned up against a

shelf full of staplers, but I tried to make it work.

"Oh yeah? What's that?" he asked. At around five foot seven, he didn't completely tower over me, but he was tall enough for a kid fresh out of middle school. I'd have to stand on my tiptoes to kiss him. If I wanted.

"I need help finding the right graphing calculator."

"A TI-84? Oh, that's nothing. I could actually give you mine. I'm going into advanced math this year and won't need it."

Okay. I peeped the door he'd just opened.

"I've never turned down free," I told him, helping him seal the deal. "But are you sure you want to lend an expensive calculator to some girl you barely know?" I propped a couple of fallen binders back up on the shelf. "How do you know I'm not into flirting with cute boys for their expensive math goods?" I stepped closer to him until I was right under his chin. "What if I borrowed your calculator and disappeared? For the rest of your life you'd be wondering—"

The boy looked down into my eyes. "I'd find a way to track you down." His breath smelled like one of those giant Fireball candies and made my nose hairs burn a little. But I didn't mind. He was one of the few boys my age around without pimples. Fair trade-off.

He plucked the green three-pack of Scotch tape off the hook on the shelf. "For one, by the time we finalize the terms of this calculator loan, we'll know each other's names." He stuck his hand out. "I'm Dev. It's short for Devrata, but—"

"Leila—"

"Right. *Then*, I would make sure I got your number before handing over anything math related." He stepped closer to me. "Since you're possibly a calculator bandit and all."

And just like that, we were exchanging numbers. Like he promised, Dev delivered on the calculator the next day, when we met up at Sweet Frog for ice cream. And before my first day at Baldwin High, Dev and I were a *thing*. Junking up Mom's living room with our laptops, pens, journals, and backpacks during our *homework and chill* sessions. Making matching Halloween costumes inspired by '90s Saturday morning cartoons. Dev teaching me to drive and then offering to drive me places when I accidentally hit a fire hydrant and vowed to never get behind the wheel again.

Lighting the candles during Diwali. Tossing colorful gulal during Holi with Dev's extended family. Riding the Metro train downtown to see the lighting of the Christmas tree on the National Mall. Easter egg hunting on the White House lawn with my mom and little sister. FaceTiming with my dad for my sixteenth birthday when his flight from Houston was canceled.

Dev was there for the regular boyfriend stuff. But he was also *there*, in the real kind of way that makes me cringe every time one of my well-meaning aunties refers to our relationship as *puppy love* or Dev as *Leila's little friend*.

Dev was *there* when I didn't get the SAT score I wanted last year. And again, when I got an even *lower* SAT score the second time around. My friends were supportive, of course, but it was Dev who missed every Friday night football game, even after our high school went to the playoffs, to help me study until I finally scored high enough to apply to the really good colleges.

Last October, for my birthday, instead of grocery store cake and cheap perfume, Dev secretly signed us up for a visit to my dream college, Brown University. While I hopped around squealing like the last bachelorette standing at a rose ceremony, Dev kicked his logical side into high gear. He found a chill day on the school schedule, printed off *very* realistic permission slips for an overnight field trip to Colonial Williamsburg, and took his mom's old minivan in early for a tune-up so there wouldn't be any mishaps on our way up I-95.

After Dev bought a case of Capri-Suns, and I made tuna wraps, we hit the highway, riding for seven hours and thirteen minutes up to Providence, Rhode Island. We toured the campus and sat in on a world literature course. I mostly kept quiet, leaning forward and chewing on my pen cap, while basking in the ninety-minute discussion on character motivation and word choice. But Dev—as a birthday bonus—raised his hand and asked a surprisingly insightful question that made the lit professor raise an eyebrow of approval. We took pics with the Brown Bear, the school's mascot, watched a few pirates walk by singing a cappella, and ate in the Ratty, aka the cafeteria—which Dev pointed out was false advertising, since the food was surprisingly delicious.

"Too bad we can't see the dorms," I said as we finished the walking tour.

"I'm sure you'll give me a private tour when I come up

to visit," he whispered, planting a kiss on my lips.

Fate had brought me the perfect boyfriend. Because, when it came to things that really mattered, Dev was my rock. Through the good times and the hard moments, like when Brown had rejected me back in December, shattering me for a solid two weeks, Dev was always there for me.

Until, suddenly, he wasn't.

FRIDAY AFTERNOON, DEV and I are stretched out in my grassy backyard, enjoying the warm spring weather and planning out the perfect summer break trip to the beach with two other couples from school. The sun is beaming down on my bare arms, I'm sitting pretty in my floral romper, and I haven't seen a bee in the last twenty minutes. All I can think about is how *perfect* this summer's going to be. No more SAT prep and college application drama. Final grades will be in soon and college move-in day won't be for another three months. Dev and I will have plenty of time to enjoy our summer vacation before everything changes. Starting with the road trip to Ocean City.

I flick Dev's arm. "Tell them we should head out there right after graduation." So far in the road trip group chat, the girls have been doing all the texting. But I don't want *my* boyfriend to look like one of those guys who lets his girlfriend do all the heavy lifting. We've always been a partnership, and our group texts should reflect that.

I'm anxious to get this summer started, because it will be the last one Dev and I share together before we become the dreaded long-distance couple. When Dev heads to Cornell in the fall and I move farther up north to Rochester, I want him to remember our last free moments as romantic, full of adventure, and deliciously fun.

"Did you send the text, Dev? I didn't see anything go through."

"Your phone's right in your hands; why don't you tell them?" Dev says, looking all grumpy even though there are literal birds chirping in the distance.

I point to his phone lying there in the grass. "Because you're not really saying anything, and it's getting embarrassing," I tell him. Not that I'm a show-off or anything, but I do like Dev and me to show a united front—especially in front of the other couple in the group chat.

Ashli Henderson, our class president, and Chad North, the class treasurer, have been going out since the last day of sophomore year. I'm not saying I'm competitive or anything, but I'm not about to have the other big couple at Baldwin High questioning the strength of our relationship.

When Dev still doesn't reach for his phone, I shoot him an annoyed look, then quickly peck out a few sentences, send, and wait for a response. I don't have time for Dev's moodiness today. We need to lock down a vehicle for the trip so the girls can move on to more important things—like swapping bathing suit links.

But when my text clears, Dev looks down at his phone and goes, "Why are you volunteering my mom's minivan?"

"I mean, you're going to be using it all the time anyway, to drive from Cornell to Rochester. Your mom won't care if you drive it to the beach."

When Dev doesn't say anything, I start to wonder if his bad mood is the beginning of heatstroke. It *is* kind of hot out here. I put my hand on his forehead to check for fever. But he instantly swats my hand away.

"Seriously?" I raise an eyebrow at his attitude. "What's *up* with you today?"

"Nothing," he says, looking off in the distance.

I scroll to the four bathing suit options I already have saved in my phone. "Just tell them you'll drive. Then you can go home to mope around in peace."

Dev lets out this long sigh. "I'm not doing that, Leila."

"What, mope around?" I pull up this neon-green two-piece that's going to slay next to my golden-brown skin. I favorite the photo so I can remember to send this one to the group chat first.

"No. I'm not driving to the beach."

I look up from my phone. "And why not?"

Dev pauses for maybe the longest minute ever. Then he looks down at his hands and sort of mumbles. "Because I'm not going."

I exit out of my photo album and glare up at my boyfriend. "Dev, stop being ridiculous. We've been talking about doing this beach trip for months. I'm looking forward to getting out of Maryland for a few days. I haven't set foot in sand since last—"

Dev suddenly turns to me, with this weird look on his face. "*Maybeweshouldbreakup*—or whatever."

I grab the bottled water lying next to me and take a nice long swig. "Boy, don't even play like that."

Everyone knows that Dev and I are basically the most unproblematic couple at Baldwin High. No screaming fights in the hall. No slamming lockers. No kissing randos to make the other person jealous. So whatever little game he's playing? Not funny.

"What do you mean, you want to *break up*?" I wait for Dev's face to crack into a smile. For him to admit that he's just trying to get a rise out of me. That maybe he's just looking for a little extra attention in all the wrong ways. That he would never think of ending what we have.

But Dev isn't laughing at all. Instead, he's nibbling away at his fingernails and looking everywhere except in my eyes.

Out of habit, I almost get up to move his hand away from his mouth. But just when I'm pushing myself up off the grass, my ten-year-old sister, Riley, of all people, pops out of nowhere, pointing her camera phone and karaoke microphone in our direction. "What's going on, you two? Any news you want to share?" My little sister basically steps over me, which forces me back onto the grass. Then she shoves her mic in my (ex?!) boyfriend's face while my heart thumps hard in my chest.

Dev gives my little sister a noogie. "*Riley*, where ya been hiding, girl?" *Super* laid-back vibes—like he's not right in the middle of breaking my heart. This whole sweet-big-brother vibe irks me a little, so I get up from the ground, brushing bits of grass off my knees. "Riley, go in the house. I need to talk to Dev privately, please."

"But I've been spying on you guys for weeks, waiting for the perfect viral moment for my new podcast and I finally get some potential footage and—"

"*Now*, Riley."

My sister takes her time inching out of the yard. "Well, if you two need a little on-air counseling, I've been taking this free online course on—"

I lunge in her direction.

"Okay, okay." Riley tucks her phone into her armpit and runs toward the deck. When she's safely on the other side of the sliding glass door, and—hopefully—out of earshot, I turn back to Dev.

"I *must* have waxy buildup in my ears. Because I *know* I didn't hear you say you want to break up."

Dev begins nibbling another fingernail. "I love you, Leila. But, like, what's the point of going to Cornell if I'm going to spend every free minute at Rochester?"

"You don't like spending time with me all of a sudden?"

"No, I *love* spending time with you. I mean, it's not just that—like, you know how I feel about my parents. They've never gone out with anyone else. Not even one date."

He side-glances me. "I just—I just don't want to wonder . . . what it's like being with someone else."

"You like somebody else?" Imagining Dev sliding into another girls DMs immediately makes my knees tremble.

"No."

"But you want someone new." The air holds in my throat as I study his face for signs of betrayal.

Dev's hands are in his pockets as he paces a few steps back and forth in front of me. "*No*—I mean, I don't know how to explain it exactly right."

Suddenly, the temperature spikes—and it's too hot. I want to shake some sense into Dev, rattle his brain a little, until he's thinking clearly again. To be honest, I don't know what to do. I've never been randomly dumped by a person who still has an *I Love You* GIF in a very recent text thread. And to be even more honest, I've never been dumped by anyone, period, because Dev has legit been my only relationship ever. I thought things were going pretty smooth. The entire senior class thinks we're perfect for each other. I do, too.

For a moment, I simply stare deep into Dev's eyes, searching for the boy who loaned me his graphing calculator four years ago. The boy who drove seven hours each way to a school I ended up getting rejected from. The boy I love with my entire heart. Whatever this thing is that's pushing him away from me—*whatever* the reason—it can't be real.

My pride wrestles with my emotions, begging me to pretend like this isn't bothering me at all—like I have at least ten guys waiting in the friend zone for their chance to come off the bench. But our history and my love for him eventually overpower my pride.

And I just say what feels right. "*Please*, Dev. Don't ruin our last summer before college."

Dev rips off another fingernail and spits it in the grass. "I'm not doing this to hurt you, Lei."

But he *is*. He *is* hurting me.

Fine.

I start walking back toward the house. Dev follows after me, up the deck, through the kitchen, and all the way to my bedroom. For a second, a flicker of hope makes me believe this is a late April Fool's joke, or that—in some cruel way—Dev's testing my love for him.

But then he reaches behind my dresser to unplug the PlayStation he keeps at my house.

I look off to the side, and take a deep breath. Then I lose it.

I start crying, right there, in the middle of my bedroom floor. Dev stops packing up his game system to put his arms around me. "I'm not trying to hurt you, Leila," he says. "But, like, I keep thinking about your mom divorcing your dad because they never saw each other—"

"My mom divorced my dad because he didn't *try*." My voice wobbles like a bike on its last leaking tire. "We were going to make it work. There's no *reason* for this."

And then I start thinking. *Was* there a reason?

I'm sniffling and sighing, and grabbing tissues from the box on my dresser. Maybe I was planning to make the long-distance thing work all this time—and Dev wasn't. I wonder if Dev secretly thinks I did the most. Googling the distance from University of Rochester to Cornell. Checking the cost of gas per mile in upstate New York. Making an Excel spreadsheet to budget the cost of making a semi-long-distance relationship work.

Did I scare Dev away with all the plans? And expectations? Did I smother him? Did I—?

My bedroom door thuds.

"Get away from my door, Riley," I shout, turning away from Dev. And even though she thinks she's doing a great job sneaking around, I hear the soft padding of my little sister's socked feet running back to her room.

And then?

I start tugging on the three-letter pendant Dev bought me for prom. DNR. Initials that I *thought* stood for Devrata Naveen Rajan. But now I'm thinking they probably meant *Do Not Resuscitate*, because Dev clearly wants me dead and gone by way of broken heart.

When I finally pop the chain on the necklace, Dev winces like *I'm* hurting *him*. He bends down to pick up the broken necklace and places it on my desk.

More tears well up in my eyes. "You had me walking around school looking like a *clown* with your initials around my neck, when you didn't even love me."

"I *did* love you, Leila—I mean, I *do*. Just because we're breaking up doesn't mean our love wasn't real," Dev says. He reaches out and wipes at a tear that's suddenly spilled over onto my cheek. "You were the *best* part of high school."

I'm unmoved by his pathetic speech, because his words are complete nonsense right now. You don't get rid of things that are the best. You keep your fridge stocked with the *best* snacks. You keep the *best* shows on your favorites list on your Fire Stick. You're always texting your *best* friend. You don't get rid of things and people that are the best.

Dev reaches for my hand, but I snatch it away.

"Come on, Leila. Don't be like that."

When I don't say anything, Dev leans in, kisses me on the cheek, like someone's *grandma*, and says, "I know this whole thing feels messed up. But once we're actually away at school, you'll see—this had to happen."

Then? He grabs his phone and his PlayStation. And he's gone.

2

MY BEDROOM IS a tomb. A cold, lonely, god-awful tomb of silence. I'm lying across my bed, nearly buried in grief. I feel like I'm attending my own funeral, except it isn't me that's passed on—it's my relationship. A relationship that wasn't even slowly deteriorating, but was instead ravaged by a surprise heart attack.

I place a hand on my chest, feeling around for the physical damage to my heart. But the soreness isn't coming from my breastbone at all. It's the area around my eyes that's raw, from all the crying and tissue wiping.

I want to call Dev, but if he doesn't pick up, I can't be sure I won't call him back twenty more times. And I worked too hard on my GPA to start college late because I spent sixty days in prison for telephone stalking.

I want to call my best friend, Bree Bailey. But then I remember that she doesn't believe in serious relationships in the first place. If I tell her I'm hurting over this breakup, she'll only tell me that love *always* has an expiration date and that if I'm not ready to throw the love away when it spoils, avoid sampling at all costs.

So I settle for stalking Dev's social media instead. I refresh Instagram. Last night, I tragically discovered Dev took my name out of his bio. Now today, I can't stop checking his page to see if he's done anything else. I check that little secret spot Bree put me on to that lets you know whether someone's online.

He's not.

Probably because *the Dev that I know* is still here in my bedroom. The little stuffed Brown bear Dev got me from the college gift shop—back when I thought Brown was the only place that would ever make me happy—is staring at me with those dark button eyes from across the room, like, *Another rejection? Sucks to be you.*

Our prom picture is literally five feet away from me, sitting on my dresser, with our names forever etched in the leather frame.

The custom-designed silver prom dress that cost my life savings is spilling from the floor of my closet because, well, prom's over now. And the necklace Dev bought me is now dangling from my desk drawer. I've been spending hours staring at it. My entire bedroom reminds me of Dev, yet I can't bring myself to leave this dungeon of torture.

I've been in here all weekend, crying, sniffling, running out of tissues and using the corner of my blanket to wipe my nose. Riley keeps banging on my door, begging for an after-breakup exclusive. And I swear, if Mom does that little struggle knock on my door one more time . . . like, are you coming in or not?

I hope she never gets up the nerve. I don't want to see her. I don't want to see Riley. I don't want Dad randomly calling just to say, "Want me to stitch your heart back together? I'm the best in the biz." (Seriously, that's the weak joke he cracked when I called him crying over getting dumped.)

I planned to live out the rest of my life alone, right here, under my blanket. But my runny nose won't let me.

So I get up from my bed to root around my desk drawer for extra tissues. While I'm there, my fingers connect with my old black-and-white marble notebook from eighth grade English class. It's beat-up and wrinkled, the pages thick with my handwriting. I page through it carefully until I get to the end.

Every day for warm-up that year, our teacher gave us a bizarre writing prompt—they didn't always make a lot of sense, but were supposed to be a way to get us experimenting with wordplay and metaphors.

But here's the thing. Eighth grade is also the year my parents divorced. So writing about lost childhood pets and my least favorite meal wasn't the only thing lurking in my subconscious. Anxious thoughts cluttered my brain with various scenarios of what life would be like with my parents not speaking.

One day toward the end of the school year, maybe a week after Dad boarded the plane to Texas to take the head surgeon position—permanently severing our family unit for good—our teacher assigned us this freewriting exercise. We were supposed to write about a time we lost a beloved childhood toy.

Instead of writing about a toy, though, I began scrawling out my innermost feelings about my parents' divorce. And how my dad was ruining my life by packing his things and heading for his new home two thousand miles away. And how I would never just throw away the person I loved for no reason.

Then and there, I constructed a set of rules to live by when it came to my future love life. Eighth grade Leila had decided that I'd rather *not* sit at home on the weekends in my bathrobe listening to sad songs. Or move to Houston, Texas, with two daughters still in Maryland. When I fell in love, I wouldn't give ultimatums, or demand too much, like my mom. And I wouldn't run from my problems or split my time up like my dad. Eighth grade Leila promised herself that no matter what, when she found love, she would work hard to make it last. She would do enough to make the person want to stay, and above all else, *never* give up.

I had just capped off my two-paragraph-long cry for help by writing a lyric from the most popular song that year—some angsty song about losing control—when a skinny kid with a goofy grin and light-up sneakers crept up behind me, snatched my journal, and began reading my most secret thoughts out loud . . . to the entire class.

"You've lost *control*?!" he yelled, doubling over, right there in the aisle next to my seat. "More like, lost the love of your life, according to this whiny journal entry." Then he broke out with his own goofy rendition of the entire song.

Of course, the class laughed. Our English teacher ordered the boy back to his seat, but even she was smiling a little bit, because the boy was tossing his head around like he was working with a wild mane of curls.

Before I could stop myself, I was out of my seat and lunging at the idiot. But he ducked right before my knuckles connected with his teeth, and I ended up smashing my fist against one of those old-school metal pencil sharpeners, breaking the skin right above the knuckle on my ring finger.

After all that, as our teacher was writing me a pass to the nurse's office, the boy went, "Now *that's* out of control."

During those last few months of middle school, sitting at my small wooden desk on one of those stiff plastic orange school chairs, I stopped writing in that journal completely. I couldn't risk further humiliation. Besides, I'd already written out the rules. And I truly believed in them with all my heart—especially when Dev appeared that summer out of nowhere.

Suddenly my phone buzzes, and for a split second I'm full of hope again. Stupid freshman-year hope. I grab my phone, fully expecting it to be Dev. But instead, it's Ashli.

Umm, Leila? Did Dev leave the chat? she texts.

I'm instantly embarrassed. Why couldn't he wait until after school ended, so we could drift apart silently? Who does this right before every major end-of-school-year event?

I'm not sure. I think something's wrong with his phone, I text back.

Oh. Okay, cool, Ashli responds.

I think I'm in the clear, at least for a few more days. But then, stupid Chad has to go and jump into the thread.

But Dev is still in our Madden League Chat. He legit just said something like two minutes ago.

I could strangle Chad. And Ashli. And *especially* Dev for humiliating me like this in the first place.

I think about leaving the group chat myself. But that will just confirm our split. And then I won't be able to get down the Baldwin High hallways without a million seniors stopping me to ask what happened.

Besides, what if Dev really did have a secret heatstroke outside on Friday, and he's home rehydrating and pulling himself together right now?

God. I could *kill* Dev for putting me in this awkward position. I feel pathetic, and the tears start up again. But just as I'm all set to grab more Kleenex, I hear a scream coming from the kitchen. *Riley.*

She yells something up the stairs about her grilled cheese catching fire in the panini press. "Seriously, Leila, if Mom comes back from the store and the kitchen's burned to the ground, I won't live to see my podcast go viral."

"*Ugggghhhh.*" I manage to make it an entire weekend in solitude, and on Sunday—the day *specifically* marked for rest—I get dragged out of bed.

With my blanket wrapped around my shoulders, I shuffle

down the glossy wood-floored hallway. I make it halfway down the stairs, skipping the step where I used to eavesdrop on Mom yelling at Dad about working too much, before I realize I don't smell smoke.

"Little girl, if this is one of your games—"

"Would I lie to my favorite big sister in the universe?"

I step into the kitchen, and—*bam*—wouldn't you know?

Riley comes around the breakfast bar, pointing her cell phone camera in my face and ambushing me with a printed-out picture of Dev and me kissing.

"Did you get that from my Instagram page?"

Riley shoves the mic on her phone closer to my mouth. "I just need to know how you went from this"—she taps the photo with her sparkly fingernail—"to Splitsville in less than a week?"

I snatch a box of cereal from the counter. "Leave me alone," I warn, pouring a heaping pile of Cheerios into my bowl. I slump down on my favorite breakfast bar stool and prepare to take my first bite of food in days—but Riley just won't quit.

"Tell me, Leila. Was it that necklace he bought you for prom?" Riley sits down on the stool next to me, props her elbow up on the bar, and leans into her fist. "Did the DNR stand for *Dates . . . Not Romantic*?"

I stab at my cereal a few times before taking my first bite. "Do. Not. Remember." I side-eye my sister in between mouthfuls of Cheerios. "Seriously, Riley. Please, don't Oprah me today."

"But, Lei, how will I get podcast streams if I don't have good *content*? I need shocking footage that forces viewers to subscribe." Riley pulls out her phone again. "Your breakup is the perfect mix of drama and heartache."

Riley isn't what you would call girly. She's what you might call *adulty*—if that was a word. She's always searching TMZ for breaking celebrity news or comparing the revenue of her favorite YouTubers. In fact, the only thing about her that screams *little kid* is her insistence on being super nosy.

I pull out my own phone to scroll the Gram for possible Dev updates—and to avoid making eye contact with Riley. I scroll past a shirtless selfie from Kai Ballard, Baldwin High's own personal influencer, and another mood board post from Ashli. I linger on some juicy Shade Room gossip for a minute before running across a Bookstagram post from Eva Martin. She's holding up *Felix Ever After* while wearing a halo of baby's breath in her hair. I heart the photo and comment, Borrow when you're done?

Eva replies back immediately: thumbs-up, winky face, heart emoji.

When I put my phone back down, Riley's still staring me in the face, waiting for answers. "You already know what's up, Riley. Wasn't that you snooping at my door?"

"Ex*cuse* me, but I don't have a team of producers to gather facts for me." Riley gets up from the breakfast bar and goes into the guest bathroom. When she comes back out, she's carrying a fresh box of Kleenex. "I have to do my own research." She sets the box next to my bowl of cereal. "Now spill it, girl. How are you feeling? You know, deep down, in your *guts*."

"Good*bye*, Riley." I'm two seconds from getting up to toss my bowl in the sink when Mom swoops into the kitchen.

"Oh, baby, give me a hug. Riley told me you and Dev had a falling out." My mom comes up behind me and squeezes me to death. With the last bit of oxygen I have left, I glare at my big-mouthed sister.

"What?" Riley goes. "I was hoping to reel her in as a potential viewer."

"*And* she felt bad her big sister's hurting. We *both* feel bad." Mom leans down for another hug. "And as a viewer who cares, I just want you to know that I'm here for you."

Then Mom slips onto the stool to my right and drums her fingers on the breakfast bar. "I won't make you talk, but if you want to share just a little bit—Riley, stop recording your sister—I'm here."

Mom's staring, and Riley's staring, but I refuse to say a word. So then Riley reaches over me to stick her mic in Mom's face. "Mom—ahem, I mean *Natasha*, what's your opinion on high school romances?"

Mom legit checks to make sure there's no lipstick on her teeth before leaning closer to Riley's mic. "Well, I'm no expert or anything, but I just don't think high school romances should last forever. Have you seen those college campus cuties? A girl about to start college should keep her options open—in my opinion, of course."

Mom looks at me like I'm supposed to do something with

that information. The problem is—I didn't ask for her hot take on love and dating.

"Goodbye." I stand and try to duck out of the kitchen, but Mom gently grabs my arm.

"Seriously, Leila. College is about to be the best time of your life. Now is the perfect time for you and Dev to get to know new people—and just have fun." Then Mom gets this faraway look in her eyes that makes me wonder who she's been matching with on Tinder lately.

I take my bowl to the sink. "You don't have to convince Dev of *that*."

Riley's eyes light up. "Now we're getting somewhere." She joins me at the sink and sticks her phone back in my face. "Spill it, Lei. Who is Dev secretly canoodling with while you're struggling to move on?"

I swat my sister out of my face. Then I swoop my blanket tighter around my body and head back to my room.

I'm halfway up the stairs when I hear the whispering start up in the kitchen. So I lean over the railing and shut things down.

"I don't remember giving my opinion when you and Dad ruined most of my eighth grade year by attempting—and *failing*—to get back together. And I definitely don't remember getting up in *Riley's* business when she suddenly started crushing on the boy who made all that weird art out of pencil shavings. This is just a trial separation. If Dev and I decide to amicably split, we will have our publicist send out a statement. Thanks."

I throw in the trial separation bit mostly to ease my own anxiety. But it doesn't help. Because Dev is gone and I don't know if he'll ever come back. I tuck my hair up under the hood of my onesie, pull my comforter tighter around my body, and trudge back to my tomb of a thousand tears.

MONDAY MORNING, I open my eyes to the sound of
Riley hassling a familiar voice just outside my bedroom door.

"I just told you, Riley. There is no secret lover. I *chose* the
single life."

"But no one *wants* to be alone," Riley says. "Have you gotten a whiff of Leila's room lately? Ever since the breakup, it
basically smells like used Kleenex and feet in there."

I stomp over to my door, fling it open, and shove my little
sister out of the way, so I can grab my bestie and pull her
inside my room.

Bree Bailey fans her nose the second she gets inside my
room. "I mean, Riley's not wrong about the smell of toes in
here." She puts both hands up. "I'm just saying."

I raise an eyebrow at my best friend. "If the smell of my

failed love life offends you, you can go on back out there with Riley and continue the discussion of your supposed happy single life."

"I *am* happily single."

Bree's entire high school experience has been dedicated to flirting and serial dating. She claims, as one of the only masculine-presenting lesbians at our school, that it's her responsibility to show the Baldwin LGBTQ+ community that being queer doesn't mean four years of loneliness and dead-end crushes. *I* just think she has commitment issues.

Anyway, the second I climb back into my bed, Bree starts yanking at my blankets, like we're in the middle of a tug-of-war contest on field day.

"Absolutely not," she says, pulling my blankets closer in her direction.

I pull the blankets back to my side. "There's only three weeks of school left. Let me drop out in peace." I give them another yank. I mean, even if I never show up again, I would still graduate with a solid B average. So is there really a point in going back?

Bree, who's dressed in her self-described school uniform of gray sweatpants, a white tee, and her ice—a clear-colored G-Shock watch and a diamond stud in each ear—jingles a set of keys in my face. "Naw, sis. I didn't beg for that Toyota Corolla outside just to be riding solo. And now that Dev isn't driving you to school, I finally have someone to sing all the background vocals to the songs on my Ride to School playlist. So get up." Bree tosses my covers into the corner of the room and points to my bathroom door.

While I'm in the shower, Bree comes into the bathroom with me and fusses with her hair in the mirror—which to me is pointless, because it always looks perfect.

Bree has just as much baby hair as me, except hers isn't swooped into a style with hair gel. Instead, she goes to the barber every Friday to get her lineup, which is about a half inch of baby hair shaved down in front of six individual twists that fall to her shoulders.

I pull back the shower curtain just in time to see her pull out her toothbrush. "Stop being vain. You look fine."

Bree traces her finger along her hairline, then repositions her twists. "And I'm trying to keep it that way, too."

"Umm, you came all the way to my house without brushing your teeth? That's nasty, girl."

Bree helps herself to my toothpaste. "First of all, you're literally next door. Second of all, I *had* a toothbrush here, until someone decided it was cool to lay their baby hair with it—"

"—I told you I didn't know you were still using that!"

"—Still, man. You know you're wrong for that. *Any*way"— Bree leans over and starts brushing her teeth—"you straight, though?" she asks, over the running water. "I noticed Dev switched up his bio."

I look around the shower curtain, and our eyes connect in the mirror. It takes everything in me to not start crying again. But if Bree sees me cry, she'll never speak to Dev again, for hurting me. And then it'll be harder to convince her to be cool with him again if we get back together. A part of me still hopes this is just a quick phase. That everything will return to normal before next weekend.

So I don't reveal how terrified I am that this is for real. That this is how it's going to be from now until forever. I do my best to sound casual, to downplay the implosion of my relationship as much as humanly possible. "Girl, don't pay that any attention. Dev must be worried about high school coming to an end or something. As soon as he stops trippin', he'll add me back."

Bree leans into the mirror to squint at each studded earring. Then she licks her thumb and smooths down each eyebrow. "All I know is, if bae ain't reppin' me in the bio, then we don't go together."

"I thought you didn't believe in serious relationships?" I yell over the running water.

"I mean, can a girl be hypothetical?"

I pull back the shower curtain just enough so I can poke my head out. "Bree?"

"What?"

"Get out, so I can take my shower in peace." I point my bestie in the direction of the door.

Good. As soon as she walks back into my bedroom, I turn up the heat in the shower and release the tears that were threatening to spill over.

After my quick cry under the running water, I try to wash away the stench of rejection before heading back into my room to get dressed.

Bree's sitting at my desk, with her feet propped up on the wastebasket, playing on her phone.

But when I reach for a wrinkled T-shirt and a busted pair of sweats, Bree puts her phone down and walks over to my dresser.

"Since when does Leila Bean wear sweatpants to school?"

"Since my reason for looking cute is gone."

Bree snatches my sweats from me and tosses them toward the wastebasket. "You're not riding in my car looking all raggedy." Then, she steps over the prom dress I still haven't managed to pick up and begins rooting around in my closet. "Cute, cute, cuuuuute—yeah, fire."

Bree hands me a plain white bodysuit I'd planned to wear on my next date with Dev, a denim miniskirt, a summer beanie, and a pair of open-toed boots. "Dev is going to be crying thug tears when he sees you looking this good," she says.

As soon as she mentions Dev, my shoulders slump.

Bree puts the clothes in my hand anyway, then sits back down at my desk, grabs her phone, and kicks her feet up again. "I know you're going through it right now, Lei, and I feel for you. I really do. But, uh, we only have, like, thirty minutes to get to—"

"*Okay.*" I quickly slip on the shirt, tuck my hair up under my beanie, step into my skirt, and throw on my chestnut-colored ankle boots.

"Is this good enough for Your Highness?" I ask her.

Bree gives me the once-over, then grabs my ChapStick off

the top of my dresser and tosses it at me. "A little something for your chapped lips won't hurt."

I roll my eyes, but I go ahead and moisturize my lips.

When I'm done, I grab my backpack. While Bree is slinging hers over her shoulders, I grab the initials pendant out of my desk drawer. Maybe out of habit . . . maybe because I'm still not ready to let go. But I slip it into my purse. Then we bounce.

I try to perk up on the way to school, but I can't help feeling like a scrub, sitting on the passenger side of my best friend's ride. It's like the word *dumped* is written all over me. And ain't *nobody* trying to holla at me.

Not that I want anyone to. I miss Dev. That's it. That's the tweet.

I pause for a moment when Bree and I get up to the main entrance. I just know that as soon as I walk through those double doors without Dev on my arm, people will look. And wonder. And the bold ones will come right up and start asking what's going on. And why.

It's bad enough I just got dumped. But there's only three weeks left of school. The teachers are barely giving us any classwork at this point, so my classmates have nothing else to do but get all up in my business.

I imagine them waiting for me at their lockers, camera phones flashing, wanting *all* the tea on this breakup. I don't want to face anyone yet. I think about calling an Uber. Or even walking the few miles back to my house. But, just as I'm about to pull up the app and check the peak time rates, Bree grabs my arm, steps through the entrance, and forces me to accept my fate.

Normally, this is the moment I would be kissing Dev goodbye before rushing to meet Bree at the locker we've been sharing all year. But now everything's different, and I can't help paying attention to whether people are noticing the change.

"See, I told you people were too busy with their own mess to worry about yours." Bree sweeps her hand out and nods toward a group of students posted up near the water fountain.

She's right. Mason King is hanging up fliers for another one of his rallies, and Kai Ballard nearly bumps into a group of girls from trying to walk and selfie at the same time. Nobody's paying attention to us at all. For a second, I think I might be able to lay low and coast my way to the end of the school year.

But then Ashli Henderson spots me and walks over. "Hey, Leila," she says in this voice that tells me she knows everything. "Chad and I talked to Dev last night . . ."

I know she's not doing it on purpose, but the "Chad and I" feels like she's choosing violence this morning. Like, if you know what I *think* you know, why would you even start off a sentence with "Chad and I"?

"I don't want to talk about it," I tell Ashli.

And I know she can sense the tense energy in the air, because she starts slinking away, going, "I get it. I get it."

But just when I think she's about to slink herself out of my face, she pauses and looks back at me for a moment. "I just wanted to say, if you ever need to talk—I'm here."

I give her a *very* forced smile, because I can sense she's uncomfortable, too, and trying to be nice about things. But I just can't pour my heart out to a "Chad and I" right now. Not when my plus-one has abruptly abandoned me.

Bree watches Ashli dart away. "Aaaand *that's* why I don't fool with relationships now. It's always a 'thoughts and prayers' warrior coming to make you feel even worse when it's over."

I don't even dispute that, because even though Ashli has been a good friend for years now—and *means* well—Bree's not wrong. We walk the rest of the way to our locker in silence. When we get there, Bree suddenly goes, "I know how you can shut down the 'thoughts and prayers' crowd."

"How?"

"By getting back in the game," she says, tossing her hoodie in the open locker. "You know the Last Chance Dance is coming up . . ."

"Nope."

"Come on, Lei—you're not going to support your girl?"

Of *course* Bree joined the Last Chance Dance committee. It's the only school tradition that actively promotes serial dating. Basically, at the end of senior year, anyone still single puts down the names of three crushes they never had the guts to ask out. If that crush happens to put your name down too, then, *boom*, you get an email saying you've matched.

Then, during Fling Week, matches get eliminated based on bad dates, misunderstandings, and overall dysfunction, until everyone has a date for the Last Chance Dance.

Trust me. It's bigger than prom around here.

But I don't care if Bree's the founder and CEO, I'm *not* participating in that self-esteem sand trap. Sorry not sorry, I'm not running around playing Tinder Jr. with Baldwin High students—I don't care how much this breakup stings.

"That's going to be a hard no for me."

"Seriously?!"

"Seriously." I check to make sure my edges are still properly swooped and laid before slamming our locker shut. "You know I'm not *that* girl."

"Everyone says they're not *that* girl. You're actually being that girl by saying that."

I push my way through a sea of kids to make it to first period chemistry on time. Bree follows after me. "*Come on,* Leila. What part of Last Chance Dance don't you get, bruh?"

"First of all, I'm not your bruh."

"Okay, well, then—*sis.* This is everybody's last chance. You might as well see what else is out there. You've been in that dry relationship for what, four years now?"

I turn back to Bree and give her a look. "Oh, so my relationship was dry, now?"

"I mean, I'm not saying it was exactly *dry.* But don't expect me to say anything good about that relationship after Dev rudely dumped you like that."

I realize shading my relationship is Bree's way of being

supportive, and I'm semi-appreciative of the gesture. But still.

"Look, this isn't *The Bachelor*," I tell Bree. "So you can count me out of your little matchmaking, Last Chance dating service."

Bree leans on the doorway of my classroom. "Look, Lei. We remixed it a little this year. We have these little questionnaire things, right? You fill it out after choosing your top three crushes. After you get all matched up, the system pairs you with a wild card match."

I break out laughing. "That's ridiculous."

Bree looks hurt. "Seriously? That was my idea. Your boy Tre' helped me put it together."

"Tre' Hillman is not my boy." Just the mention of that name makes the little keloid on my ring finger sting. "And, out of loyalty to me, Tre' Hillman shouldn't be your boy, either."

Bree shakes her head and goes, "Come on, Leila. People change. He can't be the same guy he was all those years ago."

I give my bestie a look. "Tre' is definitely the same boy from years ago."

Trevor 'Tre'' Hillman is *okay*-looking, and most people seem to like him at Baldwin. He's a tech nerd who just committed to Brown on College Signing Day. But knowing Tre'? He's going to Brown just to get under my skin.

Remember the kid who was a jerk to me in middle school? The one who basically went out of his way to make fun of the fact that I was now a part of a broken home. It was Tre'.

I rub at the scar on my finger and imagine how it good it would've felt if my right hook had been more swift.

Bree interrupts my thoughts by tapping my shoulder. "Think about it, Leila. Tre' says the wild card pick has a foolproof algorithm that will match up the perfect couples based on personality."

I snort. "And you believed that clown?"

Bree shrugs. "He's always been good with tech stuff."

Well. I guess she's right about that. But still.

"If you and Dev are really meant to be, maybe the algorithm will put you and Dev back together," Bree says. She starts walking away to her first period class. "Not that I think you should settle for the same boring relationship. But . . ."

Hmmm. Bree always knows exactly what to say to reel me in. What *if* Tre's algorithm matches Dev and me? It would prove—

No. As much as I would love unbiased proof that Dev and I should get back together, I'm still not a fan of Last Chance Dance.

"I'm good," I assure my best friend as she waves from down the hall.

But I know I'm lying to Bree and myself for the second time in less than two hours. I'm not good. My heart is throbbing so bad, I plan to just find my seat and put my head down for the rest of class. I can probably get away with it, too. Mr. Boomer, our chemistry teacher, literally drags himself into class at the last possible second, takes his time putting his stuff away, and eats an entire bowl of cereal that he brings in from home, all before officially starting class.

But of course, as soon as I take my seat, a boy with a regular fade and a dimple in his chin comes walking into the room. Tre' Hillman in the flesh.

"Tell me I'm not fine, Fivehead." Tre' strikes a chin-rubbing *GQ* pose. The squatting-down, two-peace signs-up pose. He pretends to dribble a basketball between his legs, then goes up for the three-point-shot pose, and comes back down for another nose-in-the-air model pose.

I give him a blank stare.

"No, thank you," I tell him, like I always do. I try to put my head down on the desk, but here he comes, tapping me again.

"What's wrong, Five? You missed your boy? Don't worry, I'm here now to ease the pain." Tre' swoops in for a hug.

"Bye, boy. It's too early for all your noise," I tell him, swatting him like the annoying flea he is. "And didn't I tell you to stop calling me Fivehead?"

I fake like I'm about to karate chop his rib cage, forcing Tre' to jump back a little. "Did you tell yourself to stop when you asked me for a doughnut last week?" he goes.

I try not to laugh as I turn around to strap my bookbag purse to the back of my seat. "It's not *my* fault you came to school ashy—looking like you dipped both elbows in a box of powdered doughnuts. We're Black," I remind him, pulling out my lab book. "We have to moisturize—*every* day."

"Whatever. Aye, let me get a pencil?" Trevor steps behind my chair and sticks his hand into my bookbag purse.

"Have you lost your mind?" Now, Tre' knows better than to stick his hand in a woman's purse without asking. To teach him a lesson, I scooch back hard, trapping him in between my chair and the lab table behind me.

"Whoa—whoa—*whoa*." Trevor tries to wiggle free, but I have him trapped good. "Come on, Five, let me out."

I push back harder against his abdomen. "*What's* my name again?"

"Five—*agghhhh*—Leila, *dang.*"

Then Tre' stops struggling, which is weird, because our fighting usually lasts *much* longer. I release my hold on Tre' and follow his eyes to the door. Then my heart clenches in my chest.

Dev and Darby Long are all up in each other's faces right outside our classroom door. "You better get to class, boy." Darby giggles and gives Dev a totally unnecessary hug, sending a heat wave rippling through my body.

"Wait. Did you and Dev break up or something?"

"Please walk yourself right out of my business, Tre'. *Thank you.*" I make sure my *thank you* is less about pleasantries and more of an invitation to get these hands if he doesn't leave me alone.

Tre', in a rare act of kindness, doesn't say anything more about it. But he doesn't have to say a word. The way he's shaking his head and slinking into his seat without cracking some kind of joke means that even *he* knows what they're

out there doing is dead wrong. Which piles onto my humiliation. Because *really*, Dev?

I used to ignore the heart emojis Darby Long left under
Dev's Instagram posts. Until she randomly sent him a late
afternoon selfie—and one more at 2 a.m.

There are *boundaries*. And a *code* that everyone learned
way back when we had those play crushes in elementary
school. Darby's behavior is just unacceptable. And thirsty.
And has been the only thing Dev and I have agreed to disagree about our entire relationship.

Dev thinks Darby's a harmless flirt. I know better.

How ironic that Dev and I are in the middle of a messy
high school divorce and are one step away from fighting over
custody of senior hall—and here comes Darby with the BS
again. So I guess we can chalk that up to the fact that *I knew
what I was talking about.*

Except this time, Dev doesn't smile politely and keep it
moving like I taught him. He stops and lets her hug all up
on him, right in front of my classroom door.

And it's like, *really*? You're letting *Darby Long* shoot her
shot, two seconds after we break up?

Oh *okay.*

4

THREE TIMES A week, I go to my after-school gig at the Smithsonian National Museum of Natural History in downtown DC. It's definitely more rewarding than hamburger flipping, dressing room monitoring, or other thankless grunt jobs that most teens suffer through. If you can make it through the initial sophomore training sessions, the Smithsonian gives you community service hours in your junior year. And by senior year, you get an actual paycheck and a blazer with your name embroidered on the front.

Usually I love giving tours around the dinosaur bones or taking visitors on a trip back to ancient Egypt. But Dev still works at the Smithsonian, too . . .

I reach into my purse and touch the initials necklace resting inside before heading into the Metro train terminal.

LAKITA WILSON

Dev and I normally ride together, taking the Blue Line from our Maryland suburban neighborhood to the heart of our nation's busy capital. We'd spend the entire train ride sharing music and just talking about whatever.

At the train platform, I spot Dev coming down the center of the escalator, keeping those custom Air Force 1s away from the grimy edges to avoid scuffs. My eyes linger on his long arms slipping into his blazer, and for a second I'm transported back to the many times those arms have held me close, kept me warm, made me feel—

My memory makes a sharp left, parking me right in front of an earlier image of those same arms around Darby Long— right in front of my first period classroom.

I make a split-second decision to turn my back on those large brown eyes darting around the platform looking for me, and ease myself into the sea of commuters bunching up near the edge of the platform.

Dev, to his credit, notices me dodging him, and maintains a respectful distance between us the entire time we're standing there waiting. But as soon as the train slides into the station and I find a blue pleather seat near the window, he makes it his business to sit in the empty seat next to me.

Planning to ignore him, I face the window, watching the outside scenery change from trees and traffic to pitch black as we head underground.

But Dev sitting so close to me makes it impossible to block out his familiar scent, the heavy way he breathes, the way his leg almost always spills over into the seat next to me.

Suddenly, my fingers are back in my purse, fishing out the tiny gold initials, connected into one pendant by thin strips of gold. Holding the cool metal in my palm brings me back to the moment Dev slipped it on my neck. I felt like the luckiest girl in the world when he said, "To remind you, no matter what happens, that I do love you."

At the time, I felt like I didn't even need a reminder around my neck, because Dev had spent the last four years proving how much he *truly* loved me. But now, in light of everything that's happened, Dev's words feel different. Ominous, even. And suddenly it comes to me.

"You *knew* you were going to break up with me."

Dev turns and looks at me, his silence telling me everything I need to know.

I open my palm, revealing the necklace. "You went out and bought me a necklace, with your literal *initials* on it, and you knew the entire time that we weren't even going to be together in a few weeks. Who *does* that?" I toss the necklace on his lap and get up from my seat.

I can't even find another place to sit, because the train always gets packed around L'Enfant Plaza.

Dev follows me up anyway, which bothers me even more, because usually when sudden passenger movement happens on the train, everyone throws cautious looks around, like *Uh-oh. Is something about to pop off?* Today, *Dev and I* are the reason strangers are eyeballing each other.

But I don't plan to start any real drama on this train. And I know Dev won't either. Neither of us need anything happening to keep us from walking onto our college campuses in the fall.

I wedge myself between a guy in a suit and a lady clinging on to the handle of one of those rolling briefcases. I grab one of the metal poles to keep from toppling as the train pulls out of the station and heads for Metro Center.

Almost instantly, Dev is behind me, so close I can feel his warm breath on the back of my neck. It's the kind of thing that used to feel nice.

I don't even turn to face Dev when I say, "Nobody goes from buying their girlfriend a necklace to dumping them, Dev. Like, come on. Feelings don't just change overnight."

I hear Dev sigh behind me before saying, "They don't."

And for a minute I feel like we're really getting somewhere. At least he admitted that much.

"It's not like I woke up one day and decided we needed to break up. I've been thinking it since March."

As the train slows to a stop at the next station, it lurches a little. So does my heart. I finally turn to face him. I want him to see the pain in my eyes. "You've been thinking about breaking up with me for months?" My heart beats loud over the banter of the surrounding passengers. "What was the point of the necklace?"

Dev looks down at the worn brown train carpet. "I bought you the necklace because I love you, Leila. I still do. I probably should've bought you something you could still wear. But I wasn't thinking. I mean, I liked seeing you wear my initials around your neck. I told you, this breakup has nothing to do with how I *feel* about you." Dev takes a moment to get his next words out. "I just know it's the right thing to do."

"Breaking up with me"—when the woman with the rolling briefcase stares, I realize I'm screeching over the squeal of the moving train, so I lower my voice some—"is the right thing to do? Come on, Dev. Do you hear yourself right now?"

I look at the tip of the necklace pendant peeking out of Dev's pants pocket and I suddenly feel stupid for bringing it. What did I think a piece of metal was going to do? I've been wearing it for two weeks, and he still made the decision to dump me.

"I bought the necklace for you. I want you to have it." Dev reaches into his pocket and pulls the necklace out. Then he tucks it inside my pocket. Forcing me to keep a piece of him—while letting the rest of him go.

It makes me feel like I'm splitting in two.

I think again about seeing Dev outside my chemistry class. And I swear, I don't even want that girl to be relevant. But I want Dev to know that I saw them. "You should give the necklace to your new boo, Darby."

Dev looks confused for a moment. Then he shakes his head. "I wasn't talking to Darby. She was talking to me."

"Same difference." And as the scene of the two of them all hugged up on each other plays out in my head all over again, rage begins building. "You know what? Just leave me alone."

The hum of the train speeding through the tunnel is the

only sound between us for a while. Then Dev puts a hand on my elbow.

"There doesn't have to be drama between us, Leila. We're not breaking up over something bad. I thought we could still be friends."

"Still be *friends?*" I move my elbow away from his hand. "I could never—and would never—be friends with someone who broke my heart." I think back to when I was little, and my dad used to explain the critical functions of the heart to me like a bedtime story. How once the heart stops working, everything else shuts down. Right now, Dev treating my heart like something that doesn't take forever to heal is *really* getting under my skin. "Every time I look at you, I see the person who broke my heart. I can't be friends with someone like that."

For the first time since our breakup, Dev doesn't look relaxed and easygoing. Maybe he finally understands the consequences of his decision.

"So if we're not boyfriend and girlfriend, you don't want to talk at all anymore?"

"No. I don't."

Dev's eyes widen over the finality of my words. But after a second he shakes his head and just respects my wishes, and we ride in silence the rest of the way to the Smithsonian stop.

When the Metro doors open, we get off, walk across the grass on the National Mall, and down the block until we reach the expansive stone building with its domed rotunda top, stone arches, and Roman columns lined up at the front entrance.

Right before we walk in, Dev grabs my arm and pulls me close. "I'm a jerk—okay? I'm sorry. Everything's my fault."

My wounded heart stops bleeding for one long, hopeful moment. "You mean that?" Maybe the threat of never speaking again did something to him. Maybe he's finally realizing that all or nothing isn't what he wants.

Dev lets my arm go and shrugs. "I *guess*. I'm not saying we should get back together or anything. I still think we should start college with no strings. But I *hate* when you're mad at me. And if you want me to apologize again—"

I yank my arm away. "That's what I am to you? *Strings?* You know what? Bye, Dev." I turn and stomp into the museum, letting him catch up only when I'm forced to stop to go through security.

"Come on, Leila. You're not being reasonable."

One of my favorite security guards, Annette, stands up from her swivel chair and raises an eyebrow at us. "You two okay to come inside? I can't have no mess in my building."

"I don't know about him, but *I'm* fine." I toss my bookbag purse onto the conveyor belt to get x-rayed. I step through the metal detector and get wanded down while Annette whispers in my ear, "You sure you're okay, sweetie? Isn't this your boyfriend?"

"I'm fine," I tell her, holding my arms out wide. I turn around so she can wand down my other side. "And I don't know *who* that guy is."

When my purse slides out of the x-ray machine, I snatch it up and quickly walk away before Dev can get another word in.

Our tours coordinator, Maggie, is waiting for our group under the thirteen-foot elephant guarding the museum's rotunda. I stare at the mighty beast, with her raised trunk and lowered eyes. She doesn't look like she trusts anyone getting too close, and to be honest, after Dev's betrayal, I feel her on that.

Maggie waits for all twenty-four of us to arrive before she starts handing out tour assignments. She assigns Stephanie and Claudia to the butterfly exhibit and Mark and Taylor to Ocean Hall before I raise my hand and ask, "Uh, Maggie? Can I switch with Steph? Dev and I signed up to tour the Hall of Human Origins this week, but I seriously can't stop thinking about the butterfly exhibit."

Maggie's eyes slide from Dev to me and back to Dev. "Are you kidding me? Absolutely not. Everyone *loves* touring with the dynamic Leila and Dev duo."

As much as I want to run home and bury myself back under my covers, I have a job to do. So while Maggie continues assigning teams, I throw my head back, toss my braids over my shoulders, and refuse to even look in Dev's direction. "Let's just get this tour over with."

Our group today consists of an elderly couple; a mom with her son, who looks like he doesn't want to be here; a woman with a crying baby; and two college-aged guys with huge cameras around their necks.

Dev and I kick the tour off the same as always, with the rehearsed notes we wrote together over a year ago, when we were first approved to give tours. Dev walks over to an exhibit—a mummy in a large wooden casket—and goes, "As far back as six million years ago, the human brain was noticeably smaller than it is today, about the size of a small chimpanzee's. But over time, humans and chimps evolved in very different ways."

At this point in the script, as the "heart" of the dynamic duo, I'm supposed to say something like, "Ah, the cousins of the human species. Did you know, chimps have the ability to laugh? Google it one day. It's the cutest thing!"

But I'm not in a "cute" mood today. I'm still angry over everything. And before I can stop myself, I snort loud enough for the two guys to lower their cameras. "Is that what happened to you, Dev? Did your brain somehow forget to evolve?"

Dev coughs, side-eyes me, and continues on the walking tour. "You know," he goes, in that annoying "expert" voice he only uses for tours. "Human brains have grown only slightly over the years, enough to allow us better social interactions and emotional maturity—"

"Emotional maturity, you say?" I swear, I really tried to start up the casual conversation bit Dev and I created to keep our audience entertained. But somehow I manage to go even further off script. "Is that like when someone spends all four years of high school being the perfect girlfriend, you know, using her *normal*-sized brain. And then some pea-brained guy ends a very healthy and loving relationship for *literally* no reason?"

Dev looks noticeably flustered. He doesn't like public scenes. And in my opinion, he's always cared a little too much about what others think about him. So I know for sure he'd rather *die* than give a less-than-perfect museum tour.

I'm enjoying watching him squirm. Until he says, "That's it."

Dev politely excuses himself from our tour guests, then pulls me over to a bench near the caveman display.

"Get your hands off me, you—you—*Neanderthal*," I whisper to him.

"Leila. You and I both know you have better clapbacks than that. But you can't do this here." Dev sits me down on the bench. "Stay here until I'm done giving this tour," he demands.

My butt connects with the glossy wood for all of one second before I'm back out of my seat. "Hold up. What you're not going to do is—"

"Leila—" Dev blows out a breath. "I understand that you're angry at me, but this museum is a *national* treasure, and the guests deserve a good tour." Dev points to the bench. Then he straightens his blazer, turns, and walks crisply back over to our group.

I clench my fists, burning with anger. Even I know that my emotions are running a little too high to finish this tour with him. But I know *goodness* well I'm not sitting on this bench just because he *ordered* me to.

I can't stay here a second longer. So I call my mom.

"Can you come get me from the museum?" I ask her. My bottom lip is trembling by now but I'm too exhausted from this weekend's cryfest to start the tears back up.

"Leila, baby, you can't take the train? I'm kind of—"

"Mom. *Please*."

"Okay, baby. I'm on my way."

My simmering embarrassment over being placed on a museum bench like a toddler in time-out pivots to rage by the time I spot Mom's SUV pulling up. I'm so fired up over Dev, I yank the front passenger door open without looking first—and there's some rando already buckled into my seat, smiling up at me with a goofy look on his face.

"And how are *you* today, young lady?" he goes in this over-the-line fatherly tone.

Tuh. My daddy is in Houston, Texas, probably repairing someone's heart right now, *thank you very much*.

I slam the door closed and climb into the back seat. "I *know* you didn't pick me up with a *Tinder* date in the car."

Mom turns around like, *Really?* But, since she's forced to keep it cute with *new dude* in the car, she just puts a freshly manicured hand on his shoulder and they break out laughing. "What do you know about Tinder, Leila?" Mom asks.

I click in my seat belt and fold my arms across my chest. "Enough to know your new bae probably didn't expect the end of this date to involve picking up a seventeen-year-old."

I make a face at new dude. "Or maybe he's into that sort of thing. *Even* worse."

I expect Mom's left eye to start twitching. Or send a few death stares. But instead, Mom grabs her little boyfriend's hand and goes, "Oh, Leila. Don't be such a player-hater." And they crack up laughing again.

Normally I would find Mom's outdated slang sort of amusing. But today I don't find any of this funny. This is not how this was supposed to go. I'm supposed to be in the front passenger seat, securely fastened by my safety belt and securely spilling out all my disappointments over my failed relationship to my mother. She wanted to be looped into my relationship drama so bad, well, here was her chance.

But no. Some dude I never met is riding shotgun, and I've been tossed to the back like a forgotten bag of McDonald's french fries.

Mom takes her eyes off her new boo long enough to merge into the next lane. "Leila, meet Benjamin. Yes, we met on Tinder. And no, he's not a stranger. We've been dating for three months now. I just haven't brought him around to meet you and Riley yet."

Then she winks at this dude right in front of my face. "And if you rode the train home, like you normally do, I could've introduced you the right way, instead of cutting our date short to come pick you up."

My eyebrows raise so high they almost kiss my perfectly laid edges. It suddenly occurs to me that Mom's date is riding around in *her* car. "Please don't tell me you picked this dude up for your date?" I fold my arms up and judge this bum harshly. "Let me guess—your car's in the shop?"

Bus Pass Ben turns around again, still wearing that goofy grin. "Not that there's anything wrong with being carless. Plenty of people who live in the city don't need cars." He buffs his nails on his button-up polo. "But yes, you're right. I took my BMW in for a tune-up this morning."

"Oh. Okay."

Yeah, right.

I don't call him out on his little BMW pipe dream. I decide to just let Mom have her moment. But as soon as I commit to minding my business, *Mom* proceeds to air me out in front of her little boyfriend.

"Leila's boyfriend just dumped her," she tells the man I didn't know existed fifteen minutes ago.

And before I can accidentally knee the back of her seat, *new dude* turns around and goes, "You know, I didn't think I'd get over my broken heart"—Ben grabs Mom's hand— "until I met your mom."

Mom smiles and squeezes his hand, but I'm a little too jaded at the moment to find his little *Taxicab Confession* cute. I make a mental note to keep my eye on this potential scammer. Then I get back to my own problems.

I've already caused a scene at the museum. And thanks to Dev scrubbing four years of our love from his social media, everyone knows we're broken up. At this point, with my pride in the toilet, I'm left with a pitiful set of options.

There's really only two ways to go about this to fix things.

I can either go out sad like Tia Carr when Shaina Pittman broke up with her, and literally beg on the lunchroom microphone for Dev to take me back.

Or I *could* distract myself with a few harmless dates. Not that I trust taking advice from the stranger sitting in my mom's passenger seat. But. There could be something to his little moving-on-and-meeting-someone-new strategy.

I'm not saying my feelings for Dev will vanish anytime soon. But with only three weeks left until graduation, there's only one Baldwin High event big enough to temporarily patch my wounded heart *and* make every senior forget I just got played by Devrata Naveen Rajan.

Last. Chance. Dance.

I EMERGE INTO senior hall the next day a new girl. For the first time since being coldly dumped, I'm giving luminous vibes. I am now flowers. I am hearts. I am candy. I am all the things warm, sweet, and good in this world.

I need every senior who saw me with my head down and shoulders slumped yesterday to notice my come up. I am no longer that sad, lost girl with cream pie on her face. I am a woman who stepped out of a messed-up situation, pretty much unscathed.

I purposely wave to Ashli and Chad. I square my shoulders. I tilt my head higher. For the first time since the breakup, I'm smiling my way through senior hall. Not that I'm over it or anything. I just know from my reality TV marathon days that the most unbothered contestant always comes out on top. Either she gets the guy or she doesn't get the guy, but her amazing personality earns her a loyal fandom who thinks the guy is a *mess* for not choosing her in the first place.

It takes forever for lunchtime to arrive, but when that clock finally strikes twelve, I head into the cafeteria on a mission.

As I walk, I see Bree waving ahead. I move through a group of seniors still laughing it up over Senior Skip Day antics and join Bree at the last table on the right by the windows.

Bree's sitting with a tray of chicken nuggets in front of her and a tray of cheese pizza next to her. "You were taking too long, so I got your stuff, too."

"You used my account? How did you know my PIN?"

Bree brushes her shoulder off. "I'm your bestie, girl. I know everything about you." She pops a nugget in her mouth.

I raise an eyebrow at her. "Then how come you didn't know I wanted chicken nuggets, too?"

Bree fakes an angry look. "So your bestie takes the time out of her day to go through the lunch line for you, and this is how she's repaid?"

"But you know I like the nuggets."

"Here, brat." Bree tosses a chicken nugget on my tray. "Don't say I never gave you nothing."

"Thank yooooouuuuu." I bite into my freshly gifted chicken nugget. Then I get down to business.

"Okay, let's do this," I tell Bree, with my mouth full of nugget.

"Do what?"

"This Last Chance Dance mess." I try to play it off like it's whatever, but I'm suddenly nervous about faking my way past the dumped girlfriend narrative and straight into my glow-up finale. What if my plan doesn't work, and I come off looking like I'm trying too hard?

I ignore the little voice in my head telling me this is a bad idea. Because anything that helps me ignore Dev can only be good for my ego.

Bree stops eating to stare at me for a long second. "*Seriously?* What made you change your mind?" Her eyes wander around the lunchroom for a moment. Then her gaze lands on Darby sitting next to Dev, laughing her head off about something, while he's just sitting there looking sort of uncomfortable. He's probably afraid I'm going to walk over and cause a scene. But I'm done letting *those two* ruin my last few weeks of high school.

"Ohhhh—you're on get-back status." Bree opens her juice, drinks it, and crushes the carton. "I get it. I would be salty, too. Darby is *baaaad.*"

I'm instantly annoyed with Bree for thinking of Darby in any other light than the belly-crawling snake she's always been. "Oh really? Why don't you date her—since you think she's so *bad?*"

Bree shrugs. "I flirted with her once."

My eyebrows raise again. "With my nemesis? Now, Bree . . ."

Bree shrugs. "It was before she was all up in Dev's face."

"Oh . . . *okay.*" I sneak a peek back at Dev's table, and thank goodness, Darby's finally getting up to go pester somebody else. "You're a bold one. How do you even know she likes girls like that?"

Bree starts waving her hands around in that animated way she does when she thinks she's really spitting facts. "Okay, so *boom.* If you stare into a girl's eyes and she looks away, she doesn't swing that way. Now, if she stares back?" Bree rubs her hands together. "That's bae."

I find Bree's theory shaky at best. But I have to know. "Well, did she stare back?"

Bree looks confused for a moment. "I don't know. Darby kind of stares at everybody."

Facts.

"Well, for your information," I tell Bree, "this isn't about getting back at Dev."

When my bestie gives me *the* most skeptical look, I lay it on super thick to force her to believe me. "No, seriously. Everyone already knows Dev and I broke up, and I'm sick of the pity looks already. I have three more weeks left of high school to bounce back and show everyone that getting dumped didn't break me—that I'm *that girl* whether I'm with Dev or not."

Even though my words sound confident out loud, on the inside I'm still skeptical I'll *ever* feel whole again.

Bree rubs her hands together. "Welp, before you change your mind, let's get this show on the road." She scopes the room. "What about dude over there?" she asks, pointing to Jamal—a quiet boy who sort of fades into the background whenever there's more than two people in the room.

I nibble the corner of my cheese pizza. "Him? Umm, no. That's a negative." As long as I'm bouncing back, it wouldn't hurt to show my ex that I can still pull top-tier cuties. There's no way Dev is going to be threatened by a kid he barely knows exists. I need someone a little more colorful. Bold. A tad in-your-face. I scan the room for the sexiest, most heart-crushing, soul-destroying, good-looking kid in our senior class. "More like—*him*."

Kai Ballard. Full-time senior, part-time Instagram thot. I mean, what better way to showcase my glow-up than by going on a date with the hottest guy at Baldwin High?

"Kai?!" Bree gets up out of her seat. "Are you kidding me right now? Kai? Overly filtered Kai? Fake-deep-quotes Kai? Kai, who basically begs for likes and followers with his bare abs, Kai?"

I steal another nugget from Bree's tray. "I mean, he's cute." Even I wouldn't blame Darby for flooding Kai's comments with heart emojis. I might've left one or two myself. Purely as a fan, of course. A fan of *those abs*.

"But too full of himself."

"He's full of himself because he shows off a little skin? He worked hard for those muscles."

"No. Because he's out here doing the most with that little struggle page of his." Bree swipes my apple juice off my tray and takes a sip. Her animated hands come out again. "Facts:

social media is made up of four different types of clout chasers. The body flaunters. The fake-me-out life coaches. Trolls. And the *shamefully* shameless. Kai is stepping into two major clout-chasing categories with that thirsty page of his."

"He's not that bad."

"Oh yeah? What's the difference between Kai and Darby?"

"Darby is too in-your-face. Kai is the slow burn that leaves you wanting more."

"You only have English Lit with him, where he can hide behind book quotes. I have World Studies with him." Bree holds her hand out and wiggles it side to side. "Dude is kind of *meh* in the brains department."

I side-eye my bestie. "Didn't *you* get a D in World Studies last quarter?"

"That doesn't count. I don't study."

"Well." I bite into my pizza. "Maybe he doesn't either."

Bree shakes her head and chuckles softly under her breath.

"Well, these are *my* matches and I'm putting him down as my first pick," I say while sipping my apple juice. "Do you want me to do this or not?"

Bree sighs hard and shakes her head. But she grabs my phone and types in *Kai Ballard* as my number one pick.

"Well," she goes. "Now that you just threw away one of your picks, let's get serious. Who's next?"

"Mason," I say, the second I peep him standing in the corner collecting petition signatures like a boss.

"Mason?!" Bree frowns her face up. "White-boy Mason?"

I give Bree a look. "Don't be like that."

"I'm just saying. I'm surprised Miss *I'm-voting-for-everyone-Black* hasn't chosen one Black crush yet."

"Ummm, Kai?" I give her the *duh* face.

"Kai lost his Black card when he posted that Ida B. Wells quote-caption talking about *The Way to Right Wrongs is to Turn the Light of Truth Upon Them* under a pic of the sun bouncing off his abs. I'm done with his brand of foolishness."

I try not to laugh because then I would have to admit to side-eyeing that post, too. I also might have to admit to liking the photo anyway, because—them *abs*.

So I distract her with, "Excuse me? What's wrong with Mason?" I raise an eyebrow at my bestie. "You just complained about Kai and his self-centered Insta pics. Mason's Insta is full of all that charity work. All those protests. All those GoFundMe donations for worthy causes." I smirk. "Seems to me, Mason only cares about others."

And secretly? One time, Dev got into his feelings over Mason sending me a DM. It was a whole thing, that led to a few texts from Dev and lots of reassuring that I didn't even find Mason all that cute. I *know* Dev would feel a certain way about Mason and me matching.

Bree breaks all the fun I'm having silently taking stabs at Dev's heart, by playfully shoving my shoulder. "I don't know. I just thought, after four years of being down with the swirl, you would give more brothers a chance." Bree raises her Black Power fist then types *Mason King* into my phone as my second crush.

"You know I don't really like to box myself in. I just like anyone—*nice*." I glance around the room again, my eyes settling on possibly the sweetest kid at Baldwin High.

"Like Eva."

"Eva?" Bree screws her face up. "Now hold up. I've been trying to date Eva since freshman year. I was going to put Eva on *my* list and convince her to finally go on a date with me."

"Well, who says you can't?"

"I mean, I *can*. But isn't that, like, breaking girl code or something? Both of us going after the same girl?" Bree scowls at me. "I'm more gay than you. So I should get first dibs on all the girl choices. Go run and play with them dusty boys you like so much."

I squint my eyes at her. "I told you about all that bi-slander. Don't."

"The L comes before the B is all I'm saying—"

"*No* bi-slander." I point to my phone. "Do I have to get your mom and the rest of her PFLAG buddies on the line?"

Bree puts her hands up in truce. "Please do *not* send my mom after me again. I keep telling everyone. I'm lesbian, I'm listening, and I'm learning . . ."

Bree glances across the cafeteria. "Besides, you and me are way too different. There's no way Eva's adding both of us to her list."

Bree shrugs. "And if she doesn't pick me, then it's whatever. There's a million other girls at Baldwin to flirt with."

I raise an eyebrow in my bestie's direction. "Isn't that why

Eva refused to go out with you in the first place? Because of your player status?"

Bree sucks her teeth. "I might not be ready to settle down, but I'm a fun date—ask anyone." She shrugs again. "And I never said I wouldn't settle down with the right one. I just need to play the high school field . . . and the college field. And maybe hit up all the hot lesbian clubs in New York, Miami, and San Fran first. Then when I get back to DC, if she's single—and I'm single—then . . ."

"Bree! That's terrible."

Bree shakes her head, kinda laughing, kinda serious. "*Is* it terrible, though? I mean, look at it this way. If we go on this date now, then she will already know I'm charming and just her type. So, when we're like twenty-five, twenty-six, we reconnect in the Instagram DMs and . . ."

"And why would someone wait almost a decade for you to settle down?"

Bree strikes a pose. "I mean, come on. Can you see Eva meeting a face cuter than this?" Bree sticks her fingers in her dimples and flashes all thirty-two teeth.

I side-eye my bestie's overblown cockiness. "A girl like Eva doesn't have to wait on anyone. Not even you, Bree."

I take another peek over there at Eva. "You should add her to your list, though." I smirk at my friend. "Maybe she'll be the one to make you finally turn in your bachelorette card."

Bree playfully shoves my shoulder again. "Yeah, right. So I can be crying and doomscrolling all over Instagram when it's over? Not for me, champ." She types in *Eva Martin* as my third choice, then swipes to a new screen. "Okay, now—to get your wild card match, you have to fill out this questionnaire. Ready?"

I look over at the way Dev is sipping his chocolate milk and looking all fine. "No."

"Question number one."

I let out a long, exaggerated sigh and settle in for these annoying personality questions. One thing's for sure, no personality test in the world can find me someone I'll connect with as deeply as Dev.

I look over at the lunch table where my ex is sitting. Dev must feel me staring, because he looks up and we lock eyes. For a second, it feels like it's back to the way things have always been. And I'm filled with hope. And possibility. And forgiveness.

Maybe this algorithm will match us, and it will prove to Dev—and the entire senior class—that this breakup should've never happened.

Then Dev looks away, and goes back to laughing it up with his boys and acting like he has not one care in the whole world. And I'm hurt all over again.

Boys are stupid. And I'm stupid, too, for ever thinking matching with all these randos will fix this hole in my heart.

BEFORE SCHOOL STARTS the next morning, Dev's waiting for me at my locker. And when he holds up his phone, showing me the text I sent him last night, I know exactly why he's here.

"You're really evicting me from your locker three weeks before school lets out?" he asks.

I wave him out of my way so I can open my locker door. "Yeah, so?"

"So you don't even use it. You've been sharing a locker with Bree the last four years of high school and now all of a sudden I have twenty-four hours to get my stuff out or you're going to dump everything in the stairwell?"

"I *mean* . . ."

"Come on, Leila. You know this locker's closer to my classes."

"Excuse me—why is that my problem?"

"Because there's no reason to act this petty."

"Yeah, I don't *have* to be petty. But it just makes sense, you know?" I think about his actual assigned locker—the one next to the boy's restroom with the constantly breaking toilets.

"Enjoy!" I call over before ducking into my AP Chemistry classroom.

In first period AP Chem, instead of doing actual work, Mr. Boomer has our class doing his dirty work. By which I mean he's assigned us the menial task of wrapping beakers and other chem supplies in newspaper, and carefully storing them in the supply closet for safekeeping over summer break.

Some kids grumble that storing Mr. Boomer's supplies wasn't on the syllabus, but I don't mind working on the task. It gives me time to think about where things went wrong in my relationship. The TikTok filters glossing over my memories with Dev suddenly flicker and disappear, exposing ugly little truths. Like our Netflix watch sessions, where I would be glued to the show while he was all up in his phone. Or all those FaceTimes when he'd *uh-huh* me to death because *Madden* had his attention.

But even when we were ten episodes into a new series, or Dev had only thirty seconds left on the video game clock and he was headed into overtime, somehow he never missed a shift in my mood or a moment when I really needed him.

I shake my head. Thinking about Dev makes me lose focus. And before I can catch myself, I accidentally drop a test tube, shattering it all over the classroom floor.

"Clean it up," Mr. Boomer says from his desk, between bites of cereal.

"Dang it, *Five.*" Tre' grabs the little broom and dustpan from the back of the classroom. He bends down and starts sweeping. "You're too smart to mess up wrapping beakers in newspaper. Is this why Brown didn't take you?"

And I don't know what does it. If it's Tre's mouth or my karma for being mean to Dev. But I start crying right there, in the middle of chemistry lab.

Tre's eyes go wide. He abandons the broom and dustpan to stand up and pat my back. "I'm sorry, Fi—I mean, Leila. Seriously, stop crying." He reaches over and grabs a random square piece of wax paper. "Here, use this until I can find you some Kleenex."

Tre' starts bouncing around the room, looking in lab coats and empty closets for a box of tissues. "Come on, man," he hassles Ashli. "All that sneezing you do in class. I know you got a few tissues tucked away in your purse."

Ashli glares at Tre', but she reaches into her bag and comes up with three tissues.

"Good looking out!" Tre' plucks Ashli on the arm, then runs back over to me. "Here, Leila. My bad. If I thought getting rejected by Brown would hurt your feelings this bad, I never would've said anything,"

I snatch the tissues from his hands and wipe my eyes. "I'm not crying over Brown. I'm happy about going to Rochester now."

When I open my eyes, Tre's shaking his head at me with this know-it-all look in his eyes. "All this crying over the biggest bum in our *Madden* league? Really?" He scoops back up the dustpan and disposes the shattered beaker in the trash.

I don't deny crying over Dev. Because I would be lying if I said it wasn't about him. "Mind your business, Tre'." I tuck my used tissues in my pocket. Then I snatch another sheet of newspaper to begin wrapping another beaker.

Tre' takes the newspaper from me and quickly wraps the beaker himself. "All I'm saying is, a dude that doesn't wait on line on game release day lacks true commitment in all areas of his life. You can do better."

Sick of hearing Tre's opinions on things, I walk over to Mr. Boomer's closet to start stacking beakers. "First of all, I don't want any of your relationship advice. You've never been with anybody more than a week."

"That's because you won't go out with me." Tre' squints his eyes at my forehead. "Maybe if you wore bangs—"

"That's it—"

I grab Tre's finger and threaten to bend it backward.

"*Come on*, Five. Don't play into the Black-on-Black violence stereotype—"

"*Stop* calling me *Five!*"

"*Arrrgggghhhh!*"

"Oh, stop the theatrics. I'm not even bending it that hard!"

"Mr. Hillman and Ms. Bean. Keep the *chemistry* on the lab table, please."

While the rest of the class *oops* and *mmhmm*s in response to Mr. Boomer's shade, I let Tre's finger go. I'm embarrassed, because Tre' and I are *absolutely not . . .*

But Tre' just keeps it up. "Now, last night I realized that getting dumped must have been a huge blow to your self-esteem. So I made a list of all the top-tier celebrities with big foreheads that are still pretty hot and go on plenty of dates. Let's see, there's Rihanna—*aagghhhhhhh*—" he yelps as I grab his finger again.

"The both of you, get up here now."

I release Tre's finger and follow him to Mr. Boomer's desk.

"I don't know what kind of love affair you two have going on with each other, but this ends now. How'd you like to spend the summer after senior year hanging out in summer school—with *me?*"

I highly doubt Mr. Boomer can just randomly fail two high school seniors who've been on the principal's list all four years of high school. But I'm not about to test him, so I just pretend to be really, really remorseful and follow Tre' back to our lab table.

Tre' hands me another test tube, and we settle into a workflow. Wrap and stack. Stack and more wrapping. But we only make it another ten minutes before everybody's phone suddenly goes off.

"Is this a classroom of bees or do I have students with cell phones on during school hours?" Mr. Boomer stands up at his desk. "Don't experiment with my patience."

We wait a respectable three seconds. But let's be honest here. We're literally doing our teacher a favor by packing his classroom up for him. Mr. Boomer shouldn't be reminding us of the rules. He should just be thankful for all the free labor.

The boldest senior in the room pulls their phone out first, and yells, "Oh snap, it's the Last Chance Dance list!" The room comes alive again.

"What did I say?! Turn those phones off *now.*"

But at this point, everyone's already looking down at their phone screens, scrolling past the Fling Week rules to get to their matches.

I'm too nervous to look at my matches. It feels weird going from boo'd up to planning multiple dates in a week—even if I'm only doing this to get back at Dev. So I don't pull my phone out just yet. Instead, I pretend like wrapping beakers is the most important thing in the world.

"Really? Only one match?" Halima Abdul says from across the room. She glares at the rest of us like it's our fault she wasn't magically compatible with all her picks.

Nia St. James must have gotten lucky, because she's up dancing across the room, basically wanting everyone to know she linked up with all three of her top picks. "I even like my wild card pick. Told y'all this Last Chance Dance stuff works."

She high-fives Ashli, who clearly doesn't have a list of matches since she and Chad are now officially the longest-running couple at Baldwin High. But since this dance is literally everything to our senior class, she's still all up in everyone's phones, checking out their matches.

Ashli makes her way over to Everett. "So who did you match—*oh*." Ashli freezes up and gets this awkward look on her face. "Umm, never mind." She tries to quickly dart away to someone else, but it's too late. He's slumped down in his seat, hands in his pockets, eyes on the floor. The look of humiliation and regret is written all over his face, and it's obvious to the entire class that he didn't match with anyone.

A few other kids in the class are super quiet, too. Ashli tries her best to avoid them. She sees me without my phone in my hand, probably assumes the worst, and awkwardly sidesteps me to get to Tre'. "And who did *you* match with?" she asks him.

Next to me, Tre' leans back against the lab table looking down at his phone screen.

"Chelsea. Darby. Kayla. And—*Fivehead*?! Oh, snap!" Tre' turns to me and wiggles his eyebrows. "I guess we're matched."

I figure Tre's just messing with me. But when I finally pull my phone out to view my matches? Mason—okay, not a total shock. Eva?! Washboard abs Kai Ballard? *Really?!*

For a moment, I do nothing but silently rejoice. It's like a pair of love clouds parted and introduced me to the dating heavens. Kai, *the* hottest boy in school; Mason, *the* most charismatic guy in school, who has hundreds of people hanging on his every word the second he goes live on Instagram. And Eva—literally an angel walking. Dev is going to have a meltdown when he sees my matches.

Wait—

My left eyelid begins twitching. "I *know* this list is *effing* lying."

"Oop." Ashli covers her mouth with her hand and quietly slips away.

Tre' rubs his hands together. "Leila and Tre'—wild card picks. I guess we were meant to be, Five . . ."

Ugh.

Apparently, all of my heavenly luck has run out. And now I can almost see a tiny red devil dancing across the lab table, poking me with his pitchfork and laughing at my misfortune.

Tre'. It's written right there.

Well. No one can make me go on a date with all my matches, right? I toss my phone back into my purse but Tre' won't let things go. "So when are we going on our date, Five?"

I roll my eyes. "Never."

"Why not?"

"Because you play too much." I start wrapping beakers again.

"*So?* I play around with everybody."

"Yeah, I know. And sometimes you go too far."

"Far how?"

I want to shout *Does anything from the eighth grade ring a bell?* But I'm so annoyed right now that I don't even feel like bringing that up and making myself feel worse. So I say, "Look, this Last Chance Dance stuff is dumb, okay? So count me out."

Trevor glances over at me. "Come on, Leila. You're going to just leave me hanging like that?"

I tune out Tre' to use my brain cells for more productive reasons. Like cleaning up our work space. And convincing myself that matching with Tre' won't *completely* ruin my plans. I still matched with three of the most eligible singles in the entire school.

When the bell rings and everyone rushes the classroom door, I step into senior hall—a woman with the odds finally stacked in her favor, times three.

Basking in my good fortune, I make it my business to find at least one of my matches so we can talk about how amazing it is that we chose each other.

I search for Eva first, since I know her a little better than Mason and Kai. I find her at her locker, grabbing her things for her next class.

I'm suddenly too nervous to discuss anything Last Chance Dance related. After years of being coupled up, I've forgotten what it's like to flirt with someone new. So I go with what I know.

"Hey, did you remember to bring that book you were going to let me borrow?" I ask her.

"Of course!" Eva gives me a big smile and reaches into

her backpack. She hands me the book, winks, and goes, "We can discuss what you think of the ending on our *date*."

Well. At least Eva is well versed in the flirting department. As she walks off, I'm so busy watching her toss her curls out of her face that I don't notice Mason walking up with a fresh new protest flier.

"Glad we matched, Leila," he says, showing off a set of pouty lips I never noticed before now. And for a split second, I wonder if it's the beautiful mouth that gets him all the likes and comments on his socials. But I quickly shut that idea down. I've witnessed his passionate words in too many of his live sessions to know that Mason King lives up to his Instagram bio. I watch Mason walk away with such confidence in his steps that I can't help imagining all the amazing conversations we're going to have.

But things get all the way real when I finally make it down the hall and Kai—and *them abs*—are posted up against my locker.

"I've been waiting for the day Leila *Bean* became single," he says in that deep, husky voice.

And that's it. Someone cue the party horns. I'm not saying I'm over Dev—at *all*. But having a hot guy like Kai Ballard checking for you should be on every girl's bucket list, because it feels *amazing*.

I take my time opening my locker, partially for the drama of it all, and partially because I'm still searching for the perfect flirty comeback. I check on my slicked edges, my contoured eyebrows, and my poppin' lip gloss. I creep my eyes over the entire length of Kai Ballard's perfectly sculpted body. Then I hit him with one of my favorite reality TV show lines.

"Didn't you know?" I say. "The best things in life are *always* worth the wait."

THAT AFTERNOON, WHEN Bree drives us home, I'm feeling better than when I left for school this morning, which gives me hope. No one's talking about my breakup now. All anyone can talk about are the matches. Kai, Mason, and Eva all have something special about them that could really make people forget my declarations of love for Dev all over social media a week ago.

For the first time in a long time, I'm feeling that same energy I felt the day I spotted Dev walking into that Target. Young and hopeful about my future.

Bree, though, has a funny look on her face. I naturally assume she didn't match with anyone. I mean, when you've serial-dated the entire Baldwin lesbian and bi scene by sophomore year, your options get a little thin.

But when Bree turns into our development, she goes, "Promise you won't be mad."

"Umm, I promise, I guess . . ." Then I wait for something ridiculous to drop, like Bree randomly matching with Dev or something.

"Eva's my wild card pick," Bree says with a pained look on her face.

I silently breathe a sigh of relief. "Is that all? So what?" I don't tell her I was thinking a lot worse.

"Yeah, but I checked, and you matched with her, too." Bree lets out a breath. "Look, Leila. I don't want there to be anything weird between us. I have two other matches: Chanel and Ivy. I've gone out with both of them before. It'll be nice to go out with them again. If I leave high school without ever dating Eva, it won't kill me." Bree continues to stare at the road as she drives, but now a small smile is on her face. "There will be plenty of new girls to date when I get to Howard—"

I shake my head. "Aren't you the one who said the whole point of Fling Week is dating different people and getting to know them?" I pluck Bree on the wrist. "Eva will go on dates with multiple people. It'll all come down to who she clicks with."

"Are you sure?"

"*Yes.*"

"Okay, fine."

As soon as Bree pulls up in front of my house, I notice a large white BMW 7 Series that I've never seen before parked in my driveway.

"Oh, no . . ."

"Whose car is that?" Bree asks.

"I—don't know yet."

I'm trying to keep hope alive that maybe an old friend stopped by—or one of those retro door-to-door salesmen. Possibly a very well-to-do burglar?

"Well, I'm going in with you." Bree parks behind the BMW, and follows me up the walkway leading to my porch. "I want to see who's pushing this whip."

The moment Bree and I step through my front door, my mood plummets.

Bus Pass Ben is standing in the middle of my living room, holding our Fire Stick remote, and wearing a skin-tight two-piece green-and-black spandex set.

I avert my eyes immediately, since I'm not a fan of seeing *anyone* in that much Lycra. "Uh, hey." I keep my eyes firmly planted on the ceiling, because those shorts of his are definitely above the knee.

"Leila!" Ben goes. "So good to meet again."

It is *not* good to see him in my living room, or wearing spandex, and I'm relieved when my mother finally comes down the staircase. But when I see what *she* has on, my stomach churns a little.

"What are you *wearing*?"

Mom swishes past me in the same tacky two-piece spandex set Ben has on. Riley is right behind her with her phone recording. "Okay, Mom, I just need a few seconds of you and Ben heading out. Then I can send my *Dating at Forty: It's Still Fun* episode to the editing stage."

Since Riley didn't even know Ben existed as recently as this morning, I give her the biggest side-eye for supporting this new guy situation so quickly. But she's ten—and easily influenced. Now, my bestie, on the other hand?

Bree gives Mom's outfit the once-over. "O*kay*, Ms. Natasha. The outfit is giving me eighties fitness video vibes, but you wear it well."

Mom does a slow spin for Bree. "Thank you, sweetie."

Then Bree walks over to Ben and legit daps him up. "Matching 'fits with your lady is a bold move, my guy. But shows commitment. I can respect that."

I cannot respect all of Bree's butt-kissing. So I pull on her arm in an attempt to redirect her toward my bedroom.

That's when Mom goes, "Oh, perfect. You girls are going to hang out here for a while? Ben and I were going to head out to the gym and I was hoping you could watch Riley . . ."

I make a big show of checking the time on my cell phone. "I don't know, Mom. Maybe you should make plans to hang out with your *friend* another day. I have a lot of homework and—"

Mom plants a kiss on my forehead. "Nonsense. I haven't heard you mention a homework assignment since before prom."

She makes a sad face toward Ben. "It all goes by so fast . . ."

Bree throws an arm around Riley. "You know we wouldn't let anything happen to the littlest Bean." Bree grabs Mom's wallet off the couch and hands it to her. "But you two love-birds will be back by seven, right? I've planned a huge Last Chance mixer and Leila *has* to be in attendance."

Mom gives Bree her own peck on the forehead. "No worries, my little party planner. We'll only be gone an hour." She shoots me a wink and grabs the doorknob without waiting for my response. Rude.

Then Riley comes up and sticks her mic in my face. "With four guys left holding a rose, and the dance only days away, *which* match will Leila choose?"

That gets Bree going. She's all smiling and wiggling her eyebrows.

But I brush Riley's mic away—even though I'm smiling a little bit, too. I can't help it. Dating again, especially with fine Kai on my roster, still has me boosted. "First of all—it's not four guys. It's two guys and Eva."

I squint my eyes at her, waiting for her to say something slightly homophobic so I can school her. But my little sis puts her hands up and goes, "Love is love. You won't get any judgment from me." Then she looks off, like she's counting in her head. "But you're missing a match. Did you forget about your wild card pick?"

I turn around just in time to see Bree making *don't go there* faces behind my back.

"No . . . it happened," I say, chuckling at my bestie's silliness. "So we might as well address . . ."

I turn back to Riley.

"Remember that goofy guy who stood up and whooped really loudly after my monologue in the school play last year? Tre' Hillman?"

"Yeah, what about him?"

"Well, he's my wild card pick and I'm definitely not going out with him."

"Why not? The way he whooped and cheered, he probably likes you."

"I *mean*, that's what *I* thought . . ."

I cut my eyes at Bree. "No, Riley. He only does stuff to get on my nerves—trust me."

My sister nods her head. "Yeah, like teasing you. He probably likes you."

I spin around and put my mouth up close on Riley's microphone. "Here's a juicy tidbit for your podcast. A guy who *likes* you doesn't tease you, or try to make you feel bad. A guy who genuinely likes you treats you with kindness and respect."

Riley nods slowly this time. "I get it. But it didn't seem like Tre' was being mean. He was cheering you on."

Bree taps Riley's shoulder. "Right? I mean, I don't even date guys, and I sensed a little—"

I snort extra loud this time. "If you two think what Tre' was doing was nice behavior, you *both* have a lot to learn. How do you know the rules of my high school dance anyway, Riley? You're not even in middle school yet."

Riley points to Mom's old iPad, lying on the couch. "I've

been following the #LastChanceDance hashtag since last week. I'm all caught up on the rules, and who likes who. I'll be watching to see how these dates turn out. All the drama will give me lots of content."

I laugh at the nerve of my nosy sister and get ready to head off to my room, when she clears her throat.

"Speaking of content, did you see who Dev matched with?" Riley hands me Mom's iPad, then clicks her camera phone on.

I don't bother looking down at the tablet. Once Dev discovers who I matched with, he'll come running back to our relationship. I doubt Dev makes it on even one date. "Don't care!" I sing, handing Riley back the iPad.

"He matched with that girl Darby that you're always complaining about."

Suddenly, my youthful, carefree heart turns to lead. "What?" I finally pay attention to what's on the screen Riley's showing me.

"Yes! That's it. Give me all the shock and devastation you have, Lei! That shocked face is clickbait material. I'm going to make you the thumbnail pic for my next episode."

Mom's old iPad weighs a thousand pounds in my hands as I come face-to-face with a Pic Stitch. On the left side are Darby's matches. On the right is a picture of Dev. Slapped across the whole thing is the word FATE written in neon green.

I shoot a glance Bree's way. "Did you know about this?"

She awkwardly rubs the back of her neck, which tells me all I need to know.

"Get that camera out of my face, Riley!"

"But, Lei—*content.*"

"Now!" I click on the photo, which immediately takes me to Darby's page. My eyes travel down the sixty-seven likes she's already gotten from the most disloyal senior class on the face of the planet.

I look on the likes list, to see who exactly I need to tell off tomorrow for forgetting that Dev and I were just a thing a *literal week ago*—when I see it. Right there, in the list of names that have betrayed me, is @DevTheGamingGuy.

Seriously?!

I throw Mom's iPad back on the couch and storm off to my bedroom. I can hear Bree and Riley behind me, and I swear if that phone is still in Riley's hand I'm going to—

I stop walking, planning to take my anger out on my baby sister. But when I spin around, Riley's phone is back in her pocket and she looks worried. "Are you okay, Leila?"

A wave of sadness washes over me. I squeeze my eyes shut for a moment, hoping my tears will do me a favor and evaporate before Riley has to witness her sister—who's taken honors classes since middle school—completely fail at love.

"No, Riley. I'm not okay." All those times Dev said that they were nothing—that I had nothing to worry about—that Darby was just some high school gamer groupie? And now he "likes" the fact that Darby thinks they are fated to be together? Wow.

Even Bree is shaking her head.

My eyeballs commit their own act of treason by allowing

two fresh tears to fall on my cheeks. I quickly try to brush them away before Riley sees.

"Is there anything I can do to make you feel better?" Suddenly Riley's not ten anymore. She's that four-year-old who used to hand Mom tissues, without fully understanding what divorce meant and why our mother used to cry all the time.

I'm weirdly jealous that my sister still doesn't fully understand breakups. At Riley's age, boyfriends last the duration of lunch or recess. Elementary breakups go easy on the heart. My little sister has no idea about real, true heartbreak.

"I need to talk to Bree privately for a minute, okay? I promise I'll come out and help you with your podcast in a little bit."

When Riley still looks worried, I force a small smile on my face, until her shoulders finally relax. "Fifteen minutes and I'll be back out? Cool?"

Riley gives me a small nod. "Okay."

Then I pull Bree up the stairs.

"*Seriously?!*" I go, the minute we're safely behind my bedroom door.

Bree's skin has to be sore from all that neck rubbing, "I mean, what is he supposed to do?"

I can already feel my left eyelid twitching from her lack of empathy. "We *just* broke up. You would think he would—"

Bree sighs. "Look, Leila. Dev already told you he wants to be single. What do you want the man to do? Lie to you?"

"Well, no, but—"

Bree puts a hand on my shoulder. "Getting dumped sucks—which is why I refuse to let things get that far in the first place—you already know that. But it happened, so your only real option is to move on, too."

Bree doesn't get it. No one does.

Move on, Leila.

Put a smile on your face.

I still don't want to believe that things are really over between Dev and me. But the proof keeps prying my eyelids open and forcing me to see things for what they really are. Dev and me. We're actually over.

I take a deep breath.

"You know what? Whatever . . . I'll be fine."

That's not the total truth, but I don't have any other choice.

Bree raises an eyebrow. "You sure?" She pauses. "You're still coming to the Last Chance mixer, right?"

"*Bree.* I said I'll be there . . ." I point her toward the stairs.

"Make sure to put some lotion on them knees before you arrive, Lei. This is a *classy* affair," Bree calls from the bottom of my staircase.

After waving Bree's personal brand of shadiness away, I flop back on my bed.

I should use my short break from Riley wisely. Look up a few quotes on love and heartbreak. Watch a few episodes of *Oprah's Lifeclass.*

Instead, I spend the last few minutes of solitude searching online for more kernels of evidence that Dev's officially moved on. My investigation reveals that Dev hasn't just been liking Darby's photos. He's liked two of Halima Abdul's photos, too—his other match.

Typical logical Dev. Knowing him, he probably gave both matches an equal amount of IG likes on purpose.

But why like *anyone's* posts? What message is he trying to send?

I know lurking like this will do nothing but hurt me. But I can't help it. I loved Dev for four years and this is what he does? Our entire relationship suddenly feels like a joke—a cruel prank played on me, the clown who actually believed that what we had was real.

Our prom photo catches my eye. I go over and lean in to get a good look at how closely he's holding me in the picture. His bright smile. The look of pure joy in his eyes.

I thought we were real. But somehow, in just under a week, Dev's online and acting like he's forgotten everything we had—like he forgot about us.

Well, two can play that game. I'm going to that Last Chance mixer tonight. It's time to set up my first date.

8

AT JUST PAST seven, I arrive at Party HQ for the Last Chance Dance mixer, wearing a tie-dyed midriff top, green silk overalls, and a pair of high-top Converse. Nervous energy fills me up. In a second, I'm going to be face-to-face with all three of my matches. My heart squeezes a little in my chest when I realize that going to the mixer will mean I'll have to see Dev with his matches, too—including Darby.

The place is already busy. I spot Kayla, Chelsea, Mason, Tre', Halima, and Ivy. Ashli and Chad even show up just to kick it. Then I catch sight of Darby, already flirting with everyone in sight. It's so full of people that it's hard to tell who's talking or who's just focused on games. But I'm kind of glad Darby's not all over Dev yet. Whatever happens, I can't worry about it now. I just have to focus on getting my first date locked.

Bree is running around scooting people away from tables and shuffling them over to the bowling alley lanes or upstairs to the arcade area. Tre' seems to be helping, though he's laughing his head off and joking around as he gets more kids over to bowling.

It doesn't look like Eva or Kai have arrived yet. So when Mason taps me on the shoulder and asks, with a hint of hope in his eye, if I want to get in on a game of laser tag with a few other seniors, I follow after him into the laser tag room.

As we put our little vests on, I wonder if sparks will fly with Mason, or if anything will happen. Do I want it to? Before I can think it all through, we go in and the game starts.

Chasing Mason, Halima, and Kayla around the darkened room, being guided only by squeals and flickering fluorescent lights, is pretty fun. But it doesn't really do anything to help bring Mason and me closer together.

Besides "Watch out" and "Duck!", we don't exchange any actual conversation with each other. At least nothing that would help me understand him as a person a little more.

So fifteen minutes later, I'm back in the Party HQ common area, a little out of breath and looking around for my other two matches.

Feeling a little sweaty from all that laser tagging, I pull out my cell phone to check my reflection just in case I need to reapply my makeup.

That's when I see Eva. Sitting alone, at a tall, round table in the eating area. Reading a book, like the crash of bowling pins, loud laughter, and arcade game bells aren't all around her. Just lost in her own little world.

She looks amazing. At first glance, a person could be easily intimidated by Eva Martin. She's a tall girl, with flawless ebony skin and a thick head of healthy curls that bounce back when she pulls on them to show her actual length. Her honey-blond curls frame her face, so full of volume that her hair looks like a regal golden crown resting on her head.

But while Eva takes on a queen-like aura, even sitting atop a basic restaurant stool, she has never treated anyone like they were beneath her. If anything, Eva's always been the type of person to go out of her way to treat each person she meets like they are something special. A few months ago, I helped Eva with, like, a paragraph of her English assignment, and she sent me a handwritten thank-you note. Like, who does that? Genuinely nice people like Eva, I guess.

I skip my trip to the bathroom to freshen up and head her way.

"You brought a book to the mixer?" I ask, taking a seat on the stool next to her.

Eva holds her place in her book with her finger and uses her other hand to cup over her ear.

I figure, since she didn't hear me the first time, I can just switch my question up. I mean, I'm looking right at the book in her hand. I can come up with something better than that.

I ask, "Why aren't you playing laser tag or bowling?" I cringe internally—that's the best I could do?

Eva closes her book for good this time. Her lips move a bit, but I can't hear anything she's saying over the loud music.

"What?" I try to raise my voice over the loud music.

"I *said*, I'm . . . committee . . . gift . . ." she yells.

"What?!"

Eva raises a finger, and then grabs her phone. She fast-types something and then a second later my phone vibrates in my pocket.

Her text says: I'm on the Senior Gift Committee, and this year we're donating a ton of new books to the school library. We're still narrowing down our top twenty-five choices. I have to read them all to choose!

I nod and give her a thumbs-up.

I turn her book over to view the cover. "Do you like this one so far?" I yell.

A confused look crosses Eva's face. So I repeat myself again over the loudness of the room. And again.

Eva taps the phone again, so I reach for it and type in the message. Do you like this one so far?

Eva smiles and nods—but then grabs her soda glass and mimes getting another one, waving as she heads for the snack station. Just when a sick feeling pools in my belly over the thought that I'm failing at getting to know two out of my three amazing matches, a pair of strong arms wrap themselves around me. When I turn to see who has me in a bear hug, it's Kai.

"Let's take a selfie together," he says into my ear. And

sure, I smile for the camera, and pose with the best of them. But I can't help remembering what Bree said about Kai.

Before I can stop myself, I'm asking, "Is that all you do—take selfies all day?"

Kai slips his phone into his back pocket and makes a face. "I get it. You think I'm one of those selfie kings, who can't stop staring at his reflection through his camera phone, huh?"

"Well, I didn't say all that—"

Kai pulls me to a quieter corner. "See, Leila. What some people might view as a random selfie, I look at as big business. Think about it. Everyone just spent months on college applications. Do you know how many colleges I applied for?"

I shrug while Kai makes an *O* with his hand. "None," he goes. "I'm not going to college."

I try my best not get all judgmental about his lack of higher learning aspirations, but I have to ask, "*Sooo*, just headed straight to work, huh? No community college or anything?"

Kai breaks things down for me. "See, Leila. I plan to go to New York to pursue modeling after high school. And while some people like to pretend that modeling is all superficial and unimportant, I'd like to refer them back to every major brand advertisement. *Models* help sell the jeans we wear. *Models* help us pick out the right hair products. *Models* make popular travel spots hot."

Kai shrugs. "One day, I'm going to be signed by one of the top modeling agencies—I work too hard to fail."

For the first time, I truly get where Kai is coming from. He *has* worked really consistently on his social media page. It's all specially curated, with daily themes and a whole color-coordinated aesthetic. No other senior's page looks that well thought out and put together. And he *never* steals random Drake lyrics to use for captions. I can always tell that Kai comes up with his quotes himself, even if they are a little cheesy. He puts the effort in.

Listening to Kai talk about his goals and how committed he is to his modeling career, I can tell he's not just *Kai and them abs*—and I'm here for that.

But as Kai keeps talking, my gaze drifts behind him. And hidden in the sea of arcade games, I see Dev straddling a red motorcycle arcade game, staring intently at the screen as he tries to keep his bike in the lane. And there's Darby, sitting behind him, with her arms wrapped around his waist. She's whispering something in Dev's ear, but I can't tell if his lips are moving because he's responding to her, or if he's talking himself through the game. Either way, tears spring to my eyes.

Even though Kai's in the middle of talking to me, I seriously consider heading for one of the side exits. The *nerve* of Dev to be so blatant about everything.

My house is only a block from the Towne Center, and it's still light out. I'll just text Bree later, apologizing for not staying the entire time.

But then I think about what Bree said in my bedroom

earlier. Dev's single now. And he's just doing what a single person does.

I shake my head at all the giggling Darby's doing in my ex's ear. You know what? It's time that I start acting like a single person, too.

Kai steps closer and flashes me his killer smile. "So, about our date . . . I was thinking—"

I turn back to Kai to catch the key details of his date plans. Saturday. National Harbor. BYO mat and water bottle.

"So what's up, Leila? Are you ready to say yes to our date?"

I refrain from shouting *OMG YES* loud enough for Dev to hear over the roar of his digital motorcycle. Instead, I flash Kai a casual smile—letting him know he may be cute and all, but I'm *not* one of his little Instagram groupies.

"I can't wait."

AT SCHOOL THE next day, Last Chance Dance is on everyone's minds and tongues. We have a sub in English 12. Our teacher, Ms. Amidon, left us with an assignment to read the next four chapters of *Their Eyes Were Watching God* by Zora Neale Hurston. But so far, everyone's *eyes* are watching the hallway. Every time a random senior walks by and spots the sub, they slip in for a minute to discuss their matches. Especially when they see Ms. Reeves sitting behind the teacher's desk. Everyone knows if *Ms. Reeves* is the sub, she'll be chill about extra kids coming in to hang out, as long as things don't get loud enough for one of the assistant principals to pop their head in and wonder what's going on.

Anyway, Bree and Tre' slip into the room and join Ashli,

Kai, and me, already sitting in a small group, discussing how Kai plans to woo me on our date.

I hold my hand out so Bree can bless me with some of her chips. Then I scooch over so she can squeeze in next to me.

"Okay, so *boom*," Kai says. "The question is, should I pick Leila up for our date, or should we meet at the Harbor?"

Kai puts a hand on his chest. "Personally, I think a guy should always pick a girl up on a first date. And Ashli agrees with me. But your girl Leila over here feels like that's old-school."

I pop another chip in my mouth. "I mean, it's not like I go on a first date every day. Sometimes Dev used to pick me up, and sometimes we met up places. It's not that serious to me." I reach my hand back into Bree's chip bag. "My *mom* worries about stuff like getting picked up on the first date. I thought those rules were for the thirty and over crowd."

Everybody laughs except Tre'.

When he turns in my direction, both of his eyebrows are raised. "Oh, *really*? I thought you weren't going on any Last Chance Dance dates, Leila?"

I fold my arms across my chest defiantly. "I never said I wasn't going on any dates—I'm just not going on any dates with *you*."

I smirk while Tre' basically chooses drama, by making huffing noises and looking like I just took a bat to his knees. "Oh, for real, Leila? You're just going to do me like that?"

"Just like that," I answer, popping another chip in my mouth.

Tre' slowly shakes his head, like I've actually done him wrong or something. "You stay hurting people's feelings, bruh. Like, for real."

Tre' taps Kai's shoulder and goes, "I matched with Leila, too, but she's not trying to go out with me." He sniffs. "I guess you gotta have six-pack abs and an IG following to go out with Leila Bean these days." He gives me a look like he's never met someone so shallow.

"Mason doesn't have a six-pack and I'm going out with him, too, later this week." Not that I have any solid plans locked down with our high school's official social justice warrior yet, but the intention is definitely there.

Tre' looks even more hurt now. "Really, Leila? So you're going out with everyone else, except me? That's messed up."

I *know* Tre's not about to play the victim card. Nuh-uh. *Not* on my watch.

"And *why* won't I go out with you?" I rub the little keloid on my finger.

"I have no idea, Five. You act like you can't stand me sometimes, when all I've done is work extra hard to keep you laughing all these years. Don't you like my jokes?"

Tre' flashes this cheesy grin that briefly shows off his dimple—which might have been sort of cute if he wasn't such an overall irritating person.

Bree cups her hand over her mouth like a bullhorn and goes, "Obviously not!" then she and Ashli high-five and laugh it up.

Ms. Reeves gives us a quick "All right, settle down, now."

"I absolutely do *not* like your jokes," I say in a lower tone. I try to reach my hand in Bree's bag again, but she slaps my hand away this time. "But that isn't even the reason why I won't go out with you."

"What did I do?" Tre's dimple disappears as his expression changes to serious.

I swear, the memory of Tre's treachery almost comes tumbling out of my mouth. But with multiple pairs of eyes on me, including Kai's, just waiting for me to reveal my private wounds—I hesitate.

"The fact that you don't even remember means you're not even sorry about what you did. And that is even more reason to not go out with you."

Then I change the subject before anyone else can chime in.

After school, Bree and I head out to Virginia to search for date outfits at undeniably the best mall in the entire DMV—Tyson's Corner Galleria.

On the way, Bree goes, "Leila, can I tell you something?"

I'm laid back with my feet kicked up on her dash and my eyes closed. "What's up?"

Bree knocks my feet off her dashboard. "I mean, I feel bad about your broken heart and all, but, uh, can't say I'm all that mad that you finally have a chance to do some stuff on your own."

I fold my arms across my chest. "What do you mean, finally? I've always had my own interests."

Bree throws me an amused look. "Oh yeah? Like what? As far as I know, you and Dev always did things *together.*"

I sit there and think for a while. And when I can't think of much, I suck my teeth and point at the road. "You need to focus on your *driving* activities. Your car is almost over the double yellow line." I give her my best *I want to live to see the graduation stage* face.

While Bree drives, I lean my seat back further and scroll Instagram. Since making the very wise decision to block both Dev and Darby, my timeline is now free of surprise mood-ruining pics. Instead, my timeline is full of new pics from Eva's latest book haul, along with a notification that Mason has gone live to talk about racial profiling in the classroom.

With our date taking place in less than forty-eight hours, I head over to Kai's page, crossing my fingers that he's posted something worthy of a heart-eyes emoji.

He doesn't disappoint. I like a shirtless photo of Kai playing volleyball, over a caption that reads "When it comes to social justice, you can't volley from one side to the other. You have to stand on the right side of justice."

Not quite the professional live Mason has going on his page, but . . . where's the lie? I decide not to be critical about the delivery of a good point, and focus more on the message. And Kai's message—and the way his muscles are speckled with sand—is good enough for me.

Then I scroll back a little further into his old posts from sophomore and junior year. I'm busy ogling his body and trying not to accidentally like something from two years ago when Bree waves one of her hands over my phone screen.

"Stop drooling over ab pics!"

I turn my phone over so she can't see my screen anymore. "How do you know what I'm looking at if you're watching the road?"

With her eyes plastered to the highway, Bree smiles. "I could feel thirsty energy coming from your side of the car."

We giggle as I swat at her. Then we ride in silence for a few minutes.

As we get closer to the National Harbor exit, Bree decides to get all in my business about my date with Kai.

"He's taking you to a yoga meetup? At a spot he goes to every weekend, anyway?"

"It's just a meetup to see if we like each other," I tell her. "What do you want him to do? Fly me out to the Bahamas?"

Bree turns the wheel. "I was just expecting him to get as creative with y'all's date as he does with his corny Instagram captions—that's all. No shade."

I put the passenger side sunshade down and turn it in Bree's direction to block out her judgment. Despite Bree's opinion, *I* haven't forgotten the ultimate goal here. As long as the entire senior class sees Kai's bare chest glistening in the sun with *my* smiling face in the background, I'm happy. And if Dev happens to see it too? Bonus points.

Bree chuckles from behind my sunshade. "I think I might show up just to laugh at you trying to be a fake yogi."

Tucking my sunshade back up, I make a face. "How am I a fake yogi?"

"Kai is ab blasting and doing P90X all over his Instagram page. You once Cash Apped me two dollars to get you a soda from the fridge. Y'all are not the same." Bree breaks out laughing again.

I pretend to look hurt at first. But I can't help laughing either. To be honest, I would've paid her five dollars to get me that soda. I hate getting off the couch—especially in the middle of a good show. "That was the old me," I try to explain.

"That was like a week ago!"

We break out laughing again.

"Fine. I don't care about yoga." I stare out the window for a minute. "Hopefully, he'll take me to lunch after."

"More like breakfast." Bree points out the window. In the distance is the big white Ferris wheel and all the shops that make up the National Harbor. A big sign that can be seen from the highway announces yoga Saturdays.

"It says on the Harbor's website that your yoga session starts at 6 a.m."

The horrified look on my face makes Bree scream with laughter. "You haven't gotten up that early since our eighth grade trip to Gettysburg."

"And I almost missed the bus *then*."

Panic jolts through my body. Being awake before 10 a.m. on a weekend is *not* on my bucket list. I try to push all the negative *Kai and those abs may not be worth all this* vibes out of my head, while Bree turns off at the exit.

Once Bree finally finds a parking spot, we walk together

into the mall. "Time to pick out something cute," Bree says, checking the tag on a Nike sweatsuit. "Six hundred dollars?! For just the jacket? It doesn't even come with the *pants*?" She cups her hands over her mouth. "What's up with these prices?"

A sales assistant behind a fancy perfume counter frowns at Bree while I yank her arm. "You know Bloomingdales is for people with deep pockets. This is just the shortcut to the regular stores."

We don't dare turn our heads to the left, where the Gucci section sits, or to the right, where all the Louis Vuitton luggage is on full display, as we quickly leave. While we make our way across the mall, I ask Bree where she's taking Eva on their date.

Bree rubs her hands together. "I haven't figured that out yet, but I *am* taking Chanel to see the new Marvel movie."

I try to hide my jealousy. A movie date—with a comfy chair that leans back and buttered popcorn—sounds so much better than twisting my body up like a pretzel under the hot sun. But things always work out the way they should. If my date was in a dark theater, I wouldn't be able to get a shot of Kai and those abs for my Insta story.

We finally make it to lululemon, the go-to place for athleisure, and I immediately eye a hot yellow two-piece outfit. I hold it up to my body and strike a pose for Bree.

"Too bright," she says.

"Bold colors will make sure Kai's only looking at me," I tell her.

"Yeah, but it's *neon* yellow. You'll literally be competing with the sun." Bree takes the outfit out of my hands and hangs it back up. "Do you want to blind the boy or not?"

"Fine." I grab an all-white outfit. "Cute?"

"The minute you fall into the dirt, you'll have a brown stain on your butt."

I hold up a blue outfit.

"I don't know, the color blue has always given me . . . *sad* vibes?"

I blow out a breath, starting to regret bumming a ride from Bree in the first place. "Fine, *you* pick something."

Bree carefully looks around the store. She picks up a light green, army fatigue bra-top-and-leggings set. "Sexy enough for a date, tough enough to kick his butt if he gets handsy."

I take the outfit out of Bree's hands and hold it up to myself in the tall mirror on the wall. "It's perfect," I whisper.

Imagining myself in this cute outfit reassures me that, despite the early hours, and despite the potential rigorous workout session, my date with Kai is going to look spectacular on Instagram.

And if Dev just happens to notice? Bonus points for me.

10

SATURDAY MORNING, IT'S still dark out when my phone starts buzzing and beeping me awake. I pick my phone up and check the time. "Four-thirty a.m." I groan, even though I'm the one who set my alarm this early in the first place.

My normal shower usually takes no time. But today, I'm going to be on full display for Kai and the entire National Harbor. So I carefully shave my legs, shower, and then moisturize my entire body—using a triple-threat layer of my favorite honey rose–scented bodywash, shea butter, and spray.

"It's all about the subtle layers, Leila," my mom always says. "You never want to *kablam* people as soon as they come near you. You want just a hint of your essence to linger until they want more."

With my fluffy white towel still wrapped around me, I

begin my makeup routine. It's an art form in contouring, light tricks, and feathered hand strokes, all to make it look like I'm stepping out of the house effortlessly fresh-faced, when actually, I leaned over the sink studying my face and making slight adjustments for at least forty-five minutes.

Finally, I step into my leggings and slip my bra top over my head. Checking out my reflection in the mirror, I admire my golden-brown skin, glowing back at me.

I'm taking an old toothbrush to my edges when Kai texts me that he's out front. Pressing down on my temple, I swoop tiny tufts of hair over and around my index finger, until I have the perfect Saweetie baby hair wave.

Then I grab up my keys, water bottle, and the last-minute gym mat purchase that matches my yoga outfit.

When I come outside, Kai gets out of his red Jeep and comes around to open the passenger side door for me.

"Okay, Leila. I see you," he remarks as I step inside the car. I smile to let him know that I appreciate the compliment, but I don't give him one back—I'll make him work for one.

Kai backs out of my driveway, and we head up the highway, coasting to his The Weeknd playlist. The vibe is there, for sure. Kai smells clean—like fruit—which is a nice switch up from the spicy scent of Dev's cologne. I close my eyes and take a swig from my water bottle as the sun rises just outside the car's windshield.

I sneak glances at Kai as he bobs his head to the music, really noticing for the first time that it's not just about those abs. His side profile is doing things. His thick curls bounce to the beat as he bobs his head to the music, while his perfectly squared jaw silently mouths the lyrics.

Dang, he looks good. Almost *too* good. Suddenly, I look down at my shea-buttered legs and try not to feel basic.

We turn into the Harbor with five minutes to park before the yoga session begins. When we get down to the outdoor atrium, a large group of athletic people are spread out on what I'm disappointed to find out is fake grass. Kai takes my mat from my hands and unrolls it. Then he sets up next to me as the yoga instructor starts. I don't miss a few grown women, and a couple of grown men, staring at Kai's muscles as he removes his shirt.

"Everyone's literally staring," I tell him, half in awe that he has this effect on so many people.

Kai tosses his shirt on the ground. "Staring at how good *you* look today?" Kai looks me up and down, smiling. "Yeah, I noticed . . ."

After I calm the implosion of my internal butterflies, I try my best to pay attention to the instructor's moves to avoid embarrassing myself in front of Kai out here. Thankfully, things start off pretty easy. I quickly master the chair, garland, and dolphin poses. At the point where I'm basically ready to go pro and prove Bree and all my other haters wrong, the yoga instructor leads us into firefly pose.

This new position is *nothing* like the beginners' poses. My arms have to support my entire body while my legs and feet are somewhere suspended over my shoulders. After one sad attempt, I'm laid out on my butt.

Thank goodness Kai is so focused on his own moves that he barely notices me struggling beside him. But the yogi one row up notices me dusting myself off to try again—and again. And the woman behind me can probably tell that my firefly is looking more like house fly. Once the guy beside me drags his mat a few feet in the opposite direction of me and my flailing arms, I give up and reach for my water bottle.

Kai—who has been slipping in and out of poses like a fish gliding through water—spots me slumped over in the fake grass, wipes his sweaty face with his T-shirt, and comes over.

"You all right, Bean?"

If the sun wasn't actively sizzling my shoulders, I'd swear Kai's use of my last name was the reason for this scorching heat. While I struggle to put together a simple string of words, Kai positions himself behind me.

"Try it like this . . ." Kai's chiseled arms grab me up as he positions my legs over my shoulders. Our close proximity is exciting. But also? This mess hurts.

I swallow a groan, and try not to imagine my muscles and tendons ripping in two. Because if I can look past the pain, maybe I can snap a photo of our bodies intertwined for my Insta stories . . .

Sneaking my phone from my waistband, I wait for the perfect shot.

While Kai is trying to pose me, I'm working on getting the right angles—the perfect pose that says *hot and happy*. But while I'm stretching and twisting my body like a contortionist, my calf muscle suddenly clenches. And oh-em-*gee*. "Ahhh, I think—I think, it feels like my leg muscle is— *arrgghhh—*"

Too much exercise after a lifetime membership of lounging on the couch sends my body into full-on protest mode. My phone drops to the ground as I feel a charley horse coming on. I try to squeeze my calf muscle, but the painful cramp spreads.

Kai immediately helps my leg back down and begins massaging my calf muscle through my leggings. "My bad, Leila," he says. "I was just trying to help."

I nod forgiveness through the intense pain. When the pain finally subsides, I realize that Kai's hands wrapped around my leg may be the sexiest part of our date so far. And the perfect optics for my Insta story. I snap a quick photo and add the hashtag #SomeoneCallTheMedic before uploading it to my stories.

"Hey, I don't know if my leg is going to make it to the end of this session," I whisper to Kai. "Do you mind if we slip out early and grab something to eat?"

Just thinking about all the delicious brunch options at the Harbor makes me wonder why we didn't just get a bite to eat together in the first place. Because really, what can go wrong when food is involved?

As the instructor calls out some headstand move, Kai shrugs and says, "I mean, we *can.*" He looks longingly at all the other yogis transitioning into the headstand. But he scoops up his mat and helps me slide into my sandals anyway.

As Kai walks and I hobble over a cluster of *very* annoyed yoga participants, I get excited about our date again. The heat and hell-poses are finally behind me, and the Redstone Grill is just a few more hobbles away.

When the hostess seats us in a booth, I immediately order pancakes, scrambled eggs, a hash brown, and bacon. Kai doesn't order anything. When I raise my eyebrows, he shrugs and goes, "I like to keep my body tight."

Welp. Can't argue with that. Kai's shirt is back on, but the outline of his abs still peeks through the damp fabric.

"Yeah, I pretty much cut meat out of my diet. Bread too. And sugar. And anything processed—ugh, processed foods are the devil."

"Oh, that's—nice," I say. And I mean it. Kai can do whatever he feels is best for his body. It's not going to stop me from taste-testing as many of these menu options as I can, though.

As Kai continues explaining his eating habits, I lean my head back and silently hope the tightness I'm starting to feel on my shoulders isn't the start of sunburn.

"Yeah, everyone thinks protein bars are the trick to gains, but I've come up with an organic homemade protein mix that I use on Mondays and Wednesdays. That's lift day. Cardio days, I like to—"

I tune Kai out and reposition my shoulders until they are in the direct path of the air conditioning system.

"You know, if you cut out the hash brown, and maybe the bacon, and maybe switched up to just egg whites," Kai says as the waiter sets my plate down, "and maybe lost the pancakes, it would help you build more muscle."

"I think everything on my plate is *exactly* where it should be," I tell him, grabbing the maple syrup.

Kai's eyes widen like I've just picked up a deadly weapon. "That's . . . a *lot* of sugar. Is it at least fat-free?"

"Nope!" I create a maple syrup waterfall over my entire stack of pancakes.

Suddenly, I miss Dev and our non-food-related conversations. Plus, when we went out for breakfast, he always saved me an extra piece of bacon from his plate.

Quickly, while Kai's digging around his gym bag, I check Instagram to see if Dev's viewed my story yet. So far he hasn't.

When I look back up, Kai is pulling a ziplock bag out of his bag.

"Umm, what's going on?" Seriously. I'm legit confused.

Kai holds up the ziplock bag, so I can get a clear view of the contents inside. "The breakfast of champs!" he says, like it's not completely ridiculous to bring a baggie full of celery to a restaurant.

And you know? I wasn't even going to say anything. His body, his choice—and if he wants to micro-nibble raw veggies from a baggie all out in the open at this restaurant? Whatever.

But, while I'm working my way through my hash brown, Kai leans over, grabs my knife, and *scooches* my bacon to the edge of my plate.

"That's . . . a *lot* of cholesterol," he says, in this really icky, mansplain-y voice. "Your heart will thank me later."

"Ex*cuse* me?" After I kindly swallowed back a comment about him nibbling on one end of that celery like a woodchuck?

"Seriously, Leila. It's hard for me to even look at that greasy killer on your plate."

Now annoyed and ready for this date to be over, I shoot him a warning look before grabbing for both slices of bacon.

"I'm not getting rid of bacon. Ever," I tell Kai as he stares in horror at both slices making their way into my mouth.

"But, Leila. It's the only way reach your highest fit potential."

"I'm *fine* with my body as is, Kai," I warn him, now in between healthy bites of pancake. One more hint about dieting and Kai and them abs will be driving me and my to-go bag back home.

A pang of sadness hits me as Kai excuses himself to grab more napkins from the bar. Kai is fine as all get-out, but he's *not* my perfect match. Everything with Kai comes with an IG filter. Perfect-looking abs. Blemish-free yoga poses. Evenly cut celery stalks, curated especially for the Fitstagram crowd.

I don't want to worry about being perfect for anyone. I just want to be *me*.

Cross Kai off the list, I text Bree under the table.

Cross Chanel off the list, too, Bree texts back.

What did Chanel do?

She kept talking over the movie. Asking me a bunch of questions. Telling me about what she ate for dinner last night during important scenes in the movie. Like, girl . . .

LMAOOOOOOOO

I take it Kai's abs couldn't save him this time, Bree texts. That's okay. At least you still have three more matches.

I make a face at my phone screen. Correction. Two more matches. You know goodness well I'm not going anywhere with that clown Tre'.

I'M SITTING ON the edge of my bed, nursing my sun-
burned shoulders with a ziplock bag full of ice, when Bree
comes walking into my bedroom.

"Here, try this," she says, handing me a bottle of aloe
vera. "Mom says ice is only going to make things worse."

"But the ice makes my shoulders feel better."

"Leila . . . my mom's a nurse. Can we listen to the expert,
please?"

I put the bag of ice on my bedroom floor. "Fine."

Bree looks around my room. "Now, do you have the bowl
of popcorn I requested?"

I point to a large plastic bowl behind me.

"Perfect." Bree jumps into my bed and grabs the bowl
while I slather aloe vera gel all over my shoulders. "Now,

who gets to spill the bad date details first?"

"I nominate Bree!" Riley yells from the hallway.

"Eavesdropping is bad manners, Riley!"

"Well, if you would let me in, we could all prevent rude behaviors from happening."

Bree gets up and opens my bedroom door. Of course, Riley falls right in.

"Hold up your right hand."

Riley complies.

"Repeat after me. I, Riley *Eloise* Bean, solemnly swear . . ."

My sister repeats after Bree.

". . . that if Leila and Bree let me in, I will sit quietly in the corner, cut off all recording devices, and never breathe a word of anything I hear."

I shake my head as Riley's eyes light up.

"Think carefully, Riley . . . because once you swear . . . there's no taking it back."

And I have to give it to her. Riley says, "Cross my heart" so seriously that even I believe her.

I point her to a corner of my room. "While you're over there, be a dear and fold up those clothes for me."

When Riley starts to complain, I raise both eyebrows. "Do you want to be in here or not?"

Riley grabs a rumpled shirt and takes a seat in the corner.

I turn back to Bree. "You don't get to go first. You already told me what happened between you and Chanel—"

"Yeah, but I didn't tell you about the weird date I had with Ivy today."

My mouth drops. "You went on your *second* date already?"

Bree shrugs. "I went on the second date to try to forget the first one. Except this one was bad, too. But you go first."

"Fine." I laugh. "Are you ready?"

Bree nods, so I describe my date with Kai. The hot sun. My cramped leg muscle. The bacon shade. My burned shoulders.

By the time I'm done, tears of laughter are streaming down Bree's cheeks. "Leila? You know you're dramatic, right?"

I throw a piece of popcorn at her arm. "*Am* I, Bree?!"

I yank the neckline of my T-shirt to the side, exposing my crispy shoulders—which only makes Bree laugh harder.

I toss more popcorn in my mouth. "Hurry up and tell me about this date with Ivy. I can't *wait* to laugh at your pain."

Bree sits up straighter on the bed. "Okay, *boom*. This is what happened . . ."

She gets up from my bed and takes a seat at my desk. "So we're having lunch at Uno's, right? Nothing major. Just a chill spot to rekindle things."

Bree begins reenacting the date—which is basically Bree telling a bunch of jokes and Ivy laughing. "Now, an hour in, I'm really feeling Ivy." Bree leans forward and makes an eerie face like she's telling a ghost story. "Then everything changes . . ."

At this point, I'm all in. I lean forward. "Hurry up."

Bree shakes her head. "I notice Ivy's checking her phone from time to time. At first, I didn't think anything of it.

Because, you know, everyone checks their phone. So no big deal, right?"

"Personally, I don't think phones should be out during dates, but . . ."

Bree and I snap our heads over to the corner.

"Do you want to be kicked out?" I ask Riley.

My sister runs her hand down the length of a pair of my jeans, before folding them in half. "I'm not wrong, Leila. Phones are distracting."

"No, you're not wrong. I would be mad if my date paid more attention to their phone than me. But you are just a listener—not a participator. No more comments, got it?"

Riley presses her lips together tight and grabs my favorite denim vest.

I turn back to my bestie. "And you—get to the juicy stuff, please."

"Okay, okay. So, at one forty-five Ivy starts rushing to end the date. I ask her if everything's okay. I'm wondering if I have mozzarella breath—a little basil stuck in my teeth—something, right?"

"Right."

Bree shakes her head. "Ivy says everything's fine. She even offers to pay the bill—which I would've gone halfsies on, but since she *offered*—"

I scrunch up my face. "You let her pay the entire bill? That's kind of cheap, Bree."

I think I hear someone whisper, "I agree with Leila." But since Riley's not supposed to be talking over there, I know that whispering didn't come from her. So I pretend it didn't happen.

Bree, on the other hand, waves away my comment. "That's not the important detail, here, Leila—just *listen*."

Bree stands up. "At exactly two p.m., Ivy slips the receipt into her purse, snatches my hand, and pulls me out the door . . ." Bree's eyes start darting around like she's imagining the entire scene in front of her.

"Since Ivy offered to pay the bill, I figure I'm in for another big surprise. Maybe some balloons tied to my car. Maybe a singing telegram—something."

"Okay, okay. *What* was outside?" I ask, loving the suspense.

Bree snorts. "Oh, it was a surprise all right. We're standing out there on the sidewalk no more than two or three seconds when this little gray car comes driving by, really slowly."

I clutch my heart. "Oh my god. You were involved in a drive-by."

Bree sucks her teeth. "What did I tell you about the dramatics?"

"Sorry—sorry."

"So the car window slowly rolls down, and . . . Angelina Russo is behind the wheel."

I'm back to clutching my heart. "Ivy's ex-girlfriend?!" I shriek.

I start checking Bree's face for signs of violence. "Did she hit you?"

Bree moves my hand away. "No, she didn't *hit* me . . . She just kind of stared at Ivy and me standing there."

Now I'm confused. "Why was she even there?"

"Get this. I think Ivy *told* her to come. Before I could ask what was going on, Ivy pulls me close, wraps me up in this extra-tight bear hug. Then she turns to Angelina and goes, 'I told you I was moving on.'"

My face scrunches up. "That's . . . *super* extra." As soon as the words leave my lips, I silently pray Bree doesn't call me out for being extra with the Kai photos all over my Insta stories earlier.

Bree whacks my arm. "Right?"

I flop back on my bed and let out a loud groan. "Let's just give up, Bree. Dating sucks!"

Bree comes over and sits next to me on the bed. "You can't give up because of one lousy date, Leila."

"But you just went on *two* lousy dates. Why should I suffer through a second date, when they're all bad?!"

Bree scoots closer to me on the edge of my bed. "Your first date with Dev didn't suck."

"It sucked when he dumped me!"

Bree gets quiet for a minute. "True. But you had four great years before that." Bree pats my leg. "And if you had one great first date, you'll have others, too."

My phone buzzes, and when I look down at the screen, it's Mason, asking if I'm ready for our first date.

My fingers won't allow me to text him back without a sprinkle of friend-support. "Do you promise, Bree?"

Still staring at Mason's text, I don't have to look at my bestie to tell she's smiling. I hear it in her voice when she goes, "Yeah, Lei, I promise."

Welp, here we go—*again.*

Monday after school works for me, I text Mason.

Riley, who has forgotten the rules again, comes over and gives me a hug. "I promise, too, Leila. And when you have that great first date, can you promise *me* you'll come on my podcast and chat with me about it?"

I give my sister the side-eye at first. But when I notice three stacks of neatly folded clothes in the corner, my heart softens. "Sure, Riley. And, uh, if you can manage folding *one* more stack of clothes, I'll even describe my next kiss."

Riley quickly grabs another shirt and gets to work.

12

AFTER FIRST PERIOD on Monday, all the seniors pour onto the football field, wearing white T-shirts with a snarling bulldog on the front. Ms. Mahoney, along with two guidance counselors, stands directing students to the bleachers.

"Let's go, seniors! We want to get this photo done in enough time to get you back to second period."

I could've told Ms. Mahoney before the booing even starts that no one is planning to make it back in time to finish second period inside a classroom. All around me, students are huddled up in clusters, talking, laughing, and waiting for friends to arrive before they start walking over to the bleachers. It's a sunny, relaxing seventy-six degrees out, the perfect weather to sunbathe—not sit inside some stuffy class-room, eating snacks and waiting for the bell to ring. I spot

Bree leaned up against the gray chain-link fence, talking to Ashli and Chad. Eva walks past me with a guy I've legit never seen before.

"That guy with Eva is a senior?" I ask, walking over to Bree and friends. The entire group turns to check out who I'm talking about.

"Yeah, that's Julius," Ashli goes. "You never had a class with him?"

"No. He's been here the *entire* four years?"

Chad gives me the stuck face. "Yeah, Leila. I had art with him freshman year."

I'm still trying to dig up a random memory of this kid passing me in the hall, appearing in a school play, lending me a pencil—*something*, when Ms. Mahoney's voice comes through the bullhorn.

"Let's go, seniors. We don't have all day with the photographer."

Bree looks out across the football field. "I mean, technically we do? Didn't they just pick some random kid from the photography club to shoot the picture?"

But we start moving toward the bleachers anyway. Ashli and Chad spot some other friends and quickly disappear into the crowd. Then Ivy yells Bree's name and beckons for her to join her near the back.

Bree starts patting her braids down and smoothing her eyebrows, but I shake my head.

I raise my eyebrow at my bestie. "Didn't you just spend all day Saturday complaining about her?"

I was planning to sit front and center, to make it easier to find me in the photo later on, but Bree's eyes are now glued to the top bleacher, where Ivy's sitting with her close-cropped haircut and thick hipster eyeglasses.

"Yeah, but then she sent me a cute little apology meme, and . . ." With a guilty look on her face, Bree goes, "So, uh . . . I'm not trying to ditch you or anything—"

I cut her off before she finish the rest of her blasphemous statement "Now, Bree . . . how is that going to look? The tightest besties at Baldwin not even sitting together for the senior class photo?"

But Bree clearly doesn't care about the optics. "There's, like, a billion seniors out here. We're all going to be tiny dots in the photo, anyway." She stares back up at Ivy. "Come on, Leila. I took out a full-page ad in the back of the yearbook dedicated to our friendship."

I raise an eyebrow. "I'm a little offended that you're treating our senior class photo as your own personal kickback, Bree."

"Smiling for the photo is going to take ten seconds, tops. I can use the rest of the time to flirt." Then Bree takes off up the bleachers, leaving me in the dust.

Wow.

Annoyed, I take a seat on the bottom bleacher, near the middle—leaving an empty spot next to me, just in case Bree comes to her senses and comes back over.

"Oh *good*, you saved me a spot." Tre' slides into the empty space next to me.

"Don't you have friends you can sit with?" I slide over some, so that our knees *aren't* awkwardly touching.

Tre' shrugs. "I spend all day talking to them in our *Madden* league group chat. I don't need to spend much face time with those scrubs."

He throws an arm around my shoulder—which sparks the beginning of an eyebrow raise from me. "Besides, do I want to go down in history with a bunch of guys I spend all day arguing football stats with?" He plucks a random crumb off my shoulder, which I would think is an act of shade, but he doesn't call attention to it, so I let it go. "Or do I want to make photographic history with the baddest girl at Baldwin?"

I wrinkle my nose. "And then I'll have to look at your face every time I stare at the photo? No thanks, *Trevor*." I gather my things to move but I'm too late. Ms. Mahoney gets on the bullhorn. "All right, seniors. Brighten those smiles!"

I tilt my head slightly and smize for the student photographer. The flash goes off several times, then Ms. Mahoney checks the time, brings the bullhorn back to her mouth, and announces: "Promise you'll keep it down out here, and we can spend the rest of second period out—"

The senior class is cheering before she can get the whole sentence out.

"Don't make me regret this," Ms. Mahoney says. Then she sets her bullhorn in the grass and starts up her own conversation with the guidance counselors.

I look back up at the top bleachers, and Bree's whispering something in Ivy's ear. And since I'm no hater, I decide to stay where I'm seated. Even if it's next to annoying Tre'.

"Ha ha, wait until you see the bunny ears I gave you . . ." Tre' breaks out laughing. But my blood begins to boil.

"So humiliating me is cute now? See, *this* is why . . ."

"*Chill*, Leila." Tre' grabs my hand. "I was just messing with you. *Dang.*"

But I'm still irritated. "And you wonder why I don't fool with you like that . . . It's because you don't know how to act—thinking everything is so dang funny all the time . . ."

"*Okay. I said* I was sorry." Tre' throws his hands up in surrender. "Look, just to show you I'm willing to work harder to honor your feelings . . ."

I toss him a side-eye, because this still feels like Tre's brand of messing with me.

". . . I'm going to zip my lips for the rest of our time out here."

I let out a dramatic sigh of relief.

"I'll keep my mouth shut while you spill the details on your Kai date."

I shake my head immediately. "Nope."

Tre' zips his lips with his fingers.

I smirk at how silly he looks with his lips pressed tight together like that. "I guess we're going to be sitting in silence, then. Your choice."

Tre' turns the key to lock his mouth. Then he stuffs the invisible key in the pocket of his joggers.

I let the silence linger between us for a good sixty seconds. Then boredom sets in.

"Fine. We went to the Harbor for sunrise yoga. I hated it . . ."

"You didn't look like you were that upset in that photo . . ."

I relock Tre's mouth with my own invisible key.

"We took that photo before I got the leg cramp. And sun-burned shoulders. And before Kai started eating celery out of a sandwich bag at the brunch spot."

When Tre' starts laughing, I join in. And for a moment, it genuinely feels like sharing a laugh with a friend.

"I spent all day Saturday un-liking Kai's photos, and you *didn't* end the date using his abs as your own personal xylophone?" Tre' goes, between chuckles.

I shake my head. "Trust me, *far* from it . . ." I side-eye him. "What's up with your matches? Have you been on any of your dates yet?"

Tre' shrugs. "I've actually been out with all my matches already."

"What? You went on three dates in two days?"

"*Noooot* technically," Tre' says. "I reserved a booth at Uno's and asked all three of my matches to show up."

"What?!" I whack Tre' in the leg. "Tre', who do you think you are?"

Tre' huffs. "Look, I don't have all week to sit in a diner eating curly fries and discovering someone's favorite color. I'm an efficient kind of guy. One date is all I need to know if my matches are right or not."

The unmitigated *audacity* of him to even try something so ridiculous.

"So who slapped you first? Was it Chelsea? Those volleyball-serving hands probably *tore* you up." I chuckle at the visual I'm cooking up in my head.

Even Tre' has to laugh at that. Chelsea and those hands *did* take us all the way to regionals. "Nah. She didn't slap me. She did leave, though."

I fold my arms. "As she should have. What about the other two?"

"Who, Darby and Kayla? Yeahhhh, I mean they stayed, but Darby acted like she had an attitude, and I don't know, I just wasn't feeling Kayla like that."

"Why not?" From what I know of her, Kayla's cute, earned herself a full ride to Spelman, and laughs at *anything*. She seems perfect for Tre'.

But here he is shaking his head and acting like he's too good for literal perfection. "I'm a fan of *natural* chemistry. And it just wasn't there." He reaches into his binder, slides out two sticks of gum, and offers me one. "Then again, I didn't expect it to be."

I take the one that *doesn't* look like it's been collecting dust in the pocket of his binder all semester and peel off the wrapper. "Why not?"

"Because we chose each other. I can choose three hundred different girls—it doesn't mean I know what's best for me. Now, the wild card pick, I trust that."

I make a face. "Why would you trust an *algorithm*?" I'm never trusting an algorithm again, after Instagram won't stop suggesting I follow Darby Long.

"Because algorithms take the time to get to know you—to find out what you like and don't like—before introducing you to the perfect next thing. It's fate based on science, which pretty much makes it foolproof." Tre' looks so sure of himself that I almost believe him.

Then I think of Dev and me. We didn't need an algorithm to bring us together. Based on Tre's theory, an algorithm would never match us. We have very different personalities, we don't have much in common, but . . . we worked anyway. And our chemistry was undeniable.

I shake my head at Tre'. "Real fate defies science. *Real* fate doesn't need everything lined up perfectly to connect you with—"

"People you never thought you could be with, huh?"

"Yeah."

A slow smile spreads across Tre's face. "Like me, right?"

"What?" Suddenly, I feel tricked. "Umm . . . *no.*"

The second period dismissal bell rings in the distance, and in a rare moment of mercy, Tre' lets me off the hook. We pop up from the bleachers with the rest of the seniors and head toward the building. That's when I see him.

Dev is holding Darby's hand, helping her down from the bleachers.

Forget the possibility that *I* could be in my own hand-holding situation with Mason in a few hours. Witnessing Dev's fingers interlocked with Darby's begins to crack the chill persona I've worked so hard to construct these last few days. Tre's eyes slide up the bleachers at the exact moment

Darby pretends to miss a step and slip. Of course, Dev jumps into hero mode and catches her before she falls. A few seniors close to them start clapping, which angers me even more.

I'm *this* close to losing it when Tre' puts a hand on my shoulder.

"Roll with me, Leila."

I look over at Darby and Dev walking into the school building—and you know what? There's my sign to get the eff out of here.

"Let's go," I tell Tre'.

I LOOK OVER my shoulder at least ten times as I follow Tre' away from the bleachers and across the grass. Maybe it's the fact that Tre's hands are still touching my sunburned shoulders. Or the bigger sting of watching Dev flirting with another girl. But I forget for a moment that I'm talking to my nemesis.

I blurt out. "Why would he dump *me* for *her?*"

The wound that I've been pretending has healed suddenly exposes itself all over again.

Tre' finally takes his hand off my shoulder. "Dev didn't dump you for Darby Long."

"You don't even know—"

"Trust me, Leila. Dev doesn't want to be with Darby. He wants to be with what Darby represents."

I turn to face Tre'. "And what's that?"

"I don't know. Fun? Freedom?"

Now I'm offended. "So what am I . . . *boring*?"

Tre' shakes his head. "I'm not saying that. But Dev doesn't have to put in any work with a girl like Darby. She's just kind of . . . *around*." Tre' makes a face. "You require so much more from a guy, Leila. And maybe Dev is just running from that right now."

Tre's theory does make sense. But it doesn't make my heart hurt any less.

Suddenly, I look up, and Tre' is leading me toward the parked cars.

"Wait, why are we headed toward the parking lot?" I give Tre' a funny look.

"I have something I have to do off-campus right quick."

I raise an eyebrow. "Since when have we been able to leave campus during lunch? Boy, move. I'm not getting in trouble with you."

I step forward to move past him, but he blocks my path.

"Come on, Leila. I've been slipping out for three months now. We're already almost there and no one has stopped us. Come on, live a little . . ."

Back up at the school building, seniors are still streaming into the back door. Darby and Dev are nowhere in sight, but if I had to guess, they're probably already cuddled up at a cafeteria lunch table, nibbling on opposite ends of the same french fry.

My stomach dips at the gruesome image of the two of

them meeting up somewhere in the middle of that fry.

I turn back to Tre'. "Fine," I say, and follow him to the student parking lot. I keep waiting for a teacher to call us out, but he walks with ease, like he's been leaving campus during lunch his entire life.

Tre' opens the passenger door of his cobalt-blue Tesla—and that's when I realize his family has *money*-money. "Are you driving us, or is the Tesla driving us?" I ask him.

"I'm driving us," he says. "I don't trust the autopilot yet."

"Me neither," I say, a rare moment of agreement for us.

I settle into the comfy passenger seat as Tre' backs out of the parking lot. "You leave *every* day for lunch?" I ask, wondering how he's never gotten caught.

"Yup." Tre' reaches over me and opens his glove compartment. He pulls out a granola bar and hands it to me. "Here, eat this," he goes. "You're going to need it to make up for all the missed cafeteria food."

"We're not stopping at a drive-through?" I ask. I was looking forward to snacking on a large fry and a milkshake from one of the nearby fast-food places.

"No time," Tre' says, digging around. He pulls out his own granola bar and unwraps the foil.

"Where are you taking me?" I mean, I've known Tre' long enough to know he's no serial killer. But still.

"Will you relax? I just have to do something real quick." Tre' checks for oncoming cars before heading out onto the main road. We drive up the street some before Tre' turns onto Brown Station Road.

"You're driving us to the prison?" I ask, alarmed. At least once a year, local Twitter goes crazy with reports that an inmate has broken out of jail and was found wandering around the very same road we're currently cruising down.

Tre' looks more annoyed than worried. "Do I look like a kid that visits prison often?" Just before we reach the large correctional facility, Tre' turns off the road.

"The Prince George's County Animal Shelter?" I read the sign out loud.

Tre' pulls onto a little hidden road surrounded by tall trees and a creek, and parks in front of the huge animal shelter building. When we walk inside, a woman behind the counter greets him like she's known him all her life.

"Hey, Trevor—you're here to see your guy?" she asks.

"You know it," he says, leaning over an open binder on the counter. He picks up a tiny pencil and writes his name in the visitors' log. Then he writes in mine. "I brought my big-head friend here with me—she's cool."

The woman, whose name badge says SHANNON, smiles at me. I secretly want to punch Tre' for introducing me as his big-head friend. But I smile instead and go, "My actual name is Leila."

Shannon smiles warmly and says, "The perfect name for such a lovely girl." Then she turns to Tre' and points to the back. "Go on back. I'm sure he's waiting on you."

Tre' puts the pencil down and beckons for me to follow him down a narrow hallway. We pass a room full of cats lying lazily in metal cages and two large rooms called the

BIG DOG ROOMS that seem eerily quiet. When we cut the corner, we pass a sign stand shaped like an arrow that has PUPPIES AND SMALL DOGS written in black dry-erase marker. Tre' walks me down to the end of the hall. Then he taps a hand sanitizer bottle and nods for me to do the same. After I finish sanitizing my hands, Tre' pushes two heavy doors open and leads me into the loudest, barkiest room of them all.

Little dogs yip and bark, jumping up from their cots, banging the metal cages with their snouts and pawing at the metal bars as we pass them. *Look at me, play with me, take me home*, they all seem to say. My heart breaks a little. Because the desperate look in their eyes makes me want to scoop them all up, one by one, and take them home with me.

But Tre' bypasses them all. "They're all going to find good homes, Leila," he says, almost like he can read my thoughts. "People always want small dogs." He walks me all the way to the back, before stopping at one cage on the end. He stoops down and holds out his hand, palm up. "Hey boy," he says in this low, gentle voice I've never heard before. "Ready for lunch?"

One of the shelter workers walks up to Tre' and me with a ring of keys in his hand. He uses one of the keys to open the cage. "Man, Tre'. Your boy has been waiting on you all morning."

The employee stoops down and picks up the scrawniest little Chihuahua I've ever seen in my life. His ribs stick out. So do his back and tail bones. When he opens his mouth, I can see that he doesn't have any teeth left. The skin around his eyes sags, making his big, dark eyes bulgy—even for a Chihuahua. Still, Tre' smiles warmly at the tiny dog.

"Tre's here, little guy. You can relax now." The employee hands Tre' a bottle and a sandwich bag before walking off.

The Chihuahua, who had been shaking inside of his kennel, settles down right away in Tre's arms. Tre' holds on to him, not too tight, but enough so that he won't slip, and walks me to another set of double doors. Using his elbows, Tre' pushes the double doors and leads me outside into a fenced-in courtyard. He sits down on one of the benches, cradling the dog like a baby. Then he gently puts the bottle in the dog's mouth. "Come on, Lou. I know you're going to give me at least two ounces today."

"Lou?" I could've sworn I saw the name Benji written on the dog's cage, so I'm all confused. "I thought—"

Tre' shakes his head. "Does this dog look like a Benji to you? Benji's a name for a fresh young puppy who jumps around and eats socks." He continues feeding the dog, who is taking his sweet time suckling water from the bottle. "This guy has seen some things, been places. He needs a dignified name. *Lou.*"

I scoot closer to Tre' on the bench and smile down at the calm Chihuahua. The dog sort of side-eyes me a little, giving me a weak little growl from somewhere deep under the ribs poking out of his chest. It's almost like he's saying *This is my time with Tre'—butt out.*

I give them a tiny bit of space again, but I stick close

enough to watch. "Why do you get to feed him?" I ask.

Tre' shrugs. "I've been volunteering here for a good minute now." He reaches into the baggie with his finger and scoops up a pea-sized amount of soft doggy food. He puts his finger up to Lou's doggy lips and waits for him to lick it off. "They trust me, I guess."

Tre' and I watch as Lou slowly sticks out his long, pink tongue and laps weakly at Tre's fingertip. His tongue doesn't connect every single time he goes in for a lick. But it does enough that he gets tiny bits of food.

"Plus, I'm one of the only ones who can get him to eat." Tre' spots a bit of fallen dog mush on Lou's droopy chin and wipes it off with his thumb. "They brought him here a few months ago, right around the time I was finishing up my student service hours. They were talking about putting him down because he refused to eat and wouldn't gain any weight." A sad look crosses Tre's face. "I couldn't see my boy going out like that, so I told them to let me work with him." He smiles down at Lou. "All he needed was some extra love and attention—that's all."

I look around at the small courtyard. The patches of grass peeking through the gravel on the ground. At the random balls and plush toys strewn around. "So you just come here every day during lunch?"

"Yeah."

"And you never get caught?"

"Nope."

I imagine Tre' as some sort of school-skipping bandit, able

to scale walls and slip around corners better than Spider-Man himself, when he goes, "Especially since I have a pass to come here."

I punch Tre' in the arm. "You have permission to be here?"

"From the principal herself."

I punch Tre' again. This time, Lou lifts his head up slightly, and I swear I see hints of a doggy glare on his face. So I tuck away my punching fists. "Okay, let me get this straight. I'm the only one skipping school at the moment?"

A smirk crosses Tre's face. "I guess so." Tre' slowly shakes his head in this annoying way. "Man, Leila, I thought you were one of the good ones. A girl with your kind of grades. Just out here skipping school—*ratchet*." When I curl my fists up again, Tre' ducks a little. "Re*lax*—dang. If someone asks, I *got* you."

"Yeah, you got me all right—got me out here skipping school while you rest easy on your little hall pass." I roll my eyes at Tre', but I relax a little. I mean, we *are* two weeks away from graduation. To be honest, I strongly suspect the administrators are counting down the days to summer vacation themselves. Nobody's really in school mode anymore.

I sit back and wait patiently for Tre' to finish feeding Benji/Lou. I have to admit, watching Tre' be so gentle with the dog is earning him a teeny-tiny bit of respect in my book. But not too much. This is Tre' we're talking about.

Sticking to my job assignment, I check my phone. "We have, like, fifteen minutes to get back to school, Tre'," I remind him.

"Okay, I'm finishing up anyway." Tre' squints at Lou's feeding bottle for a second, then breaks into a smile. "Ayyee, you made it to two ounces today! My dawg—" Tre' uses his free hand to sort of awkwardly fist-bump Lou. He hands me Lou's bottle and baggie of food, then he carries him back inside.

The worker comes over, so I hand him Lou's stuff. He thanks me, then looks over at Tre'. "How much did he eat today?"

"About a spoonful of food and two ounces of water."

The worker looks impressed. "We could use your talents here full time."

Tre' smiles. "I would, if I wasn't leaving for college soon."

"You'll come help out over the summer, right? Before you leave?"

"You know it, bruh."

"Cool . . . cool."

When Tre' and I get back in the car I ask, "If you love Lou so much, how come you don't just adopt him?"

Tre' goes quiet as he turns on the car. "I can't take a dog with me to college, Leila. You know that."

There's a sadness in his voice that makes me shut up for the rest of the car ride back to school. As Tre' backs into a space in student parking, I think of something. "What about fostering Lou? It's not long term, but you'd be able to keep him for a little while at least."

"Huh . . ." And by some miracle, instead of shooting

my idea down, Tre' actually looks like he's considering my suggestion.

Proud of my contribution to this blooming bromance between Tre' and Lou, I gather my things to exit Tre's car on a high note. But when I unbuckle my seat belt and open the passenger side door, Tre' cups his hand around his mouth and goes, "Yoooo, be careful . . ."

I double-check the parking lot. "Of what? I don't see the security guard lurking."

"Nah, I'm not worried about that. I am worried about you and that enormous forehead denting my doorframe on the way out."

And see? This right here is why you can't waste time helping clowns. I swat at Tre', even though he ducks and laughs. Then I grab an extra granola bar from his glove compartment before I leave.

14

I WAIT FOR Mason by the school's double doors so we can go on our date. A small tinge of nervousness hits me, but I have to go out with my next match. This date feels less about proving something to Dev and more about proving that *I* can truly do this—that I can take this next date seriously and possibly connect with someone besides the boy who lent me a calculator four years ago.

Mason comes out wearing jeans, a long T-shirt, and a gray canvas backpack with activism buttons pinned all over it. Women's rights. Trans rights. Black Lives Matter. #MeToo. All the hashtags. All the fists raised high, repped on one backpack.

Mason's not the tallest kid in our senior class, but he's

still a *presence*, with his Instagram Lives and his whole *I'm going to make the world a better place* brand.

And—o*kay!*—he smells good, too. I try to sneak another whiff of his bodywash as he asks, "Do you want to hang out at Allen Pond?"

"Sure; it's right by my house."

"Mind riding the half-day bus back to your side of town?" Mason holds up his state-issued identification card—which is basically the calling card of all teens who don't have their license yet.

As a member of the ID card/no license club as well, I don't mind that Mason doesn't have a car to drive us around. Maybe he's failed his driving test a million times like me. Or he's really good at bumming rides from friends and doesn't see an immediate need for his own set of wheels. To be honest, this kind of reminds me of the years before Dev got his license and access to his mom's minivan. The adventures we would get into—just two kids with a few dollars for the Metro bus and the ability to get creative about turning literally anywhere into a fun date spot.

A wave of sadness suddenly hits me, over the nostalgia. But also? I'm suddenly super curious to see if Mason will have Dev's ability to turn a local spot into something amazing and magical. I'm excited for what's to come.

I take a seat right behind the bus driver and pat the green leather for Mason to sit down next to me. When he gets settled, I ask the number one question on every senior's tongue right now. "So, where are you headed in the fall?"

Mason slips his backpack onto the floor of the bus. "UC Berkeley, of course."

"Why 'of course'?" I raise an eyebrow at him. "Isn't Berkeley in California? Aren't you afraid of earthquakes?" Forget the quakes. I couldn't imagine being *that* far away from home—at least, not at first anyway.

"A little shaking up might be what this country needs right now," Mason says, shrugging. "The political protesting at Berkeley is legendary. How could I *not* be a part of that?"

He has a point. UC Berkeley does feel like the perfect college fit for him.

Our conversation naturally takes a casual turn as the bus weaves through all the nearby neighborhoods. I tell him he'll probably trade in his sneakers for a pair of comfy slides the second he steps onto Berkeley's year-round warm campus. He gets me to promise I'll get a very warm hat to wear for Rochester's bitter cold winters.

When the bus makes it to South Bowie, we get off a few stops early so we can walk a block over to Allen Pond Park.

"There's a trail to the left of the pond that we could walk, if you want," I tell him. Mason puts his arm around my waist and together we head over to the trail.

As we begin walking the trail, Mason pulls me in close, which feels warm and comforting.

"Hey, I saw you comment on my post the other day. I didn't know you were interested in social justice, too?"

I give Mason a look, like, *Why wouldn't I be?* "Of course," I say. "You literally liked tons of my posts on prison reform."

"Yeah, I guess I just thought those were reposts. Because when I asked you to go live with me, you curved me."

"Yeah, that's because . . ." I don't know how to tell Mason that Dev got all jealous and shut down the idea of that collab before it even began.

But instead of going into an awkward explanation, I make something up.

"My phone is so glitchy sometimes. I didn't want to have technical difficulties in the middle of the session."

Mason doesn't even pretend like he's buying that excuse. "I bet if Dev had asked you, you would've done it."

"I mean, he's my—I mean he *was* my boyfriend, what do you expect?"

"I don't know—wishful thinking maybe." He grows quiet for a moment, then he goes, "Hey, I saw you getting out of Tre's car today. Is he one of your matches, too?"

I make a face. "Tre' will always and forever be my nemesis."

Mason lets out a slight chuckle. "I bet you didn't know you were my first nemesis . . ."

I stop walking. "What?"

Mason chuckles. "Man, old wounds cut *deep.*"

I search my head for what on earth I could've done to Mason. But I can't think of anything. So I swat him on the shoulder. Right over the patch that says ONE LOVE. "Yeah right, Mason."

"I'm serious. There's a whole story behind it. Do you want to hear it?"

Now I'm super intrigued. "Of course I do." I look around for a good spot to sit. Besides the trees, dirt path, and occasional squirrel running by, there's nothing really out here.

Mason points to a picnic bench near a tall oak tree in the distance. "We could chill over there if you want."

I mean, we could. I decide not to overthink things and just let the situation flow.

So I just say, "Yeah, why not?"

We walk over to the picnic table and get settled in. Then Mason cracks his knuckles and looks off, like he's really traveling back in time. "So it all started in the fourth grade."

"The fourth grade?" I sit up straighter. "Mason, what the heck are you talking about?"

Mason leans back, like somebody's grandfather getting ready to tell some long-winded family story. Then he jumps right in.

"So Leila Bean loves Olive Garden breadsticks . . .

"Wait. How do you know that?" I ask.

Mason smiles. "You don't remember we were in the same fourth grade class?"

I raise an eyebrow. "What does that have to do with anything?"

"So. I remember being super jealous that your family went to Olive Garden so much. Because the next day, you always brought leftover breadsticks to school, and made a huge deal out of eating them in front of everybody."

We break out laughing. "You remember that?" I ask him. No need to tell him that we ate Olive Garden so much because Mom resented the fact that Dad was never around to share cooking responsibilities.

Still chuckling, Mason goes, "How could I forget?" He grabs a pen from his back pocket and holds it up. "Look, everybody. Breadsticks again. *Nom nom nom.*"

"That was *not* me!"

"Yes, it was! You also took the time to lick the salt from your fingers to make everybody feel even worse about our own boring lunches."

I think about devouring that bacon on my date with Kai. This *does* sound like something I would do.

Mason jokingly hangs his head and says, "I low-key hated you for that."

I bust out laughing again. "For bringing breadsticks to school?!"

"No! For getting to go to Olive Garden once a week while I was at home trying to force Mom's tofu recipes down my throat."

"Aww, poor Mason. You could've just asked me for one."

His cheeks turn a little pink—which I find cute. For a fleeting moment, I wonder if he's discovering new things about *me* he likes.

"I think I'm finally ready to let my grudge go." Mason shrugs. He looks at me with those soft brown eyes again. "Especially since we're finally on a date. You showing off your breadstick privilege may be my social justice origin story."

Mason looks down at his phone for a moment. When he

faces me again, he looks slightly nervous. "Now, I know I've come across quite salty over you and all those breadsticks. But really, I think you're super awesome."

I lean back. "But doesn't that describe nearly every girl at Baldwin?"

I know I'm low-key fishing for compliments. But honestly, I want to know. Why *did* he pick me? It's not like there weren't so many other options.

Mason looks off for a moment before the ends of his lips turn up slightly. "Not every girl at Baldwin makes my heart beat faster when she walks by."

Okay. *That* makes me blush. And I'm thrown completely off, because before this week, I never really thought about dating Mason at all. It's not that he isn't cute. Or charismatic. I'd just always been with Dev.

I throw a little joke his way. "Well, I guess I should thank you for the love. Even if it did start out with a teeny bit of hate."

Mason and I share a laugh before he goes, "Trust me. You deserve *all* the love." Then we stare into each other's eyes a moment. I am definitely feeling something—and I know Mason feels it, too.

MOM AND I arrive at the African Hair Gallery at the crack of dawn the next morning, holding multiple bags of Kanekalon hair in our hands. It's a sticky eighty-seven degrees out. Humid. And days away from June. For most of the Black girls I know, all of these things mark the beginning of . . . *braiding season.*

A head full of braids means swimming without a postpool detangling session. A nightly ritual that only consists of tying the braids down with a scarf. And most importantly—if the braids are put in by the right braider, who understands the need to go easy around the edges—the natural hair gets a chance to rest while being braided up in the protective style. No heat. No tension. Less breakage. More new growth.

I should be worry free. Four weeks in a protective style

means I'll have at *least* an inch of new growth when I take my hair out.

But an inkling of guilt has been building up all morning. Last night, I went to bed pumped—the endorphins from my date with Mason still coursing through my veins.

But this morning, I woke up to the feeling that maybe it's too soon to be this excited over a new guy. Dev and I broke up just a little over a week ago. How will that look to the entire senior class—who witnessed my four-year commitment to Dev? No one will believe that what me and Dev had was real, if I'm this caught up over a new guy so soon. And that worries me.

So, as Mom and I wait outside the hair gallery for the shop owner to pull up, I stage a battle in my head over my new feelings for Mason.

How soon is too soon to feel that spark with another guy?

Mom checks the time on her phone. "It's already fifteen after. You're missing an entire school day to get these braids in. The least she could do is . . . oh, oh, there she is! Good *morning*, Sarah."

A tall, older Nigerian woman with smooth ebony skin, high cheekbones, and her own hair cornrowed flat on her scalp comes walking up from her car, carrying the largest tote bag on her shoulder. "I'm here, I'm here," she says, reaching her arms out for Mom to come closer.

Mom tucks her packs of braiding hair up under her armpit to give Sarah a hug—like she wasn't just griping about the time three seconds earlier.

But that's the beauty of the hair gallery. The tug of the love-hate relationship. We love expert fingers parting and braiding our hair up into endless styles. But we hate the wait. We love the endless chatter about a variety of topics while in the chair. But we hate the cost.

No matter the cost, though, Mom isn't letting anyone but Sarah touch her head—which is why she will wait until the end of time to make sure she ends up in her black leather swivel chair.

"What are my beautiful girls getting today?" Sarah asks, putting the lights on inside the shop.

"Senegalese twists for me," Mom says. "Leila's getting knotless braids."

Sarah runs her fingers through my hair. "Is this washed and ready to go?"

"I shampooed and conditioned last night," I tell her.

Sarah smiles. "Nice. It should be finished in about—eh—four, five hours."

I nod, even though I suspect a few more hours will be tacked on, when it's all said and done. Especially since two more women have entered the shop with bags of braiding hair in their hands.

Mom and I each get settled in our swivel chairs while a team of Nigerian women begin prepping their workstations. Behind me, one woman, Jessi, draws the Kanekalon hair out of the pack, pulling it apart and laying strips of hair out on a table, while another woman, Melissa, sections a tiny square of my hair, picks up a Kanekalon strip, and begins on her first braid. She pulls out a comb and begins lovingly parting and greasing my scalp.

While I'm enjoying the steady motion of the braiding, my phone buzzes. It's a good morning text from Mason.

"What's all that smiling you're doing over there?" Mom asks from her chair. I watch her braider wrap the Kanekalon hair around a small section of her own strands and begin to twist.

I try to tuck my smile away. "Nothing."

But Mom doesn't believe me. "Mmhmm. I know *that* look when I see it."

She smirks at Sarah through the large mirror. "I think Leila has a new crush . . ."

Before I can shoot Mom dagger eyes for being so loose with my business, Sarah clucks her tongue and taps Mom on the shoulder with the comb. "Leila doesn't have time for crushes. *Schoolwork* should be her focus."

My hair braider, Melissa, who's a lot younger than the other hair braiders, rolls her eyes at me in the mirror and mouths *Not true* when Sarah isn't looking.

But I'm still irritated Mom put me out there in front of everyone in the first place. "Sarah's right, Mom," I say loudly. "If you're telling all my business, you should've started with me being on the honor roll all year, or on the Dean's List, or receiving a nice chunk of scholarship money from the University of Rochester . . ."

That bit of information elicits a swooning noise from Sarah and the other older hair braiders.

". . . But instead you focus on crushes?" I give Mom my best embellished *shame on you* face.

But Mom doesn't seem flustered at all. If anything, her smile deepens. "I'm always bragging on how well you do in school, Leila. That's not new." She smirks at me in the mirror. "But this is the first time in four years you're dating new people. And I think it's pretty brave, if you want to know the truth of it all. I don't see anything wrong with it."

The same guilty feeling from earlier comes flooding back.

"Mom, I just broke up with Dev. It wouldn't even look right to be so into a guy so soon."

My mother raises an eyebrow. "What rule book have *you* been reading?" She leans forward in her seat while Sarah is reaching back to grab more hair. "Listen, once you get to be my age, you're going to realize that none of the rules matter. Everything you've ever heard about the ways things should be won't mean anything. The only thing that *will* matter is what makes you happy."

I give Mom a smirk of my own. "If that's the case, what took *you* so long to start dating?"

Sarah comes over and plucks me—right on my peeling shoulder. "Don't talk back to your mama, girl." She nods in Mom's direction. "This one is giving you wisdom . . ."

But Mom waves away my shade. "I started dating when I was ready, Leila. Trust me. Your heart will let you know when it's ready to accept new applicants."

Mom leans back in her seat. "If you had a good date, go on another one—and another one." She nods toward my phone. "If you get a sweet morning text—send one back. *This is what it's all about*, Leila. Figuring out what makes you smile and going with it."

While I'm mulling over Mom's advice in my head, she leans forward again.

"Holding on to hurt isn't some badge of honor, Leila," Mom says. "When you find a bit of joy, claim it. Hold on to it. And pay it forward." Mom snaps her fingers. "Because no one that cares about you will *ever* fault your joy."

With Mom's word's ringing in my ears, I search my phone's photo album for the perfect meme to send Mason. One that says *I like you enough to go on a second date, but I'm not obsessed or anything.*

The best I can come up with is a silly Google image Riley sent me a few weeks ago of two stick figures holding hands.

I regret sending that stupid random photo the second I send it off. But when Mason immediately hearts the photo, my own heart flutters. Maybe leaning into happy isn't the worst thing after all.

16

MY SCALP IS pulsating by the time Mom and I leave the shop hours later. But the time spent in the chair was worth it. Mom's Senegalese twists are tossed effortlessly over her shoulder. And I'm looking good, with fresh, waist-length knotless braids cascading down my back. Plus, all the conversation about dating between me, Mom, and the hair braiders in the shop has my heart feeling good—and ready to accept that it's okay to start over with someone new. That as long as my heart is in it, it's okay to lean into this new crush I have on Mason.

"Don't scratch, Leila. *Pat* your scalp—your braids came out so good, I don't want you to mess them up," Mom says as she lets me out at the train station.

At the museum, Maggie pairs Dev and me together again.

But this time, things are looser. Trying out this new friend-ship lane, Dev makes the first move.

"You look great, Leila," he says the moment I walk over with my long braids falling down my back.

Doing my part to make a friendship between us work, I give him a "Thanks" and a twirl, so he can catch every angle of my new look. Letting go of the bitterness I've been feeling has my heart feeling lighter, and ready to fall back into our old familiar tour routine.

And there's just no denying that there is a certain chemistry there that has repeat visitors specifically asking for us. As a duo, we flow from one artifact to the next, smoothly incorporating humor in all the right places and taking the time to help our visitors through the serious exhibits. Even I have to admit that when it comes to giving tours, Dev and I are unmatched.

I watch Dev carefully explaining to one of our four-year-old visitors how certain minerals came to live on a gray slab of rock, and my heart melts over his patience and gentleness. By the time we reach the Hope diamond, I get the sudden urge to fix the lingering awkwardness between Dev and me.

While our guests are milling around one of the exhibits, I nudge Dev's shoulder. "Hey, listen. If Darby is who you want to date, I'm going to try to live with that. I don't like it. But I guess, at the end of the day, you deserve to be happy."

There. I said it. And I'm only 65 percent ready to vomit.

Dev looks kind of surprised for a moment. Then an embarrassed expression crosses his face. "Actually, I kind of got dumped."

"What?!" I take a quick peek around the Gem Hall, praying no one heard me. Thankful, our tour is too busy staring at priceless jewels to care.

The messy side of me wants every last salacious detail of the grand opening and grand closing of this train wreck. But unfortunately, in the spirit of maturity, I simply say, "I'm sorry, Dev."

Even though I'm not.

"It's okay. Darby heard Kai was available and decided he was a more exciting match, I guess."

Huh. I guess someone must have given Darby the *embracing joy* speech early.

"I'm actually kind of relieved."

I raise an eyebrow. Because after the show these two have put on for the entire senior class all week, I was expecting matching heart tattoos by the weekend. "Why is that?"

"I mean, I know how much you hate her. And even though she was cool, I felt terrible every time you saw us together. Despite what you think, Leila, it messes me up inside to see you hurting."

I can't lie. All this tea Dev's spilling makes it a little easier to make my next mature statement. "Let's work on being friends. I know things have been awkward between us. But I'm ready to try a friendship if you are."

A smile spreads across Dev's face and for a second he just stands there, staring deep into my eyes. "I'd like that."

At the end of our last tour, Maggie gathers our group together again for an announcement.

"Don't forget the Last Night at the Museum!" she says handing us each a small postcard. Each year the museum puts together a night for the graduating seniors, to thank us for our three years of service. We get to tour the museum at night, without the public visitors who usually crowd the museum halls.

I grab my things pretty quickly from the coatroom and follow Dev across the expansive hallway and toward the exit.

"We did good today," I tell him, trying out my new casual *we're just good friends* persona.

While we walk, I think about the three years we've spent here, perfecting our museum tours together and working together as a team. A pang of sadness hits me as I realize that, just like our relationship, our time here is coming to a close, too.

"You know how we do," Dev says, fist bumping me. But when the skin of our knuckles connects, an electric charge crawls up my arm. And then Dev is staring into my eyes again. Time stops. In this moment, it's just me and my ex—and he looks like he wants to tell me something.

Does he want to get back together?

Despite my tender scalp, I run my fingers through my braids—since he did compliment me on them earlier. And I wait for Dev to say whatever's in his heart.

But he doesn't say anything else. And I don't want to push him.

So I break our gaze and clear my throat. "Umm, I guess we should get out of here."

We walk together toward the exit. But the moment Dev pushes the heavy exit doors open, I hear a car horn honk twice. I look over and a red Toyota Camry is parked on the curb behind a hot-dog vendor. The window eases down and a girl leans over.

"Dev . . . hurry up, before I get a ticket."

Chills rip through my body. I know I'm supposed to be letting go of the past, but the *past* wasn't that long ago. I plaster a fake smile on my face when I say, "Wait . . . I thought you said Darby dumped you?"

But Dev shakes his head. "No, it's Halima."

"Halima?" That throws me off for a second. For a brief moment, I hyperfocus on the fact that Halima wasn't a wild card pick. Dev actually *chose* her.

But instead of choosing hurt, I follow Mom's advice, and try my best to lean toward joy. Dev and I are friends now, and there's joy in a friend dating someone new . . . right?

An uncomfortable look crosses Dev's face. "I guess when Darby dumped me, I had one more match, so . . ."

Dev rubs the back of his neck and lowers his voice. "And I kind of wanted to let you know, before you heard it from someone else . . ."

I hold my breath, unsure of what he's about to tell me.

Dev makes a pained face. "If our date goes well, I'm probably going to ask Halima to go to the dance with me. I'm sorry, Leila. It's not like I'm in love with her or anything. But she's my last match, and—"

I let out a sigh. Here we go with my maturity bit again—even if it's creating knots in my stomach. "You don't have to apologize, Dev. If going to the dance with Halima feels right, then go for it."

Dev side-glances me. "You mean that?"

I pause for a second. Dev's reasoning isn't the most romantic reason to choose someone for the dance. But I have to admit, it feels very on-brand for him. "Yeah . . . I do."

Just then, my phone buzzes. It's Mason, sending me a selfie of us we took at the park.

I smile at the image—we look pretty cute with our faces squished together. Everything's moving forward—whether I'm ready or not. I mean, Dev's already asking someone to go to the dance with him, which means we're not getting back together. *Friendship* is our new lane.

As I watch Dev get into Halima's car, I finally let the past go—for real this time.

I pull Mason's text thread back up on my phone and begin typing. I'm ready for a second date. What about you?

17

WHEN I HOP in the passenger seat of Bree's car the next morning, the first thing I tell her is "I think Dev and Halima are going to the dance together." Before Bree has a chance to respond, I follow up with "I also think Mason might end up asking *me* to the dance."

I thought my mature feelings about Dev moving on would be fleeting. But, after my text session with Mason lasted until well after midnight last night, I'm feeling okay.

Honestly? I should feel exhausted from staying up so late. But instead, I'm full of energy from our awesome conversation.

Bree rubs her hands together and smirks. "Ha ha! That's what I'm talking about! Mason's the one, huh?"

"I *mean* . . ." I try to hide a cheesy smile behind my hand.

I can't help it. Mason's *actually* giving me butterflies. Weird.

I quickly send him a good morning text before he has a chance to beat me to it. Within seconds, he's replying back with Can't wait for our date followed by smiley face emojis.

"Oh, *really*?!" Bree goes, *clearly* all up in my text thread.

"Ex*cuse* you." I shield my phone screen from her nosy eyes. "No looking at texts and driving, please."

"Well, read it out loud to me next time . . ." Bree turns up the music in the car and backs out of her driveway, singing extra loud. She waits until we're almost at school to drop her bombshell.

"Okay, so *boom*. You know I had a little meetup with Eva last night, right?"

I raise an eyebrow. "You guys went on your date? How did *that* happen?"

Bree wiggles her hand in the air. "Well, it wasn't really a date. We both had committee meetings yesterday. I caught up to her while she was walking to her car and we ended up standing in the parking lot talking for close to an hour."

I do a little happy dance from the passenger seat for my friend. "*Okay*, Bree. So, when are you guys going on your actual date?"

"I'm taking her to Top Golf by the National Harbor to-night."

I flick my fingers in her direction until she turns and raises an eyebrow at me. "What the heck are you doing?"

"I'm sprinkling you with good vibes," I reply, laughing. I'm genuinely happy for my friend. We're both finally headed in the right direction—and closer to securing our dates for the dance.

Bree shakes her head and goes, "Okay, weirdo." But when she gets to a red light, she flicks her fingers back at me and smiles.

When we get to school, Mason's waiting for me at the locker Bree and I share.

"Do you mind if our second date is a surprise?" he asks.

I try to throw Bree a knowing look, but I think I get caught when Mason smiles. "I don't mind at all," I tell him.

"Cool. How about I ride the bus home with you again?"

"Now hold up." Bree makes a face. "I can't have Leila riding the big cheese all week. Who else is going to sing backup for me?"

Eva comes walking down the hall just at that moment. "I think I know a good temporary replacement," I say.

Bree rubs her hands together and smiles. "See, Lei, *this* is why you are on the principal's list every semester." Bree looks off past my shoulder and cups her hand over her mouth. "Hey, Eva. Wait up!"

As Bree takes off down the hall after Eva, I turn back to Mason. He's wearing a regular white tee, with a few beaded bracelets on his wrist stacked over a vintage-looking wristwatch. As a girl who pays attention to detail, I can appreciate his consistent aesthetic. "So what's up with this little surprise place you're taking me?"

Mason smiles and leans closer into me until his lips are almost kissing my earlobe. "It's a surprise."

Just the warmth of his breath on my ear sends shivers down my arms. And this time, as I watch him walk away to first period, I don't hide my smile behind my hand.

After school, Mason rides the half-day bus home with me again. I try to guess where he's taking me the entire time.

"More laser tag at Party HQ?"

"Nope. You're too good at laser tag. I don't feel like losing again."

We both laugh at that, but also—very true.

"Okayyyy, hmmm." I think of some random places. "The movies?"

"Nope."

"Top Golf?"

"Not on the bus line."

Our bus finally pulls up to the Towne Center stop.

When the school bus driver lets us off, we walk past the grocery store and the place where I get my nails done into the restaurant parking lot next door.

"The Olive Garden?!" Mason's attention to detail is giving top-tier match material.

Feeling giddy, I breeze past Mason as he holds the heavy Olive Garden doors open for me, and a hostess walks us to an empty table, where a waitress sets us up nice with plenty of bread and salad.

Over delicious plates of chicken parmesan, Mason and I talk about everything. And our IRL conversation matches the energy of our texts, which is always a good sign.

After our dinner, we walk out of the restaurant holding hands. The sun is starting to set, and the dusky aesthetic is putting pure romantic vibes in the air.

Suddenly, Mason's right up on me. His breath smells like spearmint gum, and I can hear his heavy breathing.

"I'm having the best time with you, Leila," he says in a husky voice. "I'd keep this date going another few hours, except now I finally get to kiss you good night . . ."

Every inch of my body grows warm. All I can think about is Mason's arm slowly wrapping around my waist, drawing me closer to him.

"Is this cool?" he asks.

I stare into his warm brown eyes, forgetting momentarily to actually respond to his question, until he lets go of me quickly.

"Oh, I'm sorry, Leila. I thought . . ."

"No, Mason. It's okay. Really . . ."

And you know what? It *is* okay. For all I know, Dev could be locked in a lip embrace with Halima right now. And I'm here with Mason. And he's turned out to be so fun, so smart, and most importantly, so sweet. There's literally nothing holding us back.

And then—it happens. Mason's lips are on mine. Well, almost. His lips are just kind of there, unmoving, like a dead fish. And now—oh—wait, they're moving now. Except, now he's sucking on my top lip, and I think I taste the garlic from the breadsticks? Except it doesn't taste good coming from Mason's mouth.

I pull away from Mason and go, "I need to run to the restroom."

I leave Mason on the cobbled walkway, standing there with a weird expression on his face while I dash back into the restaurant. As soon as I get inside the ladies room, I turn on the sink and splash cold water onto my lips.

But the chilly water does nothing to numb the gross feeling of Mason sucking and slobbering all over me. Who *kisses* like that?

I pull my phone out and text Bree. Meet me at my house in ten minutes.

Bree texts back immediately. Sorry, Lei. I'm still out with Eva.

Well, how long are you going to be?

There's a brief pause and then Bree writes: Well, see, here's the thing. Our date is going pretty good . . . and to be honest, I wasn't planning on leaving anytime soon. I thought you were out with Mason.

I am. And everything was going good until he kissed me . . .

You don't want to be kissed by Mason?

I wouldn't call the thing he just did to my mouth kissing.

Look, Leila, Bree types back. You like everything else about this guy. Maybe it'll be fun teaching him how to kiss?

I think about that. I *do* like Mason. And if I was able to teach myself how to blend my contouring makeup perfectly by the end of freshman year, then certainly I can show Mason how to do the same thing with our lips.

I reach into my pocket and pull out my lip gloss to reapply the layer I just scrubbed off. Then I take a breath and yank open the bathroom door, with a certain level of bravado. I'm Leila Bean, and I've overcome bigger issues than this.

Outside, I grab Mason by the hand and lead him further down the sidewalk.

"I think we might need a kiss do-over . . ." I tell him.

Mason rubs the back of his neck, clearly looking embarrassed. "That bad, huh?"

I go easy on him. "I mean, it wasn't *terrible.*" (It was.) "I just think your kisses should match your dynamic personality." I draw him closer.

I press my lips onto Mason's, this time doing my best to guide him into the right position, the right firmness, the right consistency. It seemed so easy with Dev. My heart twists.

But whatever we're trying doesn't work. If anything, now we're wrestling for control of the situation. Until finally, Mason pulls away and goes, "I probably should head home now. It's getting kind of dark." He wipes leftover spittle from his mouth.

I look down for a moment—this is enough to know. Mason's *not* my Last Chance Dance date.

And then, I swear I didn't mean to. I promise you, it slipped. *Right* at peak awkward silence, the loudest yawn ever escapes from my mouth.

Mason flinches like I've just hurled a *Worst Kisser Ever* trophy at his head. When he turns to look at me again, his eyes have hardened. "So bad kisser means bad match?"

Well. That was direct. I'd already mentally prepared to just kind of fade away from Mason, hoping he would get the hint or simply move on to another match. But now he's put me on the spot, and I guess I have to tell the truth.

How do I tell him that a terrible kiss is a deal-breaker for me? I can't do it. Mason is simply too sweet and I'm too much of a coward to hurt his feelings.

I look everywhere except into Mason's eyes. Because if I do, I'm scared I'll give in and just go to the dance with him to avoid hurting his feelings. Which is not what I want.

"It's just that we only have a week left before the dance. And I thought I was really into you, but—" I finally get up enough courage to look him in the eye. "I figure whoever I go to the dance with, I should be totally sure about . . ."

My heart pounds as Mason's face goes from confused to crushed in a matter of seconds. And I wonder for a brief moment if this was how Dev felt when he dumped me. And now, I feel a little sorry for my ex, because no matter what the reason, dumping someone sucks.

The look of despair is still on Mason's face. "I mean, no one's really going to be sure, right? *No* one's getting more than a week to get to know someone. That's what the whole dance is about—taking a chance."

"I know, but . . ." My voice kind of trails off, and now

we're in this weird silence vortex as other couples on dates walk around us on the sidewalk.

Suddenly, Mason adjusts his denim crossbody bag across his front and hardens his face. "You know what, Leila? Whatever." Then he stalks off.

18

WHILE THE TEMPERATURE outside has spiked to summer-like weather, inside, my mood has plummeted. I end up dragging myself out of bed, with only enough energy to throw on a one-piece jumper and some cute sandals. Fully committed to my moping, I have just enough time to throw a few makeup essentials into a bag, brush my teeth, and run out the door.

From the moment I fasten my seat belt in the passenger seat to the second we walk through the school's double doors, Bree can't stop talking about Eva. What she wore on their date last night, what Eva wore (a baby doll dress), how she styled her hair (parted on the side), the funny joke she told (something related to the last book she read).

"We had the *best* time at Top Golf. The food was good, they had good music playing, and having someone as cute as

Eva hanging with me wasn't bad at all," she says as we make our way to our shared locker.

Leila is not a hater. Leila is not a hater, I remind myself.

"She's not just cute on the outside though, Lei," Bree continues, "She's, like, genuinely a beautiful person on the inside."

"Well, *duh*, Bree. We've both known Eva since elementary school. She's always been super sweet."

There's no denying how much Bree truly likes Eva. So there's no way I can go out with her now. I don't care what Bree says, I'm not going to go out with someone I *know* she's into.

With the dance quickly approaching, the vibe at our school has completely changed from nervous curiosity over matches to straight-up excitement over finally choosing the one. Fragments of conversation bubble up around Bree and me as Bree opens our locker.

Date deliberations. Dance proposal ideas. And while everyone else is moving toward sealing the deal, I'm falling further away from ever finding my true match.

"So when are you planning to ask Eva to the dance?" I open our locker door and grab my textbook.

Bree gives me a look. "Who says I'm asking Eva to the dance?"

I give Bree the *duh* look. "Your Top Golf date was perfect. You talk about her like she's the best person ever. Why *wouldn't* you ask her?"

Bree's eyes follow Ivy as she passes us in the hall. "I don't know. I guess I'm just undecided. I mean, Eva's great. But so was Ivy—until her ex showed up. And yes, Chanel wouldn't stop talking during the movie. But maybe she's just the kind of person you can't take with you to quiet places—nobody's perfect." Bree grabs the rest of her stuff and turns to head off to class. "I just need more time to figure this all out."

Halfway through first period, the school intercom box begins to crackle. "All seniors, please report to the long tables in the front of the cafeteria to pick up yearbooks."

A few spirited cheers erupt all over the room as people grab their things to go.

Ashli Henderson comes walking over from her seat across the room.

"Hey," she says with a nervous look in her eye as we walk together down the hall to get in the yearbook line with the rest of the senior class. "Are you okay?"

I immediately assume Bree slipped up and told Ashli about my bad kiss with Mason. Which isn't like her, since she's normally so big on not spreading other people's business.

"Yeah, I'm fine—I guess." I'm purposely evasive just in case she *doesn't* know.

"So you've heard about Dev? He asked Halima to Last Chance Dance." Ashli gets a sad look on her face. "I'm sorry, Leila. I thought you should hear it from a friend first."

So, he *did* end up asking her. I play the unbothered role,

to avoid the further humiliation of running out of matches at the exact time my ex is securing his date for the dance.

"Yeah, he told me he was going to ask her." I shrug, and toss my hair back behind my shoulder. "I sort of gave him my blessing about the whole thing the other day."

A look of awe crosses Ashli's face. "You're such a class act, Leila. Seriously."

While I appreciate the compliment, it doesn't feel earned. Truthfully? I feel like the actress formerly known as *the girl who has it all together.*

When we reach the cafeteria, all four assistant principals are sitting behind tables, reaching into various boxes and handing off yearbooks and plastic-wrapped graduation regalia. They're checking and double-checking the names to make sure every senior gets the right stuff, so the lines are long—and moving slow.

To pass the time, various seniors are chatting it up with whoever is closest to them in line. Chad walks up soon after we get in line, scoots in beside Ashli, and soon they are deeply engrossed in a conversation about some show they watched together last night. Feeling like the third wheel, I spot Bree a little further up, and decide no one will mind if I cut the line a little.

I don't notice Eva standing beside her until I get right up on them. I squeeze in, despite the lack of space, and quickly start to regret leaving my original space in line.

We're all bunched together up here—so close I can smell Eva's peach-scented body lotion. And while I may have appreciated the nice aroma in a different scenario, being wedged between my bestie and the girl we're both matched with feels super awkward.

Maybe Eva feels the weird energy, too. Because, after a long moment of silence, she clears her throat and goes, "Did Bree tell you we went to Top Golf last night, Leila?" Eva tucks a curly lock of her hair behind her ear.

I paste a plastic smile on my face. "I *heard* . . . did you guys have fun?"

"We did—after I taught Bree how to properly hold a golf club."

Bree's mouth drops open. "So you're just going to tell all my business like that, Eva?"

Eva laughs. "My bad, Bree. I didn't know you were such a private person . . ."

Bree grins. "I just don't usually broadcast my shortcomings, is all."

Everyone laughs, except me. While Eva checks something on her phone, Bree leans in and whispers in my ear. "What's wrong with you?"

Well, let's see. Kai chose celery over me, Mason kisses like an overly eager puppy, Dev has officially moved on . . .

"Nothing . . ." I'm certainly not plummeting into the depths of bitterness over everything about Last Chance Dance going wrong for me while my bestie and my last remaining match fall in love.

Bree lets it go and eventually we reach the front of the line. It takes a while for the APs to find and check our names off the list, but once they hand us our yearbooks, everyone cracks theirs open.

Bree flips to the back and cups her free hand over her mouth. "Oh, *snap*. Yearbook quotes!"

Her eyes travel down the page and stop.

"Leila Bean: 'Love is all we need—Madonna.'"

"Ashli Henderson: 'Be a rainbow in someone else's cloud—Maya Angelou.'"

She flips a few more pages. "Eva Martin: 'We are the ones we have been waiting for—Alice Walker.'"

Bree makes a face. "I mean, these are *okay*. But they're definitely not going to go viral."

Eva cracks open her yearbook. "Don't even go there, Bree Bailey. Let's see your quote—and it *better* be good."

She skims her own pages and then makes a face. "What kind of quote is this?" She looks back down at her yearbook. "Bree Bailey: 'Dang, Bree just stole my girl again.—Everyone.'"

Bree stands up a little straighter and manages to look very proud of herself while everyone breaks into laughter again. Once again, I just sort of stand there, ready to go home.

"See, it's stuff like this that made me iffy about going out with your little player butt in the first place." Eva is too busy giving Bree the side-eye to catch the pitiful look on my face. But Bree notices.

She raises an eyebrow. "You should see your face right now, Lei. I thought you were just sick of standing in line. But something's wrong—so spill it."

I take a look around me. Ashli and Chad have now received their yearbooks and have joined our small group. Ashli already knows about Dev and Halima—so she probably already suspects why I'm feeling down. I might as well fill in the others.

"It's just—I'm already out of matches. And everywhere I look, this Last Chance Dance thing seems to be working out for everyone else. I don't know—I guess I feel like a failure."

Ashli looks confused. "What happened between you and Mason? You guys seemed cute together."

Sighing, I say, "I don't know. I guess I didn't really like him as much as I thought I did." I feel foolish saying this to her. Because days earlier I was super excited about Mason.

But Ashli simply shrugs. "Then you did the right thing." She sticks a thumb in Chad's direction. "I love Chad. But if something didn't feel right—we couldn't be together."

She puts a hand on my shoulder. "It's brave of you to know what you want and stick to it, Leila. Because what *you* want is not up for debate."

And there, for that split moment in the hall, Ashli's words make me feel proud that I *didn't* stick it out just to save face. Breaking up with Mason *was* brave—even if it was super awkward.

Bree pipes up next. "And, like, honestly, Lei? You and Dev just broke up two weeks ago. Do you honestly think someone's going to judge you for not finding a new person immediately?"

She throws an arm around my shoulder, and pulls me in. "Come on, Leila. You're awesome."

Out the corner of my eye, I see Ashli nodding. But Eva has a confused look on her face.

"How are you out of matches, Leila? We still haven't gone on our date yet."

I look from Eva to Bree and back to Eva. "It's pretty obvious you and Bree really like each other." I look down at the floor. "I'm not getting in the way of that."

Eva bumps her hip against Bree and smiles. "Yeah, I guess I *do* like this scrub. But that doesn't mean I'm not going to give all my matches a chance. That's the whole point of Last Chance Dance, right?"

She gives Bree a slight side-eye. "Besides, according to someone's yearbook quote, this Bree character has been known to be a bit of a player—so I'm still feeling her out."

Bree laughs. "Hey, I can't help it if I'm good company."

"Oh, really?" Eva shakes her head, but there's still a twinkle in her eye.

Bree smiles back at her before turning to me. "Eva's right though, Lei. Dating *all* your matches is the point of the whole thing—to try something new—get out of your comfort zone—give people a fair chance.

"Plus, as much as I like Eva—I don't *own* her. If she wants to go to the dance with me she will. Same if she wants to go to the dance with you." Bree shrugs. "I like to think that whatever's supposed to happen will happen."

A surge of optimism hits me, with the realization that, with Bree's and Eva's blessings, I'm back in the game with one more match.

In better spirits, I flip to my favorite part of the yearbook: senior superlatives.

Most of the categories are obvious.

Tre' got Class Clown.

Bree got Biggest Flirt.

Ashli Henderson got Future President.

Then my stomach drops. Right there, bottom left hand corner, is a picture of Dev and me—*together*—standing by the tall oak tree that sits in front of the gym—hugged up, with the words CUTEST COUPLE in bold typecast.

"Leila!" A familiar annoying voice cuts through the senior chatter surrounding me. Tre' exits the yearbook line with his cap and gown wrapped in plastic under one arm and holding his fresh new yearbook open with the other. He comes right over to me, taking exaggerated bows and egging people on to clap for him, while Kayla Sanders walks beside him.

"Thanks for the vote, Five." He holds his hand out to dap me up, but I'm too stunned by the photo of Dev and me to act on it. When I'm basically non-responsive, Tre' shakes his head and goes, "I'm starting to think you didn't vote for me, Leila Bean." He shakes his head. "That's okay. Here's one photo I know you can't hate on." Tre' flips a few pages and hands me his yearbook, which is open to the superlatives page.

My blood begins boiling. I just know he's going to rub that Cutest Couple photo in my face. "You can forget about me helping you with—"

I look down, but instead of the picture of me and Dev under the heading of Cutest Couple, I'm looking at a photo of Tre' and Lou. The little dog is pressed right up against Tre's cheek. Tre' is smiling so hard.

I laugh; I can't help it. The surprise—and the fact that Tre' was actually not making fun of me, but trying to make me feel better—makes my stomach flutter unexpectedly. "Where did the yearbook committee get this photo of you and Lou?"

"I ran it past the yearbook editor a couple of weeks ago . . . I mean, I'm a little hurt that we didn't make it into the actual senior superlative section, but I personally think, had we been given the chance, we would've beat out all the other options."

I can't help smiling at the one joke Tre' nailed. "I agree, Class Clown. I agree."

19

FIRST PERIOD IS over by the time all the yearbooks are handed out. So everyone filters into second period. Since Ms. Reeves is still subbing for Ms. Amidon, we spend English 12 huddled up with friends, talking, snacking, and telling jokes. About twenty minutes into class, I notice that Tre' is over in the corner of the room, biting his bottom lip and erasing something on the paper in front of him.

I walk over and thump him on the head. "What are you over here doing, Threehead?"

Tre' makes a face. "*Three*head?"

I shrug. "I mean, my forehead is big, yours is a little on the small side, so—"

Tre' rolls his eyes. "Leila, leave the cute nicknames to me, please."

"Whatever, *Tre'*." I get a closer peek at his paper. "Wait, are you *still* working on Lou's foster application essay? Come *on*, Tre', you only need to come up with one really good paragraph."

Tre' scowls. "Not everyone likes writing, Leila. You took out a full-page ad in the back of the yearbook to thank your parents. I just wrote "Mom, Dad, Brett: Thanks.""

"That's all you had to say to people who literally keep clothes on your back?"

Tre' shrugs. "I mean, they know I think they're cool. No need to elaborate."

I nudge him with my hip. "But there *is* a need to elaborate sometimes, Tre'. People might know you care. But they need to hear it sometimes. Come on, let me see what you've done." I wiggle my fingers until he places the papers in my hand. I make a big show of straightening out the wrinkles and holding the pages up so I can better see his faint handwriting.

I scan the document. "You're not doing that bad, Tre'. You've already filled in most of the questions."

"Yeah, the *basic* ones."

Tre' flips one of the pages over. "But look at this essay question . . ."

"Why do you want to foster this particular animal?" I mumble to myself, reading the question. I pause for a second to read what he actually put. ""Because we vibe'? Tre'? *Really?*" I shove the application back in his hand.

Tre' sucks his teeth. "I don't know why I have to fill this

out in the first place. They're making this just as awkward as my Brown application—asking all these personal questions, trying to get me to soul search and stuff."

I raise an eyebrow. "Don't you think it's valid that they want to pick a person who can tell them why they want Lou? They just want to make sure Lou's going to a person who actually cares."

"They see that I care every day during lunch—"

"Okay, then say that. You've spent too much time with Lou to throw him one measly sentence." I pick up his pencil and put it in his hands. "If you want to show Shannon and the rest of the animal shelter staff how much you care about Lou, you're going to have to *elaborate*." I check the time on my phone. "Ashli and I are going to chat for fifteen minutes. You should have something better on the page by then." I start the timer on my phone and set it down next to Tre'.

Tre', looking even more uneasy, says, "You're not going to help me? You know I'm bad with expressing myself sometimes—"

I suck my teeth. "I can't tell you how you feel about Lou. That's something you're going to have to spend some time thinking about."

Fifteen minutes later, Tre' slides me the application right after the timer goes off. "Killed it!"

I shoot him a side-eye. "We'll see about that . . ."

I look down at Tre's revised essay, and am happy that it's

much longer than his previous one-liner. With this in mind, I begin reading out loud with optimism.

"Lou A. Dog is an older gentleman who deserves to spend his elderly years in style. Now, I can't promise a forever home right now, but I can provide a relaxing temporary environment with plenty of access to designer dog food. My stepdad is a highly sought-after software developer—creating one of the most-used medical apps in the healthcare industry. My mom is a commercial real estate developer. As a family, the Hillmans can provide Lou with all the finer things in life. Much finer than his current life sleeping on a thin blue cot and eating generic kibble. Pick me, Trevor Hillman, and you won't be disappointed."

By the time I'm finished reading the last hideous sentence, Tre' is up out of his seat and taking a bow. "Don't hold back on the applause, ladies."

Bree's face describes my exact feelings. Total shock and disbelief.

"Are you kidding me, Tre'?" I slap his application down on the table in front of him and point him back to his seat. "This is worse than your one line about vibes. At least *that* version wasn't off topic and full of unnecessary bragging."

Bree shakes her head. "Yeah, bro, that was a bit much." She looks my way and chuckles. "Who mentions their stepdad's involvement in health care software development on a foster application?"

Tre' refuses to take a seat. "I wanted the shelter to know we could afford to take care of Lou in the way he deserves."

I shoot him a look. "Lou would be just fine with regular old kibble, Tre'. The shelter wants to know that you're going to be there for him, be his friend, and care for him like he deserves."

"—Which is why I mentioned designer dog food."

"Lou doesn't need designer dog food, Tre'—he only needs to know you're going to be there for him when he needs it most." I pick up my things. "And being there for someone takes a lot more than money."

Suddenly, I remember Tre's little attempt at making me feel better about the whole couple's superlative thing. I should do something nice for the little scrub.

I look over at the sun shining through the row of windows on the other side of the room. Birds are literally chirping out there. This classroom, however, is beginning to take on a very distinct armpit smell.

"Let's get out of here."

Tre' looks around. "Out of where?"

"Out of here, the classroom—the school building. I want you to take me somewhere." Anywhere that will get me away from this sweaty smell.

Tre' waves me off. "Yeah, right. Leila Bean doesn't skip second period—even if we've had a sub for weeks now. So just cut it out."

I fold my arms. "I ducked out early with you to see Lou at least twice . . ."

"Yeah, but that's different . . ."

Suddenly Bree leans over, and thumps Tre' on the arm.

"Just go, Tre'. Ms. Amidon isn't here. And you know Ms. Reeves doesn't care if people come in or leave." She leans back, kicking her feet up on the seat across from her. "I'm not even supposed to be here."

Tre' looks around again nervously. But he *does* start gathering his things. "Fine. But if we get caught . . ." He looks nervous as he slinks out of the room after me. "It's one thing to miss lunch. I don't like ducking out on classes."

"Oh, stop the whining," I tell him as we leave out. "We only have a few days left. No one's even going to miss us."

20

SIXTY SECONDS LATER, I'm buckled into Tre's car and he's still looking around nervously. "Okay, where are we going, Five?"

"You tell me."

Tre' looks over. "Tell you what?"

"Where we're supposed to go." I ignore the confused look on Tre's face. "I want you to take me somewhere that means something to you."

"What?"

"Seriously, Tre'. It can be a place your mom took you when you were little—or maybe your dad."

Tre's face lights up for a second. "I know a place," he goes. Then he starts the car.

He drives us to a nearby McDonalds and orders a large fry for me and a cheeseburger for himself.

"Hold the condiments, please. Actually, you can leave out the burger, too. I just need the buns."

I look at him like he's growing another head on his shoulders. "Ummm . . . ?"

But Tre' holds his finger up. "I need the bread for the place we're going."

After pulling out of the drive-through, Tre' drives us directly across the street into a large development. He pulls in and makes an immediate right, driving another minute or so before parking in front of a large lake.

"Come on, Five. It's time to show you something special."

I follow Tre' out of the car and through a grassy field until we get to the lake's edge.

Tre' immediately goes into defense mode. "This is a little embarrassing, so if you tell anybody, I'll deny I ever told you this . . ."

Tre' rips off pieces of his hamburger bun and throws them into the lake toward the squawking geese.

I throw my hands up. "I'm not about to reveal your secret bird-feeding activities." Secretly, I think it's kind of sweet.

"Nah, you can spill the beans about this part. It might actually help convince Kayla Sanders to go to the dance with me." Tre' throws out another piece of bread and the geese flap over each other to grab the morsel for themselves.

"But this other stuff . . . ?" Tre' stops throwing bread to

reach over and zip my lips with his finger. He sticks the imaginary key in his pocket.

"When my parents first separated, things got kind of messy," he finally says. "Like, they weren't punching each other or anything, but they were constantly arguing about who got to keep what in the divorce—including me."

Looking out over the lake, Tre' throws out another piece of bread. "In the worst parts of that tug-of-war, I didn't get to see my dad a lot. But whenever he did get to pick me up, he always brought me here."

He nods in the direction of the McDonald's. "We'd stop for a ten-piece McNuggets Meal deal and an extra cheeseburger." He hands me his extra bun. "Then we'd come out here and feed the geese."

Hearing Tre's divorce story reminds me of my own dad, and how grateful I was that my parents didn't argue in front of me. How, even though I didn't get to see my dad a lot, it wasn't because they were fighting over me.

"I'm sorry, Tre'."

But he shrugs. "I mean, things are fine now, though. And, like, I'm not saying my mom was like this evil ex who purposely kept my dad away. But things were just all over the place back then. Right after Dad moved out, he lost his job . . ."

Tre' throws out another piece of bread. "Mom felt like Dad needed to have more stability before he started getting me overnight. She didn't think a seven-year-old should have to stay the night in cheap motels if I didn't have to."

He throws out another piece of bread. "But I probably wouldn't have cared. I just liked being with my dad. Whenever my dad could get me, we would come out here and feed the geese, and just talk, you know—about anything and everything. About life, really. My dad was going through a lot at the time, and he didn't hide it from me. In fact, he pointed everything out." Tre' pauses for a second, looking me in the eye and then down, like he's a little bit shy about what he's about to say. I know this boy gets on my last nerves sometimes, but talking to him like this is actually kind of nice—like we're legit friends.

Tre's eyes flicker over to me for a brief second. "He said, 'Son, I'm losing everything right now. But that doesn't mean all is lost forever. Time is all I need. To regroup. And come back stronger.'"

"Did he?" I ask in a small voice.

Tre' nods and then points his finger back into the development. "He bought a house here about a year later."

"In this development?!" Through the trees, I can see the three-level colonials standing tall in front of large expansive lawns. "I thought you said your dad was in between jobs back then."

"Yeah, the cybersecurity firm he worked for went under a few weeks after Mom filed for divorce." Tre' shrugs. "But he found another job at a competing firm a few months later."

Tre' throws out another piece of bread. "The point is, Dad could've used the divorce and being out of work as an excuse to simply disappear. But he didn't. Every Saturday morning.

Just Dad and me. Here at this pond. Feeding the geese. And talking about life."

Tre' looks at me—all traces of usual goofiness gone. "My dad showed up—no matter what. The time we spent together meant everything—still does."

I understand him perfectly. "Your dad gave you lasting memories without spending a dime."

Tre' shrugs. "Well, the McDonald's wasn't free."

I whack his arm. "You know what I mean, Tre'."

We stand there quietly for a few moments, not saying anything and feeding the geese. Then I go, "You know, you and Lou are kind of repeating history . . ."

"How so?"

"I mean, you don't have a home for him yet. But same time, same place, you still show up for him."

Tre' thinks about that for a moment. "Yeah, I guess you're right." He shrugs. "I guess my dad's rubbing off on me."

I shoot Tre' a shy look. "That's what's up, Tre'. Get your essay. Because this is the stuff you need to be writing down."

Tre' looks surprised. "You want me to write about my parents' messy divorce?"

"No, you can keep that piece of business to yourself." I pluck his arm. "But write about being there for Lou, despite everything. You're always going to show up for Lou, because you care about him."

The lightbulb finally goes off above Tre's head. "I think I can pull off a paragraph or two about that," he goes. Then he heads to his car to grab his papers.

When he returns, a shy look is on his face. "Hey, I have to ask you something . . ."

I brace myself—fully expecting Tre' to use this tender moment to weasel a date out of me.

"I—I like when we talk like . . . this." Tre' looks down at his sneakers. "I guess what I'm trying to say is . . . I know I play around a lot, but you really are a good friend, Leila." Tre' looks me deep in the eyes, his gaze unflinching. "I know you don't want us to date . . . and I respect that. But do you think we could be friends?"

The sincerity of his words moves me to say, "Yes, Tre'. I would like that." I lean over and pretend to brush something off his face.

Tre's hand immediately touches his cheek. "What are you doing?"

"I'm just wiping off some of your clown makeup . . ." I tell him with a smirk. "You should go without it sometime. You might even be kind of cute under there . . ."

21

LAST CHANCE DANCE is right around the corner—and not much has changed about my love life. I mean, I'm no longer bitter about the breakup, exactly, so there's *some* progress. But I just thought I would be further along with everything—and choosing a dress right now, instead of still searching for someone that feels right. To hear my matches tell it, I have everything going for me. I'm cute, smart, fun to hang out with. So why am I so unsure about all of them?

That instant connection I felt all those years ago with Dev? Is that impossible to find with someone new? It sure doesn't look that way for everyone else. Online, you would think I was the only one left unmatched.

On our way back to school, I describe Instagram posts to Tre' as he drives.

"Ashli posted a throwback picture of her and Chad from the Homecoming Dance last fall. It's captioned *The Perfect Match. Three years and counting . . .* #SavetheDate #LastChanceDance."

Tre' nods. "I respect the longevity. You should heart the photo."

So I do, before moving on to the next post.

"All right, in this next one, Darby Long is in a photo on Kai's page. Darby's wearing a long skirt, bright red lips, and her hair up. Kai is wearing flowy pants and has a rose between his teeth. The picture is captioned *Life Is Better When You Dance.* #LastChanceDance #BaldwinHigh #CoupleGoals #BlackLove #JustDating #HighSchoolDance #DanceQuotes #Teen."

Tre' shakes his head. "Doing the most. Skip the heart on that one."

But I disagree. "You don't think these two are made for each other?" I heart the photo, happy that things didn't work out between Kai and me—even if it's one less viable match for me. Forcing something that wasn't meant to be would've kept him from finding *his* perfect match.

The next post squeezes on my heart a little. But I don't scroll by. "Okay, so Dev and Halima have kept it simple with a selfie of the two of them over the caption #LastChanceDance."

Tre' throws a glance my way. "Go ahead and heart the photo," he says. "Show off those unbothered vibes."

The next photo is from Eva and it's a breath of fresh air.

Instead of a Last Chance Dance post, she's holding up a book in front of her face, with a stack of titles off to the side. When I heart her photo, she immediately sends me a text.

I haven't forgotten about our date, she writes. I've just been stressing over this senior gift stuff.

I thought you were choosing a book collection to add to the school library? You're a Bookstagrammer. It shouldn't be too hard to come up with twenty-five books to purchase.

It's not coming up with titles that are the problem. Seriously, Leila. Have you browsed around our school library lately?

Well—no. I guess I haven't.

Exactly. Meet me in the school library right after lunch, and I'll show you what I'm talking about.

Tre' glances over again. "Why are you so quiet over there? I thought we were giving off unbothered vibes?"

I text back a thumbs-up emoji and close my phone. "Oh, sorry, I got distracted."

"Oh. Well, while we're on the subject, I guess I should tell you—"

I look over at him.

"Since I finally worked my way up to the friend zone, I guess you should be the first to know that I asked Kayla Sanders for a do-over. I asked her on a real date this time."

"For *real*?" I figured he would, after seeing them together in the yearbook line today. But it's still kind of surprising to hear it. "Congratulations," I say. And I mean it.

But instead of looking happy about the news, Tre' sucks his teeth. "Don't congratulate me. If I had known you dumped Mason Luther King, I would've asked *you* for a do-over."

I shake my head at him, laughing. "We're working on a friendship do-over, Tre'. I consider that a win."

Tre' smiles while keeping his eyes on the road. "Yeah, yeah, yeah, Five. I hear you."

But even as I'm reminding Tre' that we're just friends, a wave of sadness passes over me. I chalk it up to my dating disappointments, and let the moment pass.

When I get back to school I find Eva standing in the middle of the main hall talking with a group of friends. But, when she spots me, she waves to them and walks over.

Eva and I walk down the main hall until we reach the school library, nestled in the center of the building.

"Hey, Ms. Reeves," Eva goes, beckoning me to follow her through the double doors.

I'm shocked. Because the woman who normally subs in my regular classes is sitting behind the checkout station in our school library.

"I didn't know the school gets subs for the library."

"They do when the school has no budget for an actual librarian." Eva leads me over to one of the library stacks. "How often do you come in here?" Eva asks me.

And I'm instantly embarrassed. "Honestly, I haven't been in here since we had that ninth-grade mandatory orientation on how to use the digital research tools."

Eva gives me a judgmental look. "I thought you liked reading, though . . . you've liked tons of my book posts."

Fearing my match value plummeting in Eva's eyes, I quickly add, "I *do*. I just usually order my books online."

Eva pretends to clutch a string of pearls around her neck. "Leila. Please tell me ordering online is, like, a last resort sort of thing."

I shrug. "It's super convenient—and shipping is mostly free now."

Eva grimaces. "Yeah, but then you miss out on the *whole experience*. Okay, wait. Pause that point, because that's not why we're here."

Eva takes me by the hand and leads me down the rows of books. She glides her fingers along the spines and pulls out title after title, showcasing books that I remember reading in class over the last four years, and books I've never seen before.

When we get to the end of the last row, Eva turns to me and asks, "Notice anything?"

I try to think about the titles she showed me. But without a hint, I don't know which details she wants me to focus in on. "Not really . . . umm, didn't we read a few of those in class this year?"

"Yeah . . ." Eva nods. "What else? What did they all have in common?"

I think hard. "Umm, well. I certainly didn't see a Black person on any of those covers," I joke.

But Eva snaps her fingers. "Exactly."

I make a face. "Well, yeah. That's obvious. But the books here have always been like that. It's the *school* library. I thought they stopped ordering new books when they *built* Baldwin."

"That's the point, Leila. Without an assigned librarian here, no one's really looking at the book options. When I asked Ms. Mahoney about it, she said whichever adult has the most free time usually orders new books."

Eva's eye's slide over to Ms. Reeves nodding off behind the circulation desk. "*I* think the staff here pick out the books they read when they were kids in school—which probably weren't very diverse either."

Eva sticks a novel back in its place on the shelf. "Not having a librarian assigned to our school really hurts our student population." She makes a face. "Sure, you can just order a book online. I can drive across town to Busboys. But what about the kids that go here that don't have that kind of access?"

I shudder just thinking about that. "I mean, I can't lie, you pulled some books off the shelf that I loved as a kid—" I look around. "But if these were the *only* book options I had? It wouldn't be enough."

A slow smile spreads across Eva's face. "*That's* why it's so hard narrowing down the senior class book donation to just twenty-five books. I'm trying to reach an entire body of future students on limited funding."

I nod.

Eva snaps her fingers. "I have the perfect date idea." She

smiles and takes a step closer in the already-cramped space in the stacks. "I'm going to take you to your first indie bookstore. Then you'll feel the magical exchange of an actual person recommending books to you."

I try to use this moment to sneak in a flirty one-liner. "But I already have you and your Bookstagram page . . ."

But Eva doesn't pick up on my flirty vibes. Instead, she blows a breath and goes, "No—you . . . you just don't get—" She grabs my hand. "Meet me at Busboys and Poets on Saturday."

22

THE NONSTOP TEXTING between Eva and me is effort-less. And unlike when I first felt this spark with Mason, I don't carry an ounce of guilt. A small voice in my head reminds me that Bree likes this girl, too. But honestly? Bree likes everyone—her yearbook caption says it all. So I lean all the way in, allowing myself to think positively about the whole thing.

As chair of the Senior Gift Committee, the rest of the members are expecting me to shave five books off our list, Eva texts. But the problem is, I like all thirty.

For a split second, I imagine purchasing the extra five books in a grand romantic gesture. Eva will reluctantly cross five books off her list, and then—*bam*—I'll come through like her own bookish hero.

I'm all ready to do it, too—until I check my bank account, and realize I have just enough funding for one more round of Ubers before Dad replenishes my account next week. And I still need to make it to our bookstore date on Saturday.

So I tuck away my grand gesture, and instead offer to help Eva narrow down her list.

While Mom and Ben are in the kitchen cooking up dinner, I lounge on the couch, waiting for book pics to come through so I can give my opinion. When Mom calls Riley and me to dinner, my phone is still buzzing like crazy.

"No phones at the table, Leila," Mom goes, as she and Ben carry dishes of food to the table. Lasagna, green beans, cornbread, some other mysterious thing that still has the top on—but smells deliciously sweet.

I raise an eyebrow at the act my mother's putting on in front of Ben. "Since when?"

"Since I told you I don't want anyone checking phones at the table." Mom waves her hands in the direction of the spread in front of us. "Ben went out of his way to make us this delicious dinner. Texting with friends can wait."

"Fine." I put my phone away and work on piling my plate with delicious food. As I dig into layers of penne, gooey cheese, and pesto, the comfort food puts me into a positive space—like maybe everything could be right, if I let it. Right now, I'm surrounded by people who care about me—and I have an amazing date with Eva coming up. Nothing could be better.

Then Ben lifts the lid off the mysterious dish and reveals a three-layer chocolate cake, with fudge syrup dripping down the sides and chocolate chips sprinkled on top. One bite into my slice of this delectable yumminess, and I seriously consider taking this *cake* to the dance—what's left of it, anyway, after Mom and Riley dig in.

While we eat, Riley dominates the conversation by grilling Mom and Ben on their relationship. Eating with one hand, holding her phone with the other.

"Didn't you already do an episode about them?" I ask between bites of cake.

Riley pauses her recording. "This is for—ahem—a different project." Then she turns back to her guests.

"Tell me how it all started," Riley says.

And I pretend I'm all into my dessert, but I secretly want to hear this story, too.

Ben smiles across the table at Mom and says, "Well, we'd been matched on Tinder for three whole weeks before either of us said anything to each other."

"Why did you wait so long?" Riley asks. And I'm glad she does, because I want to know, too.

"Well, I'd been on a few pretty bad dates that month. And I was starting to give up on the idea of finding someone on a dating app."

I watch Mom lean into the camera. "And I honestly thought he was a bot, if you want the honest truth."

Ben leans back and raises an eyebrow at Mom. "Excuse me? A *bot*? Why is this the first I'm hearing about that?"

Mom laughs behind her hand. "It was the picture of you

petting the white Bengal tiger for me. I'd seen the same type of photo on every guy's profile. It just felt a little *inauthentic*."

Ben's mouth drops open. "You didn't find that photo adventurous?"

Mom presses her lips together for a second. "No, Ben. I did not."

Then she leans into the camera again. "But one day, I decided, you know what? What will it hurt to say hello? If he turns out to be a bot or some sketchy creep, I can always block him."

Ben shakes his head. "Well, thanks for believing in a guy, geez."

But in the back of my head, I'm thinking about the new chance I'm taking with Eva. Maybe this will be our origin story someday.

Mom winks at Ben. "It was the best chance I ever took on a dating app."

Again, a surge of hope races through my body.

"You see, Riley," Mom is saying. "Meeting Ben forced me to step outside of my comfort zone and to try something new. And it was scary. Your dad was the only guy I'd dated in a long time. But meeting Ben, and really getting to know him, opened the door for so many new experiences. And in the end, I'm glad I took a chance on this tiger-loving guy."

Ben smile is as bright as the sun now. "I'm glad you did, too."

Ben's goofy grin must be infectious, because all of a sudden I'm cheesing, too. And you know what? I'm glad these two took a chance on each other, too.

While we're all finishing up our meal, my phone continues to buzz with what I can only assume are more book choices from Eva. But when my phone starts ringing, I sneak a glance under the table. It's Dad trying to FaceTime.

I hold my phone screen up so Mom can see.

But she goes, "Well, call him back later, Leila. We're having dinner."

I raise an eyebrow at the shade. "Are you saying that hanging out with my mother's *boyfriend* is more important than answering my father's call? The man who gave me *life*?"

I turn to Ben. "No offense to you . . . but you get what I'm saying, right?"

Ben smiles and shrugs, obviously trying to play both sides and remain in both of our good graces.

Mom lets out a tired sigh. "Leila. Just make it quick—geez."

Riley pops out of her seat and squishes in next to me. "Dad!!!" we both shout as soon as I pick up.

"How are my favorite girls?" Dad's cheerful voice comes through loud and clear on our end. "Lei, I just purchased my plane ticket to come out there for your graduation."

"Awesome."

Riley pipes up. "How long are you staying, Dad?"

"I'm thinking maybe a few days."

Riley squeals and claps her hands. "I'm going to plan everything out. We're going to stay up late, make s'mores, watch all of my finished podcast episodes. I want *lots* of constructive feedback . . . none of that kiddie stuff—"

"Sounds like fun, honey—but I don't think my hotel room is going to come with a stovetop to make s'mores."

Riley and I share a look.

Then she goes, "You're staying at a hotel?" at the same exact time I ask, "You aren't staying here?"

An uncomfortable pause lingers in the air for a moment. Then Dad goes, "Well . . . no, girls. Mom has a new friend now. I don't want to come in and take over her personal space."

I shoot Ben a side-eye. "But this is our *family* home, Dad." Suddenly Ben's cheesy lasagna feels heavy in my stomach.

"I know, Leila. And we'll still get in plenty of family time at your graduation."

Another awkward pause follows as Ben just watches this all go down. "I'll call you back, Dad." I hit the end button on my phone and turn to Mom.

"When were you going to tell me Dad wasn't staying here?"

Mom puts a hand to her throat. "I'm sorry, I didn't know I needed to make a special announcement."

I snort. "I guess the next surprise will be Ben coming to my graduation with a foghorn and a tambourine."

Ben chuckles. "I mean, I can certainly bring the foghorn,

but I may have to order the tambourine online."

The image makes me laugh a little. "Yeah, right. Even if you *were* coming, school security would tackle you the second you pulled out the tambourine."

Mom and Ben exchange a weird glance across the table.

"What?" Then it hits me.

I whirl around to face Mom. "Ben is *not* coming to my graduation."

Mom folds her arms. "Now hold on, young lady. You don't work security for Baldwin High—"

She starts to smile but I don't find the humor in any of this. "I'm serious, Mom. I know you might be all caught up in your feelings, and *leaning* into your joy and whatnot. But Ben is *not* family."

I turn to Ben again. "No offense. You're cool and all, but you would agree that you're more of—like—a really good family friend, right?"

My eyes are pleading with him to understand. He's been cool all this time. I just need him to prove himself one more time.

Mom lets out a big breath. "Why not, Leila? You have an extra ticket, and I just thought—"

Now I'm starting to get heated. Because come on. I should *not* have to fight this hard about my own graduation. "Come on, Mom. Haven't I been supportive about your relationship? I didn't drag those tacky matching gym outfits. I didn't say anything about Ben messing up the Netflix algorithm with all those crime dramas." I push my plate away. "But this is my *graduation*—a real family moment, and you're treating this like a random backyard barbeque."

"Now, Leila . . . is it really that serious?"

I really can't believe my mother right now. "To me, it's *everything*. How often do I get to see my dad in person? I shouldn't have to share the moment with anyone else."

I turn to Ben again. "Seriously, no offense. I'm sure once I get some more reality dating shows in the queue, the Netflix algorithm will return to normal . . ."

"Ooooooooh, I *have* to get this on film." Riley whips her phone from her pocket and holds it up.

And that sends me over the edge, because *no one* seems to be taking my feelings seriously.

"Stop recording me, Riley!" I reach across the table, snatch the phone out of my little sister's hand, and slam it down on the table. "Did you know that recording someone without their consent is a crime in Maryland? Keep it up, and you're going to spend the entire fourth grade in juvie."

Welp. That does it. Riley starts crying. And now Mom's yanking me from the dinner table by my shirt sleeve.

"Pull yourself together, Leila. That's your *sister* you're talking to. I don't *ever* want to hear you talk to a member of this family like again! Got it?"

It takes me a second. But I go ahead and simmer on down—to avoid further sleeve pulling. "I shouldn't talk to my sister that way—why? Because she's family, and family's sacred, right? Why can't you see where I'm coming from with this Ben situation? Your relationship may be going well, but Ben is not family, Mom. He's *not.*"

Tears begin to well up in my eyes. And I don't mean to be so emotional about the whole thing, but no one seems to get where I'm coming from.

Mom lets my shirt sleeve go. "Look, I don't necessarily agree with what you're saying, but I hear you . . . okay?"

I nod and wipe some of the moisture from my eyes as Mom turns and walks back to the dinner table.

I take a moment to smooth down my shirt sleeve, and wipe my eyes again before heading back into the dining room. I sit down at my seat and take a long sip of water before turning to Ben.

"I really am sorry if I offended you in any way. But I'm not sorry about how I feel. I've seen you more times this month than I've seen my dad all year."

Then I turn to Riley. "And I'm sorry I made you cry. But we're going to work on the right and wrong times to record people, okay?"

Riley nods.

Finally, I face my mother. "This isn't about me attacking your new relationship. I kept my grades up for thirteen years. I joined all those extracurriculars. I tripled the required amount of Student Service hours. This is *my* day—not yours. Can't you understand where I'm coming from—even a little bit?"

Mom and Ben exchange glances.

"She's right, Natasha," Ben goes. "It's Leila's day, and she gets to decide—not us."

Mom lets out a deep sigh. But she eventually relents. "Fine. If you want this extra ticket to go to waste . . ."

"Natasha . . ."

"Fine."

I still feel bad that Ben got caught in the middle of our family squabble, but I'm glad that when it came down to it, he understood. I shoot him a grateful smile, and mouth the words *Thank you.*

23

FRIDAY AFTER SCHOOL, Eva and I plan to meet at Busboys and Poets on 5th and K for our official first date. This is it. My last chance to get it right. To feel the instant spark that will reassure me that I can feel that with someone besides Dev. And if Eva is that person, then this will have all been worth it.

Walking into the bookstore immediately puts me at ease. First of all, huge oil paintings of Black historical figures and artists are hanging on every inch of the walls. Then, Janelle Monae's latest hit plays on low from the speakers hidden somewhere beneath the many, many bookshelves lining the walls.

I resist the urge to wander immediately over to the Young Adult section. Instead, I look for Eva. I find her standing in the middle of a small group of people in the bookstore area, chatting easily and making them laugh like she's known them forever. But knowing Eva, she probably met them five minutes ago. She's always had that kind of energy. Approachable and genuinely friendly to anyone who crosses her path.

I walk up and tap Eva on her shoulder. When she turns and realizes it's me, she flashes me a smile with teeth so white I imagine she stopped by the dentist on the way to our date. "You made it!" she says.

"Yep, and I brought my tote bag just in case we needed backup carrying all these books out of here."

"*Great* idea," she says. Then she walks me over to the checkout counter.

"Esmerelda, meet my friend Leila," she says to a woman with two auburn french braids.

When Esmerelda smiles at me, I hold my tote out and go, "We're going to hang out in the book section for a while, and you might see us slip a bunch of books into our totes—but I promise you—we're not lifting them. We just need to haul about twenty-five books up here to the counter."

"It's for a special thing at school," Eva adds.

With an amused look on her face, Esmerelda goes, "Oh, no worries about that. This is a safe space here. I trust you." Then she pauses.

"You know what? One second." She holds a finger up, and walks quickly to the back. When she comes out again, she's rolling a cart.

"This will probably work a little better than the tote." She parks the cart in front of us. "And if you need help wheeling the books out to the car, let me know and I'll come help you." With a smile on her face, she says, "A mission to pull twenty-five books for a school project sounds like my kind of activity. Trust me, I'm very happy to help."

"Thanks!" we tell Esmerelda. Then together, Eva and I walk over to the stacks.

We split up at first. Eva goes over to YA Sci-Fi, while I check out YA Romance. We meet up in the middle to check out the YA Nonfiction section together. I feel like I'm auditioning for a rainbow-friendly teen rom-com when we both grab *Stamped*, by Jason Reynolds and Ibram X. Kendi, and our fingers touch.

Electric sparks ignite before I pull my hand away. I push the cart to the counter, and Esmerelda cheerfully rings up the purchases. "What kind of school project is this?" she asks, scanning *Grown* by Tiffany D. Jackson.

"Our school library is currently a little—umm, what's the word I'm looking for—" Eva goes.

I lean forward. "—Dry. She's looking for the word *dry*."

Eva giggles. "Yeah, that's the one. So our senior class is gifting Baldwin High twenty-five new hardbacks to diversify the stacks a little."

Esmerelda gasps. Then she puts her finger up again. "Hold on for a second. The owner stopped by today and he *has* to hear this."

She goes in the back and comes out with a light brown man with a mustache and a warm smile. "I told Andy what you guys are doing for your school, and he has a surprise for you."

The owner's eyes twinkle as he says, "Busboys and Poets would like to match your contribution to your school. After Esmerelda rings you up, go on back to the stacks and pick out twenty-five more."

Eva legit squeals, and after Esmerelda rings up the last book, the owner decides to do one last good deed. "Fifty books is a lot. Why don't we ship these to—?"

"Baldwin High," we both chime in.

It takes Eva and me another hour and a half to sift through the stacks. It isn't easy. We argue over which books are already in our school library and which would be most widely checked out by students.

"You don't have to pick the popular books all the time, Leila," Eva argues.

"If lots of kids check out the same book, it'll show the school that it should've already been on the shelves in the first place."

Eva thinks about that. "True. But what about the books that don't get a lot of love? The ones that aren't on the best-seller lists. I've read plenty of books that were amazing that hardly anyone's heard of. *Those* books deserve to be on the shelves, too."

I think about all the single seniors who didn't get matched. They weren't throwaways. Far from it.

"You're right," I tell Eva. Then I grab up the book in her hands and gently place it on the cart.

After picking out fifty hardback books, Eva and I are exhausted. So we grab a booth in a quiet corner of the restaurant and sit next to each other, our knees nearly touching under the table. When the server comes over, we both order hot chocolate with extra whipped cream.

While we wait, we check our phones. I scroll my feed, more out of habit than anything. I sprinkle a few random hearts around, then set my phone facedown on the table.

Since I'm right next to Eva, I look over at her feed instead.

"Hey, wasn't this one of your matches?" Eva points to a photo of Mason and—*Chelsea*?

"I didn't know that Chelsea was one of Mason's matches," I tell Eva. "Good for him!" Now I can let go of my guilty feelings for rejecting him.

Eva smiles and hearts the photo of Mason and Chelsea sitting on a fishing pier and smiling. Then she pauses. A confused look crosses Eva's face.

"Didn't Bree already go on a date with Chanel?"

I peek over at Eva's screen. Bree's IG stories are up, but Chanel's face is on the screen under the hashtag #ChanelTakeover.

The next slide in Bree's story is a wide shot video of my bestie stepping off her deck with a kickball under her arm. For ten seconds, the camera follows Bree as she walks across the grass in her backyard—under the word #Cutie. The shot is so wide, right before it cuts off, I catch Riley standing in our backyard holding her own phone up to catch a video of it.

"Riley?!" I shake my head. "That sister of mine never learns."

But Eva doesn't acknowledge seeing Riley at all. Instead she moves on to the next slide—where Riley's nosy butt must have invited herself over to Bree's backyard, because the next thing I know, the shaky video footage catches Bree using her feet to play keep-away from Chanel with the kickball.

Eva cuts her phone off and lays it down on the table. "Bree must really like Chanel . . ." she goes.

I shrug. "To be honest, I don't know what Bree wants."

The server finally comes over to our table. He sets two mugs of hot chocolate in front of us. I blow on the swirling steam to cool my drink down some. "One minute Bree was all excited about Chanel. Then it was Ivy. Then it was you." I take a cautious first sip. Still too hot, so I set it back down on the table to cool off more.

"Now, I thought you were *the one*. All I've been hearing about is how you curved her for years. So when you guys had a great date, I figured she would ask you to the dance right away." I steal a little whipped cream off the top with my spoon. "But now it's back to Chanel. Tomorrow it'll probably be Ivy again."

I chuckle and nudge Eva in the ribs with my elbow. "You know how Bree is. Whoever she goes on a date with last will probably be the one she shows up to the dance with."

"Oh, I see." Eva smiles slightly before taking a sip of her own hot chocolate.

Figuring the temperature in my own mug should've cooled down some, I take a nice long sip. Like I thought. It's perfect. "But enough about Bree. Tell me more about you . . ."

For three hours, Eva and I talk about everything, from our favorite books to our families to our hopes and fears about college.

Eva surprises me by telling me that she's attending NYU in the fall.

"Wait. I thought you were going to Pepperdine?"

Eva shrugs. "I got accepted into both, but NYU offered me a better financial aid package. Plus, I'll already be in New York when it's time to apply to The New School's writing program."

"So you want to be a writer?" I can feel the hearts shooting from my eyes.

Eva takes another sip of her drink and chuckles. "Doesn't every reader?"

My short-lived career writing fanfic from a burner Wattpad account in the seventh grade suddenly springs to memory. "You know what? You *might* be right about that."

I inch closer to her. "You seem to be right about a lot of things," I tell her.

A strange look crosses Eva's face. "Trust me. I get some things wrong . . ."

Before I can ask what she means, Eva launches into her post–high school plans. "I want to major in English, with a minor in African American Literature." She takes another sip of her hot chocolate and looks down at the table. "I figure it will look good on my grad school application. Don't call me unhinged, but it's always been a dream of mine to publish my first novel before I get married and have kids and all that stuff."

Don't call *me* unhinged, but I just want to find a date before the dance. Can't we all just get what we want?

She looks at me. "I know every girl's supposed to dream of their wedding day. But my fantasy has always been to see a story I've written on a shelf in a bookstore like this." She smiles at the shelves surrounding us. "I figure I have at least one story in me before I fully commit to other stuff like kids and a good retirement savings plan."

I secretly want to ask Eva to explain, in very simple terms, what a retirement savings plan is, but I don't want to be embarrassed if it's something I should already know. So I don't ask. But I do swoon a little—okay, a lot, over how Eva's so smart—but also so cool. So easy to talk to. So, so . . . *perfect*.

So I tell her. "You're amazing—how come I never see you boo'd up with anyone?"

Then she turns to me and gives me one of her signature smiles—and I feel it in my bones. I *like* her.

"You would think a girl who has a shelf full of rom-coms at home would crave a little romance of her own," she eventually says. "But I also watch a *lot* of reality dating shows, and they never end well." She sneaks a peek at me—and from the look in her eyes, I can tell she thinks I'm judging her TV show choices. But she has *no idea* . . .

"I don't think I've watched a reality dating show yet where the love interests make it to the reunion episode," I tell her.

"Right?!" Eva places her hand over mine and looks into my eyes. There aren't just sparks I feel—there are flames.

With Eva, it's the best of both worlds. She's so fun and easy to talk to—and just so smart. And our chemistry? Electric. I can't help staring at Eva's heart-shaped mouth, wondering how her lips would feel on mine.

24

I TEXT EVA on my Uber ride home from our date. She sends me heart emojis and tells me she had a great time, too. I send her a cute selfie. She sends me back a funny meme. I go onto her Instagram profile and like her recent posts. Then I check my IG stories and see that she's already viewed.

Yeah. Everything that I'm feeling now isn't made up. And I'm feeling pretty hype about where this is going.

When the Uber driver pulls into my driveway, I thank him for the bottled water and then hop out. And also walk right into a dark blue Tesla sitting in my driveway.

"What are you doing here?" I ask Tre'.

He leans into the passenger seat, holds up his application, and goes, "I finally dunked on all the other foster applications. Come with me to drop it off, Five."

And since I'm already feeling good about my date with Eva, I hop into Tre's passenger seat. Maybe my good fortune will rub off on him and he'll finally get his dog.

While Tre' drives, I pick up the application and read his essay out loud.

"Dear Shelter Team,

I love Lou. From the moment I laid eyes on him. He was this skinny little guy, with these large round eyes, who shook like a leaf whenever someone came near him. Some workers thought Lou might not make it. But I always believed in him. You see, Lou's been through a lot, but he's a fighter. That's one of the reasons I care about him a lot. And I—Trevor Hillman—promise that if you give me the chance to foster Lou, I will do whatever it takes to keep him safe, comfy, and happy until he finds his permanent home."

Sniffing a few times, I place the papers on my lap.

"Aww, Five. I know you're not crying over a random foster pet application! *Come on!*" Tre' turns at the light, onto Brown Station Road. A deer darts onto the road and Tre' slows his car down enough to let the animal cross over to the other side safely.

I wipe a stray tear from my cheek. "Shut up, Tre'. I get allergies in the spring."

Tre' twists his lips up like he doesn't believe me. But, now that the deer has disappeared into the woods, Tre' speeds back up and continues down the long narrow road.

"So you think they'll approve my application?"

I look back down at his slanted handwriting. "With this essay? Yeah, I think so."

A proud look crosses Tre's face as he turns onto the tiny road leading up to the animal shelter.

At the shelter, while Tre' signs me in, Shannon looks surprised, but happy to see me. "Leila. So nice to see you back again."

"It's nice to be back," I tell her.

Shannon eyes dart from Tre' to me. Then she cups a hand over her mouth, leans in, and sort of loud whispers. "You know what they say. Guys who care about animals have the most gentle souls."

Tre' smiles, almost shyly. "Go 'head, Shannon. We're just friends." Tre' beckons me to follow him to the back, picking up his pace as we get closer to the Puppies and Small Dogs room. "I know it's only been a couple of weeks, Leila, but wait until you see Lou. The on-call vet says my boy has been gaining weight." Tre' holds the door open for me to walk in. "I mean, it's only two pounds. But for a guy who was nothing but skin and bones when he got here, that's a lot."

Tre' gives me another "Just wait—" as we walk to the back toward Lou's cage. And Tre's right. Lou's eyes look a little brighter, a little less sunken in to their sockets. And he lifts his head the moment he spots Tre'.

We take Lou out to the courtyard. I'm satisfied just holding the bottle and baggie of food, but as soon as I sit down, Tre' holds Lou out toward me. "Want to try to feed him this time?" he asks.

I shake my head no. "What if I break him?" I mean, I like dogs as much as the next girl. But Lou looks like he's one strong sneeze away from snapping in two.

Tre' shakes his head. "Naw, my dude is tough. He's been through it all—I think he can survive a little Leila Bean loving."

This time when he hands Lou to me, I gingerly take him. I feel a little wobbly holding Lou in my arms. Despite Tre's claims that he's gained weight, he feels lighter than a loaf of bread in my arms, and I can feel his bones poking into my arm. I run my pointer finger down the length of Lou's body, marveling over every bump I'm able to feel in his spine.

"Careful," Tre' goes, now looking a little less sure that I should be holding Lou. "Make sure he's able to burrow into the crook of your arm a little." Tre' adjusts Lou in my arms, until I gain a burst of confidence.

"I got him, Tre'. Stop being such a helicopter mom—or dad," I say with a slight giggle.

I mean, at first I was nervous about holding such a fragile dog in my arms. But now that he's here, the warmth of his tiny body soothes me, making me feel more confident that I can hold and feed him. "Hand me the bottle," I tell Tre'.

He hands me the bottle. When Lou begins to suckle, Tre' lets out a huge breath. And that's when I realize he's been holding his breath since passing Lou over to me.

"Really, Tre'?"

Tre' scoots closer and tips the bottle higher in my hand. "If you had seen what this little guy looked like when he first got here, you would be like that too. I just worry about him."

Tre' watches me closely while Lou sips from his bottle. And when Lou refuses to lick anything from my finger, he dips his own finger in and holds it up to the dog's mouth. "Don't take it personal," he says, when I look hurt over Lou's rejection. "He's like that with everyone—even me sometimes." He dips his finger in the baggie several more times, gently coaxing Lou to try more using a soft and gentle voice. A few moments later, he checks his cell phone.

"Dang, we gotta go. You're going to Ashli's party, right?"

When I nod, Tre' scoops Lou up, kisses his forehead, and goes, "You did good today, my dude."

Tre' looks over at me next. "You did too, Leila."

I wrinkle my nose. "Yeah, right. He only drank an ounce today."

"That's more than he drinks with other people." Tre' strokes the top of Lou's head with his thumb. "The bond Lou and I have doesn't come around often. It's one of those things that doesn't seem like it makes sense but just does, you know?"

My heart clenches for a second—and I almost stop to ponder why. But Tre' cuts into the moment by thumping me on the arm. "Come on, we have to go now. You're going to need all the time you can to get that big head through Ashli's front door."

I chalk the weird feeling from earlier up as nothing more than random heartburn from all the hot chocolate I drank at Busboys earlier. Then I swing for Tre's stomach, but he dashes just outside of my reach, and my punch never lands.

"HOW WAS YOUR date with Eva?" Bree asks on the way to Ashli's party. Either she's truly okay with me dating Eva, or she's doing a great job of keeping the salty vibes hidden.

"Oh my gosh, we had the *best* time!"

Bree smiles. "Did you?"

I give Bree the quick rundown on everything that happened, including our book haul doubling, the delicious hot chocolate, and even the moment we peeped Chanel in Bree's backyard.

I shoot my bestie a smirk. "You didn't tell me you were inviting Chanel over . . . I thought you crossed that match off the list a long time ago . . ."

A sheepish look crosses her face, and Bree goes, "Yeah, she texted me last minute—and I just figured, why not?" She turns onto Ashli's street and slows the car to a crawl. "Since you and Eva were hanging out . . . I figured I'd take another chance on my other matches."

"So how was the second date?" I press.

"I mean, it was regular. We played with the kickball for a while—then Riley forced us into an impromptu interview on love."

We both shake our heads at my sister's journalism. "So what did you say in your interview?"

A smile creeps up on Bree's face, and she goes, "I told her that people are too worried about *love*. And, like, love isn't the problem—it's just, people only look for it in romantic relationships. Like, dude, you can find love almost anywhere. With your family, with your friends, with a mutual you met on social media two years ago . . ."

"Bree, are you sure that @KickballLover99 isn't a catfish? Like, they've never posted a selfie—not *one* selfie to their profile, in all these years—you don't find that a *little* strange?"

"Lorraine is a real person! You can't know that much about kickball—"

I throw my hands up. "Okay, okay . . . don't bite my head off . . ."

Bree smooths her edges down. "Like I was saying . . . you don't need a whole relationship to get and receive love." She shakes her head. "And at that point, Chanel got all huffy, and was like, 'Oh, so you're not interested in a relationship?' And when I told her no, she was like, 'Well, why am I here?' and I was like, 'I mean, I thought we were just hanging out?'"

I shake my head. "Bree . . ."

"Leila, I don't lie to people. I tell them exactly where I'm at on things, and if they don't like it, it's cool."

"Yeah, but she was probably expecting you to ask her to the dance . . ."

"And that's fine. I wouldn't have minded going to the dance with Chanel—she's cool. But I don't want a relationship—not right now, at least."

I pull down the mirror to check my makeup. "Okay, Bree. Whatever you say."

I can't believe I was ever really worried about Eva and Bree. Despite all her talk about last chances, my bestie's clearly still in player mode.

When Bree finally gets her parallel parking together, I swipe on an extra layer of lip gloss, and make sure my lashes haven't suddenly flapped away in the wind, before we hop out the car.

I'm not going to lie, I feel like a VIP—all eyes on me, as we make our way to Ashli's front porch. My newest 'fit is serving a whole look and I'm looking forward to the festivities.

Kids from our senior class are leaning over the deck in the backyard, waving and calling our names. Friends are meeting us at the front door, dapping us up. This is the energy I've been waiting for. Six more days until Last Chance Dance. A week until graduation—I just spent four hard years keeping my GPA right and tight, and now I'm ready to relax, kick back, and celebrate.

Ironically, Eva is the first person Bree and I run into—and she's all smiles.

I put a lot of thought into my outfit for tonight. A cute little matching three-piece set in pastel pink. Eva looks effortlessly amazing. She's dressed in a little gray baby doll dress that stops well above her knee. She's wearing some cute chunky jewelry on her fingers and wrists and a necklace around her neck that's so thin you barely see it—unless you're looking extra close.

And I am.

"Finally!" Eva goes. "I've been waiting for you guys to get here," she says, giving both of us an individual hug.

For a brief moment, I wonder which one of us she's more excited to see. But I quickly tuck away any lingering insecurities when memories of our Busboys date pop up in my mind.

This doesn't stop Bree from practically stepping on my baby toe to get all up in Eva's face to strike up conversation.

"Ex*cuse* you, Bree!" I roll my eyes, but I go on and let Bree have her little moment. There will be plenty of time for Eva and me to pick up where we left off once the party really gets started.

I leave those two to continue their conversation while I check out who else has already arrived.

More kids are sitting on the couch, listening to music and talking. I drop the sodas I brought in the kitchen and head out to the deck. Kai and some of his friends are there. He hands his phone to Darby, then he takes his shirt off and hops up on the banister, and leans back until the sun is bouncing off every inch of his torso.

"Make sure it's on Portrait mode," he tells Darby. But she's already happily snapping photos.

I don't want to interrupt his impromptu photo shoot, so I decide to say hi later. But then I see Mason on the other side of the deck huddled up with friends.

"Leila—what's going on?" he says. Ever since he posted Chelsea as his date for Last Chance Dance, the dirty looks have faded. But I haven't forgotten. I give him a quick, barely there hug when he opens his arms wide, like he didn't just hate my guts a few days ago.

A small commotion erupts inside the house, and when I peek through the double glass doors, I spot Ivy coming in, dragging a large red cooler on wheels.

"I have something special for the seniors!" she yells, getting some cheers of appreciation.

Perfect timing. As soon as I pull off this quick swap, I can have Eva all to myself.

I walk back into the house and tap my bestie on the shoulder. "Hey, Bree. There's *Ivy*."

Bree gives me a funny look. "Okay . . ." Then she goes back to her conversation with Eva.

"*And* she's struggling to carry that huge cooler in the house."

Bree gives me a funny look. "Fine, let me go help her."

As soon as she walks away, I scoot in closer to Eva. "Hey."

"Hey," she says right back, her beautiful brown eyes sparkling as I step closer.

"Can we talk for a moment—just the two of us?" All the noise floating in from the deck is giving off Party HQ vibes—which is cool, if I'm ready to turn up. But, with Eva, I want to get that Busboys and Poets feeling back. Quiet, intimate, and personal.

I grab her hand, and lead her deeper into the house. I open a few doors, looking for an empty room so we can have a little peace and quiet. But so far, I've only found the laundry room, and now the bathroom—which is a little *too* intimate for the vibe I'm going for.

The third door I open has steps leading down into an unfinished basement.

"Okay, this looks creepy," I joke to Eva.

But she acts like the darkened basement is no big deal, and grabs my hand as she steps over the threshold. "We can sit on this top step if you want," she says. "That way, if the boogie man jumps out, we're right here by the door."

"Good idea." I sit down next to Eva and ease the basement door closed behind us.

"So I had a nice time at the bookstore," I tell her even though I already texted her that the moment we parted ways.

Eva smiles. "Didn't I tell you indie bookstores were on a different level?"

I nod. "I'm definitely going back there soon, for sure."

"Make sure you call me when you go," Eva says. "Because I'll definitely go with you."

"It's a date," I say—which, yes, I know makes me sound like a complete cornball. But in this moment, it feels right. She smiles again and I feel butterflies. I scoot closer to Eva on the step.

Normally, I would give things more time—at least a week or so. But, I've known Eva since we were in elementary school. And these last few days have brought us closer—in a different way.

So I tell her all of that. And more. "I guess what I'm trying to say is . . . I like you, Eva." Then I go with what I'm feeling. I close my eyes . . . lean in . . . then ease my lips onto hers.

Suddenly, a firm hand is on my chest. And not in the second base kind of way.

I open my eyes and Eva has a worried look on her face. "Leila, I've been thinking . . ."

I sit up straighter, embarrassed that my best little move just got curved hard. "About what?"

Eva runs the toe of her shoe across the tweed carpeting on the next step down. "I—I know that none of this is going to make sense. But . . . I still like Bree—a *lot*." She turns to face me. "More than I think I should, actually."

The light beneath the basement door trickles in enough for me to notice a pained look crossing Eva's face. "Have you ever had feelings for someone, and it didn't quite make sense—but you liked them anyway?"

That weird heartburn feeling is back—but I ignore it.

Eva stares off into the darkness. "I see Bree with lots of girls. She's cute, she's charming, and the girls at our school know it. It's why I've held off on dating her for so long. But—"

Eva turns and looks at me, with a hint of sadness in her eyes. "When I'm around her, there's this connection I can't deny."

Eva's words gut me. It's exactly how I feel about *her*.

I fidget with the bracelet on my arm. "You don't get that feeling when you're around me?" The words sound pathetic out loud and I'm instantly embarrassed for saying them. But also? I have to know . . . why not *me*?

Eva comes closer and grabs my hand. "I had the *best* time with you at the bookstore. You love books just as much as I do. We have so much to talk about. You're really sweet. I feel a special connection between us, too—as friends . . ."

Eva drums her nails against her knee. "I don't know, maybe I would be open to something more if I didn't have these feelings for Bree—but . . ."

As soon as Eva says the word *more*, I instantly know how to fix things.

"Okay, let me stop you right there," I say. "If it's more you're looking for, then I don't know if Bree is the girl for you."

Eva gets a funny look on her face. "What do you mean?"

I choose my words carefully. I don't want to throw my bestie under the bus—but I know how Bree is. And Eva is my friend, too. I can't have her peeling egg off her face, like I did with Dev.

"See, Eva. Bree is good at playing the friend role. She's really cool and chill to kick it with—have fun with. She's always the one cracking jokes, life of the party. And she's a true friend. Like, she'll always be there for you. Bree's a good person—but—"

Eva looks at me . . .

". . . I know for a fact Bree's not looking for more than just friendship."

"Did she tell you that?" Eva asks in a small voice.

"She literally says it all the time, including on the ride over here," I say, thinking back to all the times in the past few days Bree has told me she's not ready to settle down. And in all our years of knowing each other—Bree has never once gone out with anyone more than a few times. When Eva's face falls, I try to soften the blow. "Look, I'm only telling you this now because I just went through something similar with Dev. As much as I loved Dev, he didn't want a relationship anymore." I stare off into the darkness. "And to be honest, trying to convince him he should be in a relationship with me would've been a disaster."

Eva nods. "I agree. Love can't be forced."

"Yeah." I wait a couple of beats, then I shoot my shot again. "So, like, I don't know if that changes anything for you." I can hear the hope in my voice, bordering a little on desperation. But so what? Eva's my last match—my last chance. And I really like her . . .

But Eva's back to drumming her nails again. And the pained look on her face tells me all I need to know. "I'm *really* sorry, Leila. I still think we're better off as friends."

Now my neck is *really* burning with embarrassment. Clearly, she was trying to let me down easy. I didn't see it— and only pushed harder. A sick feeling puddles in my belly, and I can't help feeling stupid. And disappointed.

I try to play off my humiliation by acting like Eva's rejection is no big deal. I tell her I understand. But I don't mean it.

Then I give her a hug, and try to keep my eyes focused on the darkness at the bottom of the steps, as she gets up from the basement steps and rejoins the party.

26

AS I WALK out of the basement and back into the party, Tre' walks through the front door, wearing a pair of Balenciaga sneakers that I've never seen him wear to school and a crisp white tee that looks a lot nicer than the regular three-in-a bag undershirts. I would check him out a little harder, if this wasn't Tre' we were talking about.

"I know y'all didn't start the party without *Tre*'," he yells, before making his way over to Ashli's kitchen island, where I'm sitting—alone, wallowing in self-pity.

Eva, Mason, and Kai. None of them were what I thought they'd be. Even Tre' is back on the dating scene with Kayla—who quite honestly feels like the perfect girl for him. Ugh. Even though we're happily moving along in the friend zone, Tre' still feels like a waste of a wild card pick. If the algorithm had matched me with someone else, I would still have a crush to give me hope.

Tre' slams a large bag of chips onto the granite top next to me. Still feeling bitter over Eva's rejection, I turn my nose up at the off-brand label. "You couldn't spring an extra dollar for the name brand? What are *Floritos?*"

Tre' rejects my public shaming of his chips entirely. Instead, he points to the red cooler sitting near my feet. "Do you see how much beer Ivy brought? People are going to be begging for these Floritos after they kick back a few." He opens the bag and hands me a chip.

"First one's on me, Five."

"Boy! Get that cheap chip out of my face." I smack the chip out of his hand—a little too hard. It flies through the air, hits the floor, and slides under the fridge.

Tre' slowly shakes his head. "We're at a party, Five . . . act like it."

Then he turns and dances his way into the crowd.

"Probably searching for his boo, Kayla," I grumble to myself. I slouch over Ashli's kitchen island with my head in my hands, feeling matchless and alone.

From where I'm sitting, I have a clear shot of Bree whispering in Ivy's ear, then dancing with Chanel, and chatting it up with Eva—and all the other girls who swoon over her like she's next season's Bachelorette. And look, I'm no hater. I can acknowledge why everyone loves Bree. She has a certain brand of *charisma* that I, too, enjoy. But right now, I'm down bad—and my bitterness is taking over in the worst way.

At least Ivy's red beer cooler hasn't completely abandoned me. I open the top and dig through ice to get to one of the pink cans of flavored beer. If I'm going to drink a beer, I may as well be color coordinated.

I hold my pink can high in the air—to officially toast to all the failures I've accumulated this month. Then I sit at Ashli's kitchen island and shady-stare at the rest of the party.

Everyone has someone to dance with. Ashli and Chad. Kai and Darby. Eva and Bree. The front door opens, and in walk Dev and Halima—their fingers locked together tight. They come into the kitchen together, drop off more cases of soda, then breeze on by me like I'm the ghost of girlfriends past.

I crack open my third can of beer while they saunter onto the makeshift dance floor Ashli's created in her living room. When Bree and Eva step closer, staring into each other's eyes, I decide I've had enough. Time to call my Uber.

I get up from the barstool, but the kitchen suddenly tilts hard, and I'm forced to cling on to the edge of the island top to avoid falling on my face.

I wait for the kitchen to steady itself before stumbling off in a random direction, my stomach churning and threatening to send strawberry-flavored bile back up my throat. What was I thinking? Did I really think I would find someone I connected with in three measly weeks?

I almost want to cry—if the walls would just stop spinning.

Everything has gone wrong. I'm a total mess. And I don't

think I'll ever find someone who really likes me—someone who I like back—again.

It happened with you and Dev, a little voice in the back of my head reminds me. *You both felt the chemistry from day one.*

I push through couples left and right, and using the wall as my guardrail, I almost make it to the bathroom, when . . . Ivy's cheap beer decides it doesn't like settling in at the bottom of my belly.

The second I start making retching noises though, Tre' comes out of nowhere, swoops me into his arms, and runs me to the nearest bathroom.

"Please, Five, try to hold it in," Tre' whispers into my ear. "Not the Balenciagas—not tonight." He fumbles for a second, trying to get the bathroom door open without dropping me on my head.

Then, lucky for Tre's Balenciagas, he dumps me off close enough to the toilet that I'm able to let the chunks fly in the bowl, instead of all over his expensive footwear.

Tre' pinches his nose and covers his mouth like he's going to throw up next, anyway.

I wipe more sweat off my forehead and try to force myself into a standing position. "Is it really that serious?" I nod toward the toilet bowl. "Look, I already flushed. You can barely smell anything."

Moving my head, even a fraction of an inch, makes everything around me spin again, so I lean against the bathroom wall to try and center myself.

Tre' takes one look at me, hunched over, forehead all

sweaty, and shakes his head. "Choosing to ignore our eighth grade oath to be drug and alcohol free almost ruined an iconic pair of sneakers tonight . . ." Then he sighs hard, slings my arm over his shoulders, and helps me off the wall.

"Where are you taking me? I don't want to *dance*." At this point, even I can hear my slurred words. But Tre' bypasses the dance floor and heads straight for the front door.

The blast of cool nighttime air feels good on my sweaty forehead. And I take a couple of wobbly steps forward, lose my shoes, and nearly stumble off the top step before Tre' catches me and helps me down into a sitting position.

Weird. I thought only Lou received the Super Caring Tre' treatment.

"Wait right here, Five." He retrieves both shoes, then kneels down to slip them on my feet like I'm a toddler.

"Ooooh, Kayla's not going to like this . . ." I say in a singsong voice.

Tre' stops what he's doing momentarily to look up at me and shake his head. "Kayla's going to the dance with someone else, so I doubt she cares what I do with your feet."

I wiggle my toes at him. "Well, how did you mess that up?"

Tre' makes sure my shoe is on tight, then he helps me back up. "I guess I took too long to make an honest effort, and gave her plenty of opportunity to fall for someone else."

Tre' shakes his head like he's trying to rid himself of the idea of someone he likes falling for someone else. Then he shoves a bottled water at me. "Drink."

"You don't tell me what to do." I glare defiantly at him.

Tre' rolls his eyes. "Just drink it. Your puke breath is starting to make my stomach hurt."

I cup my hands over my mouth, confirm that I do in fact have vomit breath, and then take a large swig of water.

"You get on my nerves," I grumble, wiping my mouth with the back of my hand.

"Me? The guy who just risked getting puked on by the entire senior class gets on your nerves?" Tre' shakes his head. "I guess the good guys really do finish last . . ."

I cover up a stray laugh with a cough behind my hand.

"Stop laughing." Tre' reaches up and wipes the sweat from my forehead. "Before I change my mind about giving you a ride home."

"I don't need a charity ride from you." I fold my arms in defiance.

Tre' rolls his eyes. "Just come on."

Trying to salvage my last shred of dignity, I try to flip the script, like I'm doing him a favor. "Only if we stop for McDonald's fries, first."

Tre' nods. "You're going to need something in your stomach, after drinking all that cheap beer." He thumps my shoulder. "Here. Let me tell Bree I'll take you home. Wait here."

My head is spinning too hard to protest. So I wait while he runs in the house. He comes out with my purse and my phone. "All that drinking has you about to get your phone stolen."

"Let's go . . ." I say, but as I start to get up, my head spins. I grasp for the railing to steady myself before pretty much falling right back onto the step. I sigh, feeling so pathetic. Tre' leans down, scoops me up in his arms, and carries me to the car.

After Tre' stuffs me into his passenger seat and buckles my seat belt for me. I lean my head back and close my eyes while he drives carefully down the street.

"I hope you're not drinking and driving," I grumble.

"You think I'm about to throw away my Brown scholarship on some cheap drinks at a high school party? That's not me, Five. You should know that." Tre' looks almost insulted that I'd even accuse him of something like that.

He gets to the McDonald's drive-through and orders my fries.

I mumble a quick "Thanks" and then proceed to devour the entire large box, four or five fries at a time, while he drives me the rest of the way home.

"You all out of matches, too?" I ask Tre' as he turns onto my street.

"Yep."

Then I say what's been lingering on the edge of my thoughts all night. "If you didn't get on my nerves so much, I would've told you you looked cute tonight in your little 'fit, or whatever . . ." I take another peek at his Balenciagas. I always *have* been a sucker for nice footwear.

Tre's head goes on immediate swivel. "You *must* be drunk . . . talking like that . . ."

I shrug. "Maybe . . . maybe not."

Silence follows, until Tre' pulls into my driveway. "Leila, you really don't want to go on a Last Chance date with me?" He tries to say it in a joking way, but something real is woven in there.

I slump against the passenger door, a little too tired to sit up straight, but mostly feeling weird about the direction this conversation is headed. "You know that's not us, Tre' . . ."

Tre' winces like I've just sucker punched him, he actually seems . . . sad. "All I know is you're okay with us being friends but can't stand the thought of us dating . . ."

The old memories of what Tre' did back in middle school bubble to the surface. Whatever part of the brain alcohol messes with to impair judgment also pushes me to finally tell Tre' the truth.

"You want to hear *my* parents' divorce story?"

Tre' looks confused. "What does this have to do—?"

"*Do* you?"

Tre' sighs. "Sure."

I fixate on the floodlight on the garage shining into the car, trying to keep myself steady.

"My parents were actually supposed to divorce my seventh grade year. But they didn't. They called the whole thing off, telling us they loved each other and wanted us to be a family. Then the next year, my dad missed every major holiday, my parents' wedding anniversary, Riley's birthday, and then . . ."

The outline of the floodlight fades, and suddenly all I can

see is me on the night of my fourteenth birthday, kneeling at my bedroom vent, listening to my parents argue.

"Dad missed my birthday dinner after he promised that another surgeon would cover any emergency surgeries that came through the ER. I believed that he was still coming— because he *told* me he was. I refused to leave my birthday dinner until he arrived, even after they started cleaning off the rest of the tables at the restaurant. It was so late that I fell asleep. Mom had to carry me to the car and buckle me into the back seat like a toddler.

"That night, Mom said that she never wanted to see Dad break another promise to me or Riley again. That it was over—for good this time. Dad said that being married to a surgeon meant learning to sacrifice. Then Mom said that the look in my eyes at my birthday dinner opened her own eyes—that sacrificing her children's happiness was never an option again."

I finally look over at Tre'. "Do you remember hearing that before?"

Tre' shakes his head.

I look back at Tre'. "You don't remember snatching my journal in Ms. Mealey's English 8 class?"

Tre' shrugs. "I mean, maybe? I snatched a lot of people's journals back then."

He gives me a strange look. "Didn't you write some kind of super-emotional letter about your stuffed animal or something?"

"The letter wasn't about some silly toy, Tre'! It was about

my parents divorcing and my father leaving us to move to Texas!" I stare down at my hands. "And you read it out loud to the entire class—all to get a cheap laugh."

Suddenly, all the dots connect for Tre'. Once he realizes what he did all those years ago, he covers his face with his hands. "Leila, I'm so sorry . . . I didn't—"

Anger boils up inside of me all over again. "You know what? I'm going to go . . ." I snatch off my seat belt and open the car door.

But, as my foot hits the pavement, Tre' goes, "Leila, wait."

I don't know why, but I stop and turn to face him.

"You know I wouldn't purposefully try to mess with you while you're going through stuff, right?" he says softly. "Remember, I went through the same thing, Leila. I know what it feels like . . ."

A twinge of sadness hits me, as I remember that out of everybody, Tre' probably does know how I felt. But that doesn't change what he did. "All I *know* is that you'll do anything to get a laugh—even if it's at someone else's expense."

I don't want to hate Tre'. I know he has another side to him—the more vulnerable side that hardly anyone else gets to see. So I focus on that as my own voice softens. "You may not have hurt me on purpose, but you did."

Tre' looks near tears when he says, "I'm sorry, Leila. I know I play around a lot—too much sometimes. But I'm not cruel, Leila. You know that."

I shake my head. "People do hurtful things they don't mean all the time, Tre'. It doesn't make what they did any less painful." I take a few steps back and stumble a bit. My phone and purse fall in the wet grass.

"Need help to the door?" Tre' asks.

"Nah." I grab my purse and phone off the ground. "I got it."

As I walk across my front lawn, I realize, mournfully, that I actually "got" nothing. No more matches and no date to the Last Chance Dance.

27

I WAKE THE next morning with an upset stomach and a pounding headache. Even the buzz of my text notifications makes me want to puke. I grab my phone and tap the screen. It's Tre'.

I'm sorry again, Leila. I couldn't sleep last night. I couldn't stop thinking about what you told me.

I'm immediately embarrassed about telling Tre' all my business. Let's not talk about that anymore, I text back.

The three texts dot appear on the screen for a minute. Then another text from Tre'. You cool?

No, I type back.

You'll be all right. You just need to drink water and sleep it off.

For a moment, I'm sort of touched that Tre's checking on

me. I know everyone saw my top-tier clown behavior. But so far, only Tre' has texted me.

A knock at my bedroom door interrupts my cringe session—sitting up makes my head feel like it's splitting open.

"Come in!"

My mom knocks on my bedroom door and opens it. "You're giving me a preview of what sending you away to college is going to look like?"

"No," I mumble, embarrassed that my mom even knows I've been drinking. Even if it was just those awful flavored beers.

She goes into Mom mode, feeling my head with the back of her hand and checking me over like I've suddenly grown two horns since last night. "You know that's dangerous, right?"

"What?"

"Getting drunk like that and getting into a car with some boy."

"It was just Tre'—"

Mom gives me a look. "—and thank goodness this Tre' had good intentions. The wrong boy would've spotted a girl drunk off her *behind* and thought of a way he could take advantage."

I look down at my fingers, embarrassed at being so stupid. "Tre' wouldn't do something like that," I mumble.

My mom rubs my shoulder. "Thank goodness." She pauses for a moment. "You know, it was commendable of him to bring you home. Young people aren't always so considerate." She looks off for a moment. "I remember going to a college party in high school and drinking whatever was put in my hand. Besides swinging from the banister and waking up in a pool of my own vomit, I was, thankfully, not attacked or creeped on by some older boy. But all my so-called friends who I came with weren't even thoughtful enough to make sure I got home safe."

Mom gives me a serious look. "That moment taught me a lot about the people I was hanging out with. Tre' looking out for your safety like that says something about his character."

I mean, maybe. But, she also doesn't see all the times Tre' clowns me at school, so . . .

Mom raises her eyebrow. "And where was Bree while all of this was going on?"

My shoulders slump. "Busy tending to her adoring fans." And just so Mom doesn't suspect Bree could *ever* be anything like her bad friends who left her, I quickly tell her, "Tre' told her he would take me home, before she could offer to help."

Mom nods her approval, before saying, "Now, *that* sounds like our Bree-Bree. By the way, she's downstairs now."

Mom kisses my cheek, before scrunching her nose. "Just make sure you brush your teeth before leaving this room. You don't want to be in company's face with your breath smelling like that."

I smile as she shuts my door quietly.

I slip into a pair of shorts and a T-shirt and run a toothbrush over my teeth. Then I go downstairs, where Bree's waiting, holding a box of Krispy Kreme doughnuts— my absolute favorite breakfast treat.

I reach for them, but Bree snatches the bag just out of my reach. "I have something important to tell you."

I reach for the bag again. "I already know—Eva likes you . . . blah, blah, blah. So tell me, are you going with two girls to the dance, or three?" I reach for the bag again, but Bree yanks it away again.

"I'm hopefully only going with one girl."

Now I'm growing impatient. Because I need to sink my teeth into one of those delicious sugary treats . . . "It better be Eva. Because if I got curved just for you to end up at the dance with Chanel, I'm—"

"Leila, Eva's more than a date to Last Chance Dance. I want Eva to be my girlfriend."

I stop reaching for the box. "Yeah, *right*. Weren't you the same person who said you weren't looking for anything? That you didn't *believe* in relationships?" I raise a judgmental eyebrow at my bestie. "You just went on second dates with both Chanel and Ivy!"

Bree hands me the box of doughnuts to pace the room. "That was because I've been trying to talk myself out of feeling this way. A whole relationship is *scary*." Bree rakes her twists back with her hand. "But, I can't help it, Lei. Eva has everything. Beauty, brains. She's *sweet*. I don't know—" Bree looks at me with this almost bashful look on her face. "I guess I see how people end up in love."

"Love?!" I toss the box of doughnuts on the couch. "You're *in love* with Eva Martin?"

Bree looks down at her sneakers. "I think so."

I shake my head. "No, Bree. When you're really in love—it's something you know."

Bree pauses a moment. Then she meets my eyes again and goes, "I know it, Leila. I'm in love with her."

And I'm floored. Like, completely taken aback. All crush-worthy feelings I had about Eva go out the window, because this is one of the most important moments in my best friend's life. She's found someone she's willing to trust with her heart.

Tears come to my eyes and when I reach for Bree, I hug her tight. And even though my head is still killing me, my heart feels lighter—because my bestie is finally in love. "I'm so happy for you, Bree," I tell her.

And that's when I remember everything I said to Eva last night. And all the things I said about Bree being a player—what if I ruined everything?

For a second, I consider telling Bree. But telling my bestie what I said would mean spilling the tea on completely embarrassing myself going for that kiss. And I decide that some things are better left unsaid.

Besides, Eva already told me about her feelings for Bree. And they danced together all night. Once my bestie works up the nerve to tell her she feels the same, everything will fall into place.

And I can work on forgetting all my embarrassing moments at Ashli's party.

"I'm going to ask Eva to the dance after school tomorrow. And if she says yes, I'm going to ask her to be my girlfriend."

I throw my arms around my bestie in one last celebratory hug. Cue the party horns. Our girl is finally growing up, and settling down.

28

ON MONDAY, INSTEAD of heading to second period, all seniors are scheduled to report to the school gymnasium for graduation rehearsal. When I reach the athletics hall at the very back of the school, the gymnasium's hyped. The rehearsals are just another event reminding us all that graduation is just around the corner. Five more days, to be exact.

I find Bree and sit down next to her, since our last names are just as close as our friendship. We wait for our assistant principal Ms. Mahoney to get through her speech about not embarrassing her on graduation day.

"Remember, you are Baldwin Bulldogs for the rest of your lives. Don't get out there on graduation day and show off in front of your loved ones."

Quiet laughter ripples through the rows of chairs, because isn't that what you're supposed to do on graduation day? Show off a little? There's been whispers for weeks of which dances students plan to perform as they cross the stage. Secret air horns. And a persistent rumor about a certain student from chess club who plans to go clothesless under his gown.

Anyway, Bailey and Bean are called pretty quickly, and Bree and I are forced to sit through the rest of the alphabet of names. I'm thinking about taking a nap until Marie Zane is finally called, when a bunch of noise spills in from the hall.

"All hands on deck." We all hear it from Ms. Mahoney's walkie-talkie. "We have a physical situation between two sophomores at the vending machine near the gymnasium. We need all hands on deck. Copy."

Ms. Mahoney rolls her eyes and mumbles, "Every dang year around this time. Every *dang* year."

"Sit down, students," she demands, as we all crane our necks for a glimpse of a possible WWE match in the hallway. "Just sit yourselves here while I go see what's happening." Ms. Mahoney lets out another long sigh, then shuffles to the hall.

For a moment, we all trade possible scenarios about what could've led to the tenth-grade fight. I'm busy telling the section behind me that it's probably over some dusty tenth-grade boy, when I feel the slight breeze of someone walking by me.

I turn just in time to catch Tre' walking up to the pretend

graduation stage (really just a folding table and a withering houseplant). He grabs Ms. Mahoney's mic and goes, "Ahem, a*hem*, is this thing on?"

Everyone stops talking about the fight to see which way Tre' is going to "entertain" us all today. Even I pay attention—eyebrows raised.

"A*hem*. I just wanted to say, before our last week of school is over and I only catch up with you scrubs on social media every now and then, that I need to apologize—to a very *special* scrub in my life."

"Yeah, Tre'!" one of the football players yells from somewhere in the T section.

"Leila Bean thinks I can be a little insensitive at times." Tre' takes the mic and begins pacing in front of the fold-up table. "And at least one time, I took things way too far."

Tre' stands there a long moment trying to make sure everyone gets a good look at the regret on his face. Please.

"Look, I don't want to be remembered as the guy who was a jerk to Leila. So to make things right, I'm inviting her up to the mic right now to say something really mean about me, as payback."

"Yeeeeeaaaaaaaah!" all the senior varsity members of the football team, sprinkled across several rows, start cheering, and all of a sudden the entire gym breaks out into a chorus of "Do it! Come on, Leila. Get him back!"

And while this whole thing is turning out to be wildly entertaining—being mean to someone on a random Monday morning is just not my thing.

So I stand up, take a bow in front of my adoring fans, and call out, "You're good, Tre'! No need for payback."

When the entire senior class begins booing my decision, I yell out, "I said *no*. Now move on!"

I sit back down and try to get back to discussing the fight, when another *ahem* comes from the mic. This time it's Halima.

"Leila might be above payback, but I'm not," she goes, and the gym starts cheering again.

"Remember freshman year, when you kept calling my Birkenstocks Jesus sandals?"

"It was a joke!"

"Well, your joke had upperclassmen laughing at me for the rest of the day. I never wore those sandals again because of you. I'm *another* victim of your stupid jokes and *I* deserve payback."

"Fine—whatever. I can take it." Tre' hands the mic to Halima, then faces the entire senior class with his chest poked out.

Halima leans into the mic. "I just want to say—yourhead-isshapedlikeakidneybean. That's all." Halima shoves the mic back in Tre's hands while the gym erupts into another round of laughs.

In between chuckles, I look over at the gym doors, and spot the security guard perp-walking an angry looking sophomore toward his office.

Back in the gym, four kids are lined up to the side of the folding chairs waiting for their turn at the mic, including—
Bree?!

Tre' is holding the mic hostage and shaking his head at the growing line. "I know I haven't hurt all of your feelings. Now you guys are just trying to take free jabs at your boy Tre'."

Ashli snatches the mic from Tre'. "Oh, this isn't a free jab at all. Remember when you said that Chad and I looked like the broke version of Ciara and Russell Wilson? Well, I'm here to tell you that you shouldn't be talking because you haven't had a girlfriend the entire time I've known you."

The gym is roaring by now.

Right before Ms. Mahoney comes walking back in to break up the fun, Bree manages to get in a "your jokes aren't that funny" and "didn't you laugh so hard you peed your pants in the eighth grade?"

Ms. Mahoney snatches the mic from Bree's hand and points her back to the B section. "Get your tail in your seat, young lady. And Mr. Hillman?" Ms. Mahoney looks down her glasses at Tre'. "Maybe if you had worked on your *decorum* a bit these past four years, your friends would be able to find nicer words for you." She points him back to his seat too.

Tre', looking physically battered, takes the long way back to the H section by wandering past my row. "You happy now?" he says to me.

My stomach hurts from laughing so hard. "Boy, nobody told you to do all that! You brought that on yourself."

"Yes, key point. I didn't *have* to take a public beating like that. But I did—all for you."

I roll my eyes at him because he is nobody's martyr. But secretly, I'm touched by his grand gesture.

"Mr. Hillman! Get your butt in your seat, so we can finish rehearsals."

Tre' reluctantly walks back to his seat. But after Marie Zane crosses the mock stage, he's back in my face again.

Bree raises her eyebrows. "You're back over here for more jokes?"

But Tre' waves her away and gets all in my face. "So are we friends again, Five?"

I hold back a giggle. His head *is* shaped like a kidney bean. "Yeah, Tre'. You are officially my best frenemy."

Tre' breaks out into a smile. "Good. Because I can't have you walking around holding a grudge." His dimples deepen. "You know too much."

His eyes travel down to my hands. "Now. If I'm going to be your *best* frenemy, I have to ask. Are you planning on doing something about that busted fingernail? I have to be honest. That ripped fingernail isn't keeping up with the overall Leila Bean aesthetic."

I look down at my full set and notice the pointer fingernail on my right hand is chipped and the tip is broken off.

"When did this happen?!" I don't care what anyone says. A girl needs her full set intact.

Tre' lifts my hand up and grimaces. "Probably when you were busy whooping and clapping at my public humiliation." He shakes his head. "Now, was all of this worth breaking a nail?"

I wipe the smile off my face long enough to deadpan my best frenemy. "Yes. Yes, it was."

Tre' shakes his head at my pettiness. "Fine. Grab your things. I'm taking you to get it fixed."

As I get up to follow him, Bree cups her hand over her mouth and calls out, "Hey Tre', I recommend you visit the restroom before you leave. I wouldn't want any more . . . *accidents.*" Halima and a few other kids sitting nearby crack up laughing.

29

TRE' DRIVES US to Bowie Towne Center and the Spa 1 nail salon. "One full fingernail, please," he tells the man at the front desk.

I roll my eyes at Tre'. "*Please* excuse him. I actually need this nail filed and repolished." I hold my pointer finger out for the receptionist to inspect. Then I peek over at Tre's mitts.

"I *know* you're not talking about my one little fingernail, Tre'." I make a face. "Have you ever heard of a nail clipper?"

The receptionist looks over at Tre's uneven fingernails. "Manicure?" he asks.

"Yeah, a simple cut down and clipping of the cuticles should be enough." I tell her.

But Tre' hides his hands behind his back. "Now, hold on,

Leila. I'm just the sidekick in this situation. I didn't come here to get *pampered*."

I smirk as a woman comes from the back with a basket of nail polishes and other supplies. "Are you really going to end your high school career with . . ." I make a show of looking at his nails again. ". . . *Hot Cheetos* residue under your nail bed?"

I point Tre' to the nail station next to me. "Come on, Tre'. Just one little manicure and you'll be hooked."

Tre' sighs. "Fine."

Two nail technicians sit down on the other side of our stations and turn on bright lamps to get a better look at what they have to do to our nails. Then they get to work.

Tre's technician is finishing up his pinkie finger when his phone buzzes. He reaches for his phone with his finished hand, taps the screen, then goes, "Oh, snap!"

"What?" I say over the whirring of the nail buffer.

Tre's eyes widen. "The shelter just sent me a message. Lou's foster application just got approved. They want to know if I can come get him before they close."

My heart jumps. "Oh my gosh, Tre'. That's amazing. Congratulations!"

Tre' drums his freshly manicured nails on the nail station tabletop, while staring at my finger. "How long is that nail going to take? We only have"—Tre' checks his phone again—"an hour."

I carefully pull my fingernail from under the blue light. "Okay, fine. Let's go now. But drive carefully, Tre'." I give him a pointed look. "My nail is still drying."

I nod for Tre' to pull my card out of my wallet to pay the nail shop, then with Tre' carrying my things, and with my pointer finger propped in the air so it won't bump into anything, we run out of the shop and into Tre's car.

"Buckle my seat belt for me, Tre'?"

"What are you, a toddler?"

"My nail, Tre'!"

"Fine, fine." He reaches over and latches me in. Then he starts up the car.

Tre' speeds down the road toward the large shopping center a mile from the animal shelter. While Tre's parking the car in front of the PetSmart, I give my nail a final blow and a cautious tap to make sure it's really dry. Then we get out.

We walk around the entire store arguing over what to get Lou.

"Tre'. Lou does not need a hundred-dollar doggy bed."

"He's old, Leila. And he's been sleeping on cheap cots for weeks. His fragile bones deserve a little luxury."

"Tre'! That bed is too big and too soft. You're going to smother the poor thing as soon as you get him home."

"Fine, well, you pick something better—oh, that *is* kind of nice. Fine, throw it in the cart."

Up and down the aisle we push the cart, arguing the whole way about dog food, bedding, his harness, even whether or not he needs a doggy toothbrush.

"He doesn't have any teeth, Leila."

I throw the green doggy toothbrush in the cart. "I counted at least two—near the back." My face dares him to take the toothbrush back out. Good for him, he doesn't.

But when we get to the register, Tre' holds his hand up, and I high-five him.

"Now tell the truth, Tre'. Could you have done this without me?"

"Nope!"

I bask in the glory of Tre's props, and, with our arms full of doggy supplies, we head back to the car and Tre' drives back to the animal shelter.

When we get to the animal shelter, Shannon comes around the information desk and hugs the both of us. "This is a special day," she says, her eyes all misty. Shannon walks us to an office and introduces us to Meera, an adoption counselor at the shelter.

"Where's Lou?" Tre' asks, looking around the room.

Meera smiles. "He's in another room, getting last minute shots and his release papers from the on-call vet. He'll be ready shortly."

Meera produces a stack of papers and places them on her desk. "In the meantime, I have some official business to go over with you."

Meera walks Tre' through all the rules and procedures that come along with fostering a dog. I listen closely in case he forgets anything. Tre' signs what looks like a hundred documents promising to do his best while Lou is in his care, and then the moment comes.

Meera walks out of her office and comes back in carrying Lou. I pretend not to notice the tears welling up in Tre's eyes. Which does something to me. And now I can't tell if I'm getting emotional over Lou or watching Tre' get so emotional over Lou.

When we prepare to leave, with Lou in Tre's arms, and me carrying the free cans of wet dog food the shelter gifted us, a little voice in my head stops me when we get to the double doors. Acting on instinct, I block Tre' from stepping forward with my arm. "Let him walk out," I tell Tre'.

Tre' shakes his head. "He's too old, Leila."

I give old Lou the once-over. I think about the odds stacked against him. How no one predicted he would even live to see this day. And I believe in him enough to go, "He's a fighter, Tre'. Give your boy a chance."

Give your boy a chance bounces around my thoughts for a moment—but I shake it away. "Come on, Tre'. He can do it."

So Tre' clips Lou's leash to the new collar we bought him and gently places Lou on the ground. And slowly but surely, Lou starts walking out of there—his rib cage protruding with each gallant step. He moves at a snail's pace, but that's okay because Tre' and I are both taking baby steps, careful not to make Lou and his slow stroll look anything less than regal.

And when Lou takes his first step out of the shelter and onto the warm sidewalk, my heart is filled with hope—for all things that once seemed impossible.

With Lou taking confident strides across the sidewalk,

my focus once again returns to Tre' and the little voice still bouncing around in my thoughts.

Give your boy a chance.

Tre' pulls up to a huge house with a circular driveway, immaculate grass with a crisscross design mowed in, and two water fountains on either side of the huge front door.

In other words, Tre' is basically living like The Fresh Prince of Bowie. I resist the urge to ask to borrow a dollar.

While we haul Lou's items into his house, and work together to arrange everything nicely inside Tre's surprisingly neat bedroom, Tre's mom peeks her head in and squeals at the sight of Lou, before pulling her phone out and snapping nearly a hundred pictures of Lou. And then Lou and Tre'. And then Lou, Tre', and me.

Unlike Tre', Ms. Hillman has a quiet charm about her that draws me to her instantly, and I wonder how she could've birthed such an attention-seeker. So I ask her in my own sneaky way.

"Oh, Tre's always loved the spotlight." She places a hand on my shoulder. "He gets that from his father's side of the family," she says, giving me a knowing look.

We share a laugh and Tre' goes, "All right, all right. Break it up." But he's smiling hard, looking at us, then back down at Lou. My stomach flips, and I check on my freshly dried fingernail to avoid addressing this building feeling.

When his mom eventually leaves out to make a quick run to the store, Tre' and I find ourselves left alone with just Lou staring up at us from his newly purchased, perfect doggy bed.

"Today has been so perfect," I blurt out.

Tre' doesn't bother looking up. He's too busy kneeling in front of Lou, staring into his eyes and stroking his short fur. But he says, "Yeah, I have to agree with you on that."

"My sister would love Lou," I say, making a kissy face at Lou.

"How old is your sister?" Tre' asks.

"Ten."

Tre' shrugs, then finally turns his head to look up at me. His brown eyes almost sparkle. "I don't have much else to do today. Do you want to take Lou to visit her?"

Awww. "Sure."

I walk over to Lou's bed, scoop him up, and tell Tre' to follow me out the door.

30

NO ONE'S MORE surprised than I am to see a gray minivan parked behind my mother's car, when we get to my house.

Dev's car.

"What is *he* doing here?" I mumble to myself.

Tre' glances at the minivan and turns to me. "You sure you still want me to come in?" A worried look crosses his face. "I just thought about something. What if your mom hates me?"

It's my turn to look confused. "Why would my mom hate you?"

Tre' twists his lips, like the answer is so obvious. "Come on, Leila. I know you've been talking big junk about me all these years . . ."

I laugh. "I'll smooth things over—don't worry."

It doesn't miss me that I'm telling Tre' not to worry at the same time my knees are shaking a little bit over the sight of that minivan in the driveway.

Tre' grabs Lou and follows me up to the front porch. I do a quick check inside the minivan as we pass it. There's no driver inside—which can only mean one thing.

When we walk through the front door, Dev is sitting in my living room with Riley.

"Ummm . . ."

Dev's gaze briefly flickers over to Tre'. His forehead crinkles for a moment before smoothing out again. "Riley asked if she could interview me for a special project."

I raise an eyebrow. "And you just came right over? Didn't check with anyone or anything?"

"Well, she said your mom said it was okay, so . . ."

But did I say it was okay? I think to myself.

If I had known Dev would be laid back with his feet kicked up on my couch when I arrived home, I never would've invited Tre' here. I mean, it's not like Dev and Tre' are friends, but they are in the same *Madden* league and usually say "what's up?" when they pass each other in the hallway. They haven't said one word to each other today, though.

Thank goodness Riley eases some of the tension, when she stops recording to ask, "Whose dog is that?"

Tre' finally speaks. "It's mine."

Riley drops her phone on the couch next to Dev and comes over. "He's so cute! Can I hold him?"

Dev lets out a nervous chuckle. "What am I, yesterday's news?" His short laugh is strained, though. Forced.

"Come on, hand him over." Riley holds her arms out, and Tre' gently hands over Lou.

I raise an eyebrow at my sister. "You're not even going to ask who this is?"

"I recognize Tre' from Instagram. He's the guy you said you would never go out with, except, according to Tre's stories, you guys have been to the animal shelter together a million times." Riley goes back to petting Lou.

Dev lets out another uncomfortable chuckle.

My mouth drops open. "You little snoop." I glance over at Dev. "Friends hang out together sometimes, Riley, in case you didn't know."

But Riley is too focused on Lou to care about the particulars. She stops petting Lou for a brief moment to stick her hand out toward Tre'. "I'm Riley. It's nice to meet you, and I would appreciate if you could subscribe to my podcast on YouTube."

Tre' shakes my sister's hand. "Nice to meet you, Riley." Then he pulls his phone out. "So do I just google the name of the podcast or—?"

While Riley gives Tre' the details, I marvel at how caring he is with her—very similar to how he is with Lou. It warms my heart that, as goofy as he is, when it comes down to it, Tre' knows how to be gentle with the people who need it most.

Just then Mom and Ben come walking into the living

room. "Did I hear a dog out here?" Mom goes. She stops short when she sees Tre'. "Oh . . . hello." Her gaze shifts to Dev. And back to Tre'. Then to me.

I shrug.

Mom sticks her hand out. "Nice to meet you . . . ?"

The nervous look is back. "Umm, some people call me . . . Trevor?"

I roll my eyes at his attempt to slip under the radar. "This is Tre', Mom."

Tre' looks relieved when Mom smiles instead of throwing him out of the house by his collar.

Out the corner of my eye, I peep Ben hanging back. He stares at our little group, but doesn't come closer. I know it's because I completely bit his head off about including himself in family stuff.

He looks so pitiful, staring into the living room, half standing in the dining room, that I feel bad and go out of my way to say, "Tre', this is my mom's boyfriend, Ben."

A huge smile appears on Ben's face and he finally walks all the way into the room to shake Tre's hand.

Later on, Dev does a little fake yawn. "Well, I guess I should get going, too."

He looks right at Tre', but Tre' is so deeply engrossed in a conversation with Ben about sports that he never even looks up. A weird looks crosses Dev's face.

He throws a glance my way. "Walk me outside?"

"Okay." I slip into a pair of my mom's slides and follow Dev out the front door. The second we step off the front porch, Dev turns to me and goes, "So, you and Tre'? You guys are a thing now?"

I raise an eyebrow at his questioning, but on the inside? I'm asking myself the same thing. Because, what *is* this? "I mean, we're just friends—*good* friends—as far as I know."

But even I know that friends—even good friends—don't feel quite like this.

And now I'm wondering why Dev is digging. Isn't he going to the dance with Halima? Why does he care what I do?

Dev makes a face. "I thought you couldn't stand that guy."

I shrug. "He's all right . . ." Something gnaws at me, urging me to look deeper, to figure out whether Tre' is more than all right. If—

A look of surprise crosses Dev's face, but he doesn't say anything more about it. Instead, he bites at one of his fingernails and goes, "So I know I probably should've sent you a text about Ashli's party. But I didn't know what to say." He finally looks me in the eyes. "What was all that drinking about the other night? Is everything okay?"

I look down for a second before meeting Dev's eyes again. So he *did* notice. Now I'm even more embarrassed about how I acted. I try to laugh the whole thing off. "It was nothing," I assure him. "It's just—I kind of got curved by Eva. And my ego took a hit."

Mentioning Eva to Dev reminds me that Dev was the

first person I confided in that I might be bisexual, back when we were sophomores. I remember being so afraid that he would break up with me—that he would think my attraction to girls changed how I felt about him. I worried that he would start acting suspicious that I would cheat. That he would think he wasn't enough for me. But none of those things happened.

When I told him, Dev simply shrugged and said, "Sexuality's always been sort of a spectrum to me anyway. I don't think anyone fits neatly into any box."

I remember eyeing him, before asking, "Do you have something to tell me?"

And he was all like, "No. I'm straight—as far as I know." Then he chuckled easily, like he always did, and grabbed my books to finish walking me to the next class. Easy. That was the word for everything Dev-related. There weren't any issues—until he decided to create one.

"So you haven't announced who you're going to the dance with—" Dev suddenly blurts out.

"I don't even know if I'm still going." I keep my expression as steady as possible and I try not to think about how much easier things would be if we were still together. We would've laughed at this whole Last Chance Dance—and used it as an excuse to go on extra dates.

"That's too bad. But, you *are* still going to the Last Night at the Museum thing tonight, right?"

"Oh my gosh, I forgot all about that!" And that's the truth. Picking up Lou today didn't give me a moment to think about what else I might have going on.

"I guess I could throw something on and go," I tell Dev.

Dev nods. "Cool . . . well, I guess I'll see you there?"

When I nod, he suddenly reaches over for a hug. "Hey, I don't want you to think I'm going to be the weirdo ex who randomly pops up at your house," he says into my ear.

When I hold back a smile, he grins. "But you know how I feel about Riley. She's the closest thing I've got to a little sister. And I would do anything for her."

I smile at how genuine Dev has been with Riley over the years. "I know you would, Dev. That's part of the reason I fell for you."

We share one last lingering stare. It's almost like how it was between us—yet totally different at the same time. But the moment breaks as I look back toward the house and go, "Well, if I'm going to make it to the museum tonight, I guess I'd better get back inside and get ready."

Dev nods and goes, "Yeah, yeah, of course."

Then he gets into his car, starts the engine, and pulls off.

As I walk back up to the front door, I think about how nothing is ever really cut and dry. That people come and go from our lives; their roles change. That what we think about a person can change over time. That nothing is ever set in stone. That there's always room for evolution.

Mom and Ben are in the living room when I get back inside, listening to some raw footage of Dev's interview.

"This is going to be really great once you finish with the edits," Mom is telling Riley.

"Yeah, this kid is making some pretty good points. I'll definitely be listening once you finally publish the episode," Ben says.

The smile on Riley's face melts my heart.

And then I think about Ben.

No, Ben isn't our dad. Nobody will ever replace him. But Ben is still an important addition to our family—in his own way. He clearly makes Mom happy. And from the looks of things, does his best to make us happy, too.

"Hey, Ben . . ."

Ben looks up.

"I was thinking of asking if you wanted to go to my graduation."

Mom breaks out into a huge smile as Ben goes, "I would love to attend your graduation, Leila."

Feeling pretty evolved and mature, I'm practically floating out of the living room.

Then it hits me. I don't want to attend the museum night penniless. I'm not even sure if the event is catered.

I lean down into my mother's ear. "Umm, I'm kind of broke. Do you think you could lend me . . ."

I don't even have to look into Mom's face to know she's rolling her eyes. "Really, Leila?"

"I mean, it's just a loan until Dad Cash Apps me my allowance."

Mom chuckles. "Your grand gesture was enough. I'll pay for the tickets."

And with that settled, there's only one person still on my mind—Tre'.

The postcard Maggie gave us for the event tonight says we can bring a friend. I'm pretty sure Dev's bringing Halima. And there's no way I'm going to make it there on time by Metro train.

"Do you want to go to this museum thing with me, Tre'?"

Tre' glances over at Lou. "I would, but I don't think they're going to let me bring a dog inside the museum, though . . ."

"I'll watch him, I'll watch him!" Riley yells. She runs over to Lou and scoops him up into her arms.

I inspect Tre's outfit, and quickly decide he's looking cute in his fitted polo and jeans combo. "Just give me a few minutes to change," I tell him.

I've been wanting to wear this purple oversized hoodie I've repurposed into a minidress for the longest.

Cute, sort of new, and unexpected.

The perfect outfit to wear on my official first date with Tre'.

31

EVEN THOUGH IT'S still rush hour, traffic heading into downtown DC isn't so bad. The commuters are heading home and most of the Smithsonian museums are beginning to shut down for the day. But the lights are still on at the Natural History Museum, welcoming all the graduating seniors of the program.

"Do you think we should call Riley to see how things are going with Lou?" Tre' asks as we walk up the stone staircase together. He's had a nervous look on his face the entire car ride, and now I know why.

"You don't know my little sister that well yet," I tell him. "But trust me. Riley Bean is guarding that dog's safety and well-being with her life." I'm happy to see Tre' finally let out the breath he's *clearly* been holding in. "Besides, Mom and Ben are there, in case of an emergency."

I pull Tre' by the arm closer to me. "Relax. Tonight, we get to hang out with the exhibits."

Tre' gives me a gentle—almost shy—smile, and asks, "Where are we going first?"

As we walk up to the giant elephant guarding the museum's entrance, I brace myself for another one of Tre's jokes. Will he compare my forehead to the woolly mammoths? Will he turn his arm into an elephant's trunk and create his own version of what she may have sounded like in the prehistoric age?

But to my surprise, Tre's wisecracking jokes are gone. He looks awestruck by the space. I watch his eyes quietly sweep over the long empty hallways, marvel at the marble floors, and take in the long columns reaching the skyscraper ceilings.

"Leila?"

I turn, and there's Dev. Halima is standing next to him with her arm looped through his.

"Hey, Leila!" Halima says, looking genuinely happy to see me—until she recognizes my plus-one. "Oh, *hey*, Tre'."

Halima sends a smirk my way. "I *knew* there was some flirting behind all those arguments." She loops Dev's arm in a little tighter. "*I* think you two look really cute together. Right, Dev?"

An uncomfortable smile crosses Dev's face. "Yeah, I guess so."

Halima smiles, then smooths down a lock of Dev's hair. "Well, I guess we'd better get out of here. Dev promised me we could visit the diamond from the *Titanic*, first."

As Dev and Halima wander off, Tre' nudges me. "*Dang*, all in *our* business . . ." I bust out laughing, for once one hundred percent appreciating Tre's smart mouth.

Tre' and I cross the atrium and wander down one of the exhibit halls. With the dim lights illuminating our backs, we move easily from room to room, exhibit to exhibit. I carefully explain why most people are more fascinated with the dinosaur fossils, yet I'm obsessed with the ancient whales. The lights shining off the priceless gems help me tell him the majestic origin story of each jewel resting in a security case. Together, we run our fingers over the shiny wood banisters, staring into the glass cases and retracing our steps through history. We journey through time until the *Homo sapiens* finally uncurl their spines and stand up tall and straight, on their own—no help needed.

Tre' listens better than I thought he would, especially when I repeat the story of the polar bears who were once grizzlies, except, against the snow, the ones with white spots lived longer because they could blend in better.

"Over time, as the white spotted bears mated, their offspring had more and more white spots, with the whitest ones surviving the most. With the whitest bears surviving, the grizzlies who lived in these snowy climates quickly evolved from brown bears to white polar bears," I explain.

Tre's eyebrows dip a little—like he was thinking about

something. "You think that's what happens at these PWIs and Ivy Leagues?"

"What's that?"

"The Black kid gets there, and because he doesn't blend in, he's the easier target—and doesn't survive as easily as the others."

My heart aches over the worry I see in his eyes. It's the same one I have, coming from Prince George's County—one of the richest Black counties in the country—and being thrust into a mostly white college landscape, where so many well-meaning white people will automatically assume you're there on financial aid or because of affirmative action.

Like Tre', I'd been thinking about the fall, too. About surviving in a new place with not very many people around who share my skin color.

"That—and the fact that systemic racism and gatekeepers keep us from attending in the first place."

Tre' gives me this look, one I haven't seen on his face before. "You're the smartest girl I know, Leila. Brown was dumb for not giving you an acceptance letter. We could've gone together."

I shrug. "Rochester's where I'm supposed to be, apparently." I tell him simply. Then I grab his hand and pull him into the Hall of Fossils. Tre' seems surprised at first, then he squeezes my hand and smiles. Together, we stare up at the towering bones of a massive T. rex.

"It's wild to think that, in a moment, the entire world can change out of nowhere," Tre' says quietly.

I sneak a glance in his direction. His words feel loaded, like he means so much more. And I completely understand. If I'm being honest, I'm feeling so much more than I want to admit.

"Come on, I have one more exhibit to show you." I pull Tre' into the museum's newest pop-up augmented reality exhibit, about twenty-four endangered orca whales living in the Pacific Ocean's Salish Sea.

"*I* haven't even seen this one yet," I say, handing Tre' a headset. "So this will be new for both of us."

I don't expect to be so moved by the experience, but I find myself tearing up a little as six-year-old Kiki and her pod of orcas struggle to hunt for food, despite the many obstacles humans have now put in their way. Climate change and the human need to transport goods are killing off the type of prey that these massive whales like to eat. But unlike other orcas, these Pacific orcas refuse to change their diets to other types of prey. And now they're endangered.

"I just don't get why those orcas didn't find something new to snack on," Tre' says after the viewing. He shakes his head as we hang our headsets on a hook and step back out into the Deep Blue Sea exhibit.

I frown. "You're acting like exploring new territory is easy. Making a huge life change is scary, Tre'."

A flashback of me crying alone in my room the weekend after Dev and I broke up pops into my head. At the time, losing Dev felt like being cut off from a critical resource.

Tre' side-eyes me. "Come on, Leila. If someone took away

your resources, you would not just shrivel up and die . . ."

"Honestly, when Dev broke up with me, it felt like I did . . ." I admit. My stomach swirls a little at how hopeless and depleted I felt. How even just going on *one* new date felt unimaginable.

When Tre' snorts, I double down on my truth. "*Seriously,* Tre'. That's what it felt like. I couldn't see a future without Dev."

"Well, what do you see now?" Tre' asks quietly.

I shake my head. "Trust me. I'm not doing much better than those orcas."

Tre' raises an eyebrow. "What do you mean?"

I let out a soft chuckle. "You've been around for the whole thing, Tre'. You already know I've been in struggle mode ever since Dev broke up with me—like Kiki."

Now Tre' looks at me like I've grown two heads. "Are you listening to yourself right now, Leila? You think you've been *struggling?*"

I nod. But Tre' shakes his head *no.*

"You're right, Leila. I've been watching from the side-lines this whole time. And from what I can see, you've been *thriving.*"

Suddenly Tre' goes from quiet to animated. "Okay, let's compare your love life to Kiki's. Your love life could've been straight-up endangered after Dev dumped you. But you didn't let that happen. You created new lanes for your love life."

"But none of those lanes worked out . . . Kai. Mason. Eva. None of them."

"But think about it. *You* decided Kai wasn't right for you. And *you* broke things off with Mason." He pauses a moment. "I mean, you *did* get curved by Eva—but hey, you win some and you lose some. The point is, since Dev broke things off, you've been dating on *your* terms."

The Deep Blue Sea exhibit is dark, save for a smattering of backlighting on the walls. I've been in this room a hundred times giving tours. But somehow, standing here at night, with Tre', the vastness of the space feels majestic. And I get it. I can remain in my tiny known world. Or I can take one step outside my comfort zone and discover how endless my possibilities truly are.

I don't know what does it. If it's the deep blues of the room. Or the moonlight trickling in through the windows. But suddenly, I sense Tre' moving closer. And he's tilting his head. And I know one second from now, he's going to kiss me. And, as crazy as it seems, I just . . . might . . . let him—

"Ahem." A loud cough comes from the whale exhibit entrance. And then a bright light shines on Tre' and me. When my eyes adjust to the bright light shining in our faces, I realize it's Annette, the security guard. "We're closing up in fifteen minutes," she says.

And just like that, the magic of the moment dissipates, and I'm left wondering if I'm only swimming to Tre' because I've run out of resources everywhere else.

Gently pushing him away, I tell Tre', "I don't want us to give this a shot just because I don't have any matches left."

And when he nods, I know that he doesn't want to be my fallback plan any more than I do.

"Hey, do you want to go grab a Big Slice?"

The thought of an oversized slice of cheesy pizza warms my spirit. We walk over to the nearest Big Slice and wait in line outside the little pizza stand. The entire time we wait, I mull over Tre' and me—and what's happening between us.

I've been wrong before. About Kai. Mason. Eva. Even Dev, when you really think about it. Why would Tre' be any different?

I think about the times Tre' and I hung out at the animal shelter, the times we bonded over our divorced parents, Tre' rescuing me from the party, showing up for me in ways that only a real friend would.

Besides our misunderstanding in middle school, Tre' has been there for me when I needed it most—being a true friend. And if I'm being honest, those dimples certainly don't hurt the situation.

As Tre' and I grab our pizza slices from the stand and devour them on the way to his car, under the stars, with the cool summer air whipping past our shoulders, I take a chance—on Tre'. But most of all, on myself. I throw all my trust in making the right decision to move forward with a guy who put our friendship first.

"Let's go to the dance together," I blurt out.

"What?"

I grab a few napkins out of his hand to wipe the grease

from my fingers. "I'm serious, Tre'. We've gotten so close these past few weeks. It's only right that we go to the dance together."

"But we haven't gone on our date yet."

I point at the Smithsonian building directly behind us. "Umm, do you see where we're standing? I'd call this a date, Tre'."

The smile on Tre's face quickly spreads. "Yeah, Leila," he says. "I would love to go to the dance with you."

32

AT THE BEGINNING of our car ride home, Tre' makes a big show of showering me with compliments and listing all the ways we would make the perfect couple, now that I've given him a chance.

He even makes a big show out of holding his hand out at chest level and proclaiming, "Girls I've had a crush on for years. Rihanna . . ."

Then he raises his hand high above his head. "Leila."

"Okay, Tre'. Enough. Have you ever heard of the term 'love bombing'? Keep it up, and I'm not going to believe any of this is real," I tell him.

So Tre' shuts up. But not before proclaiming that the next song on his playlist will be "our song" since it'll be the first piece of music we listened to after I agreed to go to the dance with him.

Unfortunately for Tre', the next song on his playlist is "The Star-Spangled Banner."

I crack up laughing. "Rules are rules, Tre'!"

Tre' fumbles around with his car's shuffle button, trying to quickly skip the national anthem. "Okay, next song, next song . . ."

But I don't let him off so easy. "Why is 'The Star-Spangled Banner' even in your rotation, clown?"

Tre' sucks his teeth. "*Excuse me* for actually wanting to hit the correct musical notes in band recital last month."

I'm still cracking up when Tre' pulls into my driveway. I get out of the car and head straight for Bree's house to tell her about finally finding my date for the dance. It's a little late to knock on her front door, so I head around to the side of the house, slip off my ballerina flat, and hurl it up at Bree's window.

Bree finally comes to her window after three solid throws and one miss. "Can't you take a hint, Leila? I'm trying to ignore you."

There's a bass in her voice hinting at big attitude, but I don't really pay it any mind, because she's always cranky when woken up.

"Let me in!"

Bree gives me a death stare, and then goes, "No."

I give her the stuck face. "No?"

"Exactly what I said. No!"

Suddenly my big mouth, and what I said to Eva, comes

barreling toward me. "Uh, why not?" I ask, in a shaky voice.

Tre' lowers his window and leans over the passenger side. "Really? You guys are going to have a full-blown conversation outside at eleven p.m.?!"

I wave him away. "It's all good, Tre'! You can go."

"Are you sure?"

"Yeah."

Tre' leans over further and yells up at Bree, "Nice nightgown, Muscles!" before pulling off. I *really* have to teach him to tone down the jokes some.

I turn back to Bree, dreading the inevitable.

Bree glares at me. "Because. Like your corny boyfriend over there, you have too much mouth."

"How do I have too much mouth?" Who am I fooling? I already know what I said—what I did. Dragging this out is making things worse. I know this, yet . . .

Bree huffs extra loud, and pull the window up higher. "Let's see. You tried to kiss Eva. Then when she curved you, you warned her that I was just another player?!"

Bree stops to give me the most evil smirk I've ever seen from her. "Then, after you were all loud and wrong, you didn't even have the decency to warn me you said all that junk. You just set me up to look stupid."

Okay, okay. I deserve this. Now I just have to make things right. "But, Bree . . ."

My bestie points her finger at me. "Oh no. Don't even try to come up with excuses. I put myself out there, in a real way, for the first time ever. I didn't just ask Eva to the dance: I asked her to be my girlfriend. And the whole time, you had already sabotaged me!"

I send a pitiful look up to the second floor of Bree's house. "I didn't know how to tell you—"

Bree shakes her head. "That's funny. Because I know exactly what to tell your sorry butt. Stay out of my love life!"

Then she slams her window shut.

I send Bree three middle-of-the-night apology texts, and one more at the crack of dawn. I'm not only left on read, Bree's car is gone the second I walk out the house for school the next day.

You left me?! I text Bree.

Use that big mouth and ask somebody else for a ride.

Okay. So I finally got a text back . . . but this is going in the *opposite* direction of forgiveness.

I said I was sorry, Bree!

Actually, you never apologized. You just stood there making excuses.

Bree!

Leila!

I check the time. Tre's probably already left by now. Plus, I don't want to have to explain why Bree suddenly ditched me. So with no ride to school, I'm forced to wait at the morning bus stop with all the underclassmen. I try not to make eye contact with any of them, but I catch their pity stares anyway. They don't have to say a word. I already know a senior riding the big cheese puts a neon-green sign on my forehead that says friendless and alone.

I have a lot of time to think once I settle into a seat on the school bus. I figure, since Bree's already mad at me, it won't make thing any worse to ignore her directions and jump back into her love life—just this once—to fix things.

While the school bus is hitting every pothole imaginable, and quite possibly giving me whiplash, I reach out to Eva.

Are you just saying all of this so I'll go out with Bree, Leila? Eva texts. Because I'd like to make it out of high school without getting seriously played.

I promise, Eva. She really likes you.

When the school bus pulls up to the bus circle to let us all out, Bree is waiting for me on the sidewalk. "I hope your bus ride in was as annoying as I remember it," is the first thing she says to me.

Now, I could just ignore Bree throwing salt in my wounds. But whatever. If it gives her satisfaction to see me suffer, I guess I'll throw her a bone.

"It was terrible." Then I make sure Bree knows that I'm truly sorry for what I did.

"I know how much you must like Eva to take such a big step like this, Bree. And it was wrong for me to tell Eva who I thought you were. I didn't consider the fact that people grow and evolve, and that you are the only person that can speak for you. I should've just minded my business, and let things play out." I look up into Bree's eyes, so she can see how much I wish I could take back what I did. "I'm sorry I ruined things between you and Eva."

Not even a second passes before Bree throws an arm around me and grins. "Lucky for you, Eva just called and agreed to be my girlfriend *and* go to the dance with me."

I would jump for joy, but my neck is still hurting from that bumpy bus ride. So I squeal instead. "Does this mean I get my passenger seat privileges back?!"

Bree rolls her eyes. "We'll see about all that."

"Don't play that tough girl role with me, Bree. You know you can't stand to see me suffering for too long." I pull Bree in for the biggest hug, certain that we're both about to end senior year on a high note.

33

ON FRIDAY, BREE shows up around three to hang out while I get dressed. The last dance I prepped for was prom. Things were so different then. Dev and I were still together and in love. I never would have imagined going to Last Chance Dance with someone else—Tre', of all people!

I shower and slip into a strapless dress that's fitted at the top and billows out at the bottom. I purposely picked the color purple because, after spending the last few weeks feeling like a lady-in-waiting, tonight, I finally feel like royalty again. I carefully apply my makeup, contouring my face to highlight my cheekbones. Then I amp up the drama with a smoky eye.

Bree admires my look and showcases her own tux-pants-and-blazer look. Then she rummages around in my jewelry chest. "I'm not about to be out here looking like a Disney princess all the time, with a bunch of necklaces and bracelets." She holds up a golden bangle. "But tonight's special enough to add a little extra glam." She slips the bracelet on her wrist and one of my dangly necklaces around her neck.

When the doorbell rings, I rush to the door. Eva is standing there, looking breathtaking in a pink jumpsuit 'fit. But my eyes don't stay on her for long. How did I know Tre' would go all out? Of *course* he didn't settle for the regular black-tux look. Only his pants are black. But he's ditched the plain white dress shirt for a dapper baby blue. His neck is looking icy. His freshly faded haircut looks amazing. And he's obviously decided to give *himself* flowers with that custom-looking hand-stitched floral tux jacket. O-*kay*.

Of course, Tre' strikes an immediate pose. "Admit it, Leila. I look *good* in a tux."

My eyes travel from his head to his shoes one more time. "Fine. I'll admit it, just this once." Forget the games, I take a step closer to take in a whiff of his cologne.

Bree comes up behind me, takes Eva's hand, and low whistles at the sight of her stunning girlfriend.

Bree takes a break from admiring Eva to jingle her keys. "Aight, are you guys ready to take a spin in my Bree-mobile?" She eyes Tre'. "Unless, of course, Tre's trying to let me take the electric whip for a spin . . ." She wiggles her eyebrows at him.

Tre' tosses his keys to a very excited Bree, and I climb

into the back seat with him, while Eva takes the passenger seat next to Bree.

Before she backs the car out of the driveway, Bree smirks at Tre' in the rearview mirror. "Let's see what this auto-drive feature does . . ."

I whack Bree's shoulder from the back seat. "You better not!"

Bree turns around in her seat. "Come on, Lei. You already took a chance on love. Why can't we take a chance on the auto-drive feature?"

I glare at her. "Look, either you drive with your own two hands, or you and Tre' are switching spots."

"*Ughhh.* Fine." Bree puts on her seat belt and plugs her phone into the auxiliary. By the time we hit the corner of my street, Drake is blasting through the speakers, relaxing us all, and we slip easily into laughing and talking about all the fun we're about to have.

We arrive right on time at this old, rustic-looking lodge sitting up on a hill overlooking a lake. It's all going to sound corny when I try to explain everything to Mom later. But right now, experiencing the vibe firsthand? It feels just right for a group of kids who've bought into the whole fairy tale ending.

Bree negotiates a compromise, and we all watch in amazement while the Tesla parks itself. Then Bree throws the keys to Tre', grabs Eva's hand, and heads over to the front entrance of the lodge, leaving Tre' and me alone in the back seat.

Tre' grabs my hands and stares deep into my eyes. "Ready?"

I can't lie. Just yesterday, I was still questioning whether or not to take things out of the friendship zone with Tre'. But looking into his eyes now, I'm sure I've made the right decision. Raising an eyebrow, I shoot him a coy look and go, "Boy, I've *been* ready."

Senior year has been full of great memories—and painful moments. But all the pain I endured eventually led me to right now, and Tre'. For the first time, my breakup from Dev feels more positive than negative. It kicked off a fresh start for me. And now, I'm ready to embrace the butterflies, the tenderness, and all the happy moments that are coming from simply being around him.

Tonight, I don't want to pick apart the past. I don't want to worry about the future. In these secluded woods, with the lake shimmering under the moon's gaze, I just want the space to embrace what makes me happy. And in this moment, *Tre'* is who I want by my side.

Tre' opens the car door and lifts me up by the hand out of the car. I feel like a princess as I practically float toward the front entrance.

A slow song is playing as we walk through the doors of the lodge. And everything's right. The white and silver balloons. The darkened room, illuminated by strobe lights and fake stars splashed across the ceiling and walls. The smoke machine gathering fog at our feet. And most importantly, I have the most unexpectedly thoughtful, *genuine* guy leading me out to the dance floor. I catch a quick glimpse of Dev out of the corner of my eye, chatting with Chad. But I don't linger too long. At least for tonight, Dev belongs to Halima. Let her focus on him.

For me? Tonight is all about Tre'.

Tre' pulls me close to him, and slowly we begin swaying to the music. Careful not to ruin his rent-a-tux with my makeup, I nestle into his shoulders, not believing that I'm here with a guy this smart and, I can't believe I'm even thinking this, handsome. A guy who—okay, I can admit it now—has a little flair for comedic timing, but most of all, is open enough to wear his heart on his sleeve. Who saved an old dog from a lifetime of loneliness on the same day he saved my heart. Today, Tre' is what I'm looking for—even if it took me forever to see it.

As the song ends, I get so wrapped up in the moment that my breath catches. I look up into Tre's eyes and find that he's already staring down into mine.

For a brief moment, the digital stars glued to the walls flicker, and I'm so wrapped up in this magical moment that I assume fate has instructed the stars to twinkle—just for Tre' and me.

And then, just when I'm just beginning to tilt my chin upward, positioning myself to accept a kiss from Tre', Dev appears.

"Umm, can I cut in?"

What?!

I raise an eyebrow at Dev.

"Just one, Leila. Then you two can go back to—*ahem*—your date."

Tre' steps back. "It's cool. I was going to go get something to drink anyway." He looks nervously from Dev to me and back to Dev again. "Uh, anyone want anything?"

I shake my head *no*, and Dev goes, "Just one dance, Tre'."

Tre' nods. "Cool."

Tre' disappears into the sea of seniors before Dev steps closer, placing his arms around my lower waist. "You look really good tonight, Leila," he says."

I look around for signs of Halima—because—what?! "Uhh, thanks."

A brief moment of awkwardness passes before Dev blurts out, "I barely got any sleep last night. I couldn't stop thinking about you and Tre'."

The words stop me cold. I squint my eyes at my ex's sudden confession, because really, Dev?! You're just going to blurt this out in the middle of my date *with Tre'*?

"Well, I mean. It would've been us here tonight. But you dumped me, remember?" I don't tack on a polite little laugh at the end of that statement. Because there's nothing particularly funny about being sucker punched in the heart three weeks before the end of high school. But, here we are.

"I know—and I was stupid," he says, going quiet.

I mean—he's not wrong about that. But I don't say anything. Because it's still super weird that he's saying all of this and Tre' will be back from the punch table any minute now.

"I know I said I wanted to date, that I didn't want to be

like my parents . . . But nobody compares to you, Leila."

I side-eye that statement. *Plenty of people compare to me, Dev. And you went on dates with both of them,* I think to myself. But I don't say it, because—I don't even know what he's trying to do. Ruin things between me and Tre'?

I look around again. "Where is Halima?"

Dev sighs. "Last night, I sent Halima a message telling her that I couldn't come with her to the dance—that I'm still in love with you. And she didn't take it well at all . . ." Dev looks behind him again. "Not that I blame her . . ."

He looks back down into my eyes. "But I can't help how I feel, Leila. I *love* you."

My heart skips a beat. So many times after the breakup, I wanted so badly to hear those exact words—needed Dev to right what I felt had gone terribly wrong. But now that he's finally said them, I have a whole date here with me at the dance, and . . . I'm standing here, stuck. I don't know what to say. But I do know I have to see this thing out with Tre'.

But Dev apparently has more to get off his chest. "I know I messed up. I know it's probably too late. But—I had to tell you that."

He looks up at the decorations. "This is what tonight is all about, right? Last chances?"

I don't get a chance to respond, because Tre' suddenly reappears.

He and Dev exchange an awkward look, and then Dev releases his arms from my waist and takes a step back.

As Dev slips away, Tre' takes back his spot in my arms, his

arms circling my waist. "What was that all about?" Tre' asks.

I let out a snort. "Can you believe he came over here apologizing for dumping me?" I shake my head. "He was acting like he wanted to get back together. But, like, I'm at a dance with a whole other person—a person I had time to hang out with while he was busy seeing what else was out there."

I make the air quotes sign with my fingers and try out my best Dev impression. "Uh, sorry, Leila. I made a mistake— *honest.*"

Tre' cringes a little. "I mean . . . people do make mistakes sometimes."

"Yeah, little mistakes, like bringing me back the wrong dipping sauce for my chicken nuggets—not dumping me after four years of relationship perfection."

Tre' goes quiet again. "Okay. So what *if* Dev made a huge mistake? You said so yourself—in every other way he was a really good boyfriend."

I look up at Tre'. I don't know why he's asking me this.

Tre' keeps going. "What if he's owning up to what he did? He can't feel genuine remorse for a mistake?"

"I mean, I—guess." I give Tre' the side-eye. "Did Dev pay you to help him win me back, or something? Why are you all of a sudden Team Dev?"

Tre' shakes his head. "Nah. It's nothing like that. It's just—" Tre's voice trails off for a moment. "Sometimes people mess up—and—"

And when Tre' finally speaks again, hesitancy clouds his voice. "Leila, there's something I need to tell you . . ."

I bury my head into his shoulder, figuring whatever he has to tell me can't be any worse than Dev trying to walk back three weeks of curving me.

Just when I'm really getting into the slow song playing through the sound system, Tre' leans into my ear. "Leila . . . I . . . I—it wasn't fate that matched us. It wasn't even the algorithm. I . . . I . . . switched the results so that we ended up as each other's wild cards."

Wait.

I raise my head from Tre's shoulder and untangle myself from his embrace. "Why would you do that, Tre'?"

"I—I liked you for years." Tre's voice is now frantic. "I didn't know how to make you see that—to make you give me a chance. I didn't—"

"You shouldn't have to *make* me do anything." I shake my head sadly. Then the act of betrayal sets in. "We were *friends*, Tre'. I *trusted* you. How could you do that to me?"

I shake my head. "I was confiding in you about all my matches—all my dates." I pause a moment. "Who was I matched with before?"

Tre' looks down, his face streaked in shame. "Dev," he says quietly.

"Dev?" Nausea rises from somewhere deep inside me. "What do you mean, *Dev?*"

"I didn't think it mattered," Tre' says quickly. "You'd just broken up. It's not like getting matched would have made you get back together."

Dev's apology. Professing his love. It all sounds different

in my head now. "You don't know that . . ." I take another step back. "You don't know *anything* about Dev and me . . ."

Tre' may have been on the sidelines looking in. But he was just that. An outsider who couldn't possibly understand the connection Dev and I shared. How could *Tre'* determine whether Dev and I would've gotten back together. He wasn't there for the secret conversations, the special moments, all the threads that made Dev's and my relationship so solid.

Despite everything Tre' and I have been through these past weeks, I feel so confused . . . and hurt. "You had no right to do that . . ."

"Leila, I'm so sorry . . . you have to believe me . . ."

"You said you *cared* about what I liked—what made *me* happy." I shake my head, almost in disbelief that Tre' could do this to me. "Then you took away my opportunity to get back the person who made me most happy."

Matching with me would've made Dev see that he was wrong so much sooner. That we *did* belong together. That he did make a terrible mistake breaking up with me.

Tre' grabs my hand, his eyes pleading with me to see things his way. "Come on, Leila. I know what I did was wrong. But admit it—we're good together. I've loved spending time with you—getting to know you for real. Who cares how we got together?"

"*I* do," I say. The stars digitally adhered to the walls begin flickering again and I see them for what they truly are. Plastic stars with faulty wiring. And suddenly I'm even more sad. Because this whole time, I thought I was moving toward the Leila who made her own decisions. When this whole time, Tre' had completely manipulated things to get what he wanted.

"You just asked me why I couldn't forgive Dev for his one mistake, Tre'—when everything else about our relationship was good. And you're right. Dev *was* a good boyfriend. And this *was* one really big mistake. So who knows? Maybe I can forgive him."

Hope rises in Tre's eyes. "I made a mistake, too, Leila. You can't forgive me?"

Every emotion is coursing through my body right now. The Tre' I knew these past weeks has been good to me, has been someone I thought I trusted. But if it all started with a lie—then what do I really know?

"I can't." Even the sight of Tre' is making me physically ill right now. "Dev was honest with me from the very beginning—even if he risked breaking my heart."

I take a step back. "But you let our friendship grow over weeks, and didn't consider telling me the truth until you got what you wanted.

"I can forgive a mistake, Tre'. I can't forgive dishonesty."

I take one last look at Tre'—who looks completely crushed. Then I turn and walk away.

34

WEAVING THROUGH THE crowd of dancing seniors, I think about Dev putting his heart on the line for me, admitting he was wrong, and fighting for our love. And even though it meant possibly looking like a clown in front of Tre', Dev was willing to take that risk—for me. Maybe *fate* was desperately trying to bring us back together. Why else would things end so badly with Tre'?

With tears blurring my vision, I make my way over to the exit doors.

"Leila, what happened?"

I turn, and there's Dev again, making his way over to me with concern in his eyes. "Something's wrong. I can see it in your eyes."

It makes sense that Dev can tell something's bothering me—he always knows.

"Tre' switched my matches around. He put himself as my wild card pick, instead of . . . the right person."

Dev raises an eyebrow. "Who did you actually match with . . . ?"

I stare up into my ex's eyes. "You, Dev . . . You were my wild card pick."

Dev winces like he's been sucker punched. And honestly? I know the feeling.

I try not to think of all the time I missed repairing things with Dev. I didn't need to go on dates with Kai, Mason, or even Eva. I especially wouldn't have gone *anywhere* with Tre'. The fact that I spent the last few weeks of school entertaining anyone, when it was Dev and me the entire time, messes with my head.

I feel like crying all over again. I know Dev shouldn't have broken up with me. But matching with each other would've proven it. And now—*now*?!

"I knew it . . ." Dev mutters to himself.

I shoot him a funny look. "You knew Tre' switched the match?" I brace myself for the looming double betrayal. But Dev shakes his head.

"No." He places a hand on my arm and stares deep into my eyes. "I knew we belonged together." Dev looks behind him like he's expecting someone to show up. "I've been feeling like a terrible person for weeks. I knew I should have come to you and said something, but I didn't want to be that person—pulling you back and forth, and playing with your heart."

My heart right now squeezes hard in my chest.

Dev makes a fist. "I'm not that person, Leila. I *love* you."

Then Dev leans in and kisses me. And just like four years ago, on our first date at the Sweet Frog, just like on my living room couch, his basement couch, at Diwali, at Christmas, on Valentine's Day, at every pivotal moment of my high school life, Dev is the perfect fit.

In this moment, with those dumb stars above our heads, with magical music playing in the background, with everyone clinging to their last chance, it's been Dev—the only guy worth me taking a chance on—all along.

Dev pulls me closer, searching my lips with his, finding his way back home. His lips cling to mine, feeling warm, familiar, and comforting. And I let him stay right where he belongs.

I only break away to come up for a little air. And that's when I see him. Tre'—a few feet away on his way to the door, clearly searching for me.

I try not to think about how this all looks—me kissing my ex two seconds after ripping myself from his arms. And, honestly, I don't even know how I feel.

But I do know that Tre' betrayed our friendship. I didn't tell him to go messing with the Last Chance results. I definitely didn't advise him to keep it all secret for weeks. Despite everything, Tre' brought this on himself.

He knows it, too. Because he doesn't yell. He doesn't charge in our direction. He doesn't even ask *why* I'm locked in an embrace with Dev.

Tre' simply hangs his head and walks away.

The moment Tre' disappears from sight, Dev pulls me in close for a follow-up kiss. But this time, I swerve quickly, a thought coming to my mind.

"Wait, Dev. You just canceled your plans with Halima—at the last minute?"

Dev nods. "Well, yeah. Like, I told you . . ."

This time I take a step back from Dev. "But she probably spent money on a dress, and her hair. She probably spent all day at the nail shop . . . Dev, that wasn't fair."

"I don't love Halima, though . . ."

"Halima's still a *person*, Dev. And it's wrong to just toss her to the side like that . . ."

Dev hangs his head for a moment. "Listen, I get what you're saying. But why string Halima along? She isn't you . . ."

"But I wasn't even available, Dev. I came here with someone else—with Tre'."

Dev makes a sweeping motion with his hand. "I mean, who cares about Tre'? I came here for my girl—and I was going to win you back—no matter what . . ."

For the second time tonight, an admission brings up a wave of nausea. "But I liked Tre' a lot, Dev. And if he didn't do what he did, we would still be on the dance floor—together."

Dev makes a face. "You've been into this guy all of what? Three days?" Dev does his little barely there laugh under his breath. "A few measly days could *never* compete with four years of what we had."

"Which *you* decided you didn't want anymore . . ." I take a step back from Dev. Suddenly, Dev's attempt to win me back doesn't feel shiny, or heroic. When it came down to it, this whole thing—the breakup, and his attempt to win me back—are all on *his* schedule. Based on *his* feelings, and what *he* wants.

I reach into my formal purse and pull out my cell phone. "I'm about to call an Uber to take me home."

Dev reaches into my hand and turns my phone over. "Why would you do that when I can just take you? I do still know where you live . . ."

He grabs my hand, but I pull it away almost instantly. "I know, but *I* want to go home in an Uber, alone—so that's what I'm going to do."

Then I turn and walk away from him—now even more confused.

35

I SHOOT BREE a quick text letting her know that I'm leaving the dance early. I tell her to enjoy her night with Eva, and that I'll explain tomorrow.

Then, I burst into tears.

My Uber driver glances at me in the rearview mirror, but I wave him away. "I don't want to talk about it," I tell him, just in case he thinks he'll get a higher rating for talking me through my heartbreak.

I'm grateful my driver doesn't pry. But it doesn't make my ride home any easier. A piece of me feels guilty that Tre' saw me kissing Dev. But—Tre' lied to me. Another piece of me feels guilty for leaving Dev. But again, Dev is acting on pure selfishness.

Yet I can't deny that I really like Tre'. And a *huge* chunk of my heart still belongs to Dev.

My face is streaked with tears when I walk into the house, and all I want to do is run up to my room and be alone.

"Leila, is that you?" Mom calls from somewhere in the house.

I follow her voice to the kitchen, and find her standing at the sink washing dishes.

"Back so soon?" Mom glances at the clock. "It's only nine."

Maybe it's the sight of me reaching into the freezer to grab the tub of ice cream. Maybe it's my droopy shoulders. Maybe it's the dried tears streaked across my face. Whatever it is, Mom cuts off the running water and wipes her hand on her jeans.

"What's wrong, Leila?" Mom grabs two spoons from the kitchen drawer and leads me into the living room.

For a few moments, I don't say anything. I can't say anything. There are no words to describe the feeling of wanting multiple people, but also no one at all. So I slouch down into the couch and stuff spoonfuls of ice cream in my mouth, while I collect my thoughts.

Finally, I decide there's no better way than the absolute truth—no matter how embarrassing—or how much it hurts.

I let it all spill. My dates with Kai, Mason, Eva, and Tre'. How I thought Tre' was the one until he turned out to be a liar.

Mom rubs at the back of my hand with her thumb. "Maybe Tre' made a mistake—at least he told you . . ."

Feeling bitter, I snap back at Mom. "Was it a mistake when Dad worked too much?"

Mom doesn't let my bitterness faze her. Instead she says, "Your dad and I didn't get divorced the first time he came home late. Or even the first year that he spent more time at the hospital than at home." Mom sighs. "Real relationships are about understanding, and patience, and forgiveness. Nobody's perfect," she says.

I give my mom a sad smile.

Mom folds her arms and raises her eyebrows. "Now, if you start to feel like your patience is wearing thin, and your forgiveness is being taken for granted—when your unhappy starts to outweigh your joy, then it's time to kick the buster to the curb."

My heart skips a beat over having to make such an impossible decision. Who would I even kick to the curb, when I truly have feelings for both guys?

Mom shrugs. "But I don't know. I like this kid, Tre'. He seems to really care about you."

"But Dev does, too," I tell Mom. "Dev and I? We have history. And even though he hurt me, he always kept it real with me. Remained honest, even when the truth hurt me to the bone. Despite our issues these past weeks, maybe we *do* belong together. Even the Last Chance Dance algorithm matched us."

Mom grabs my hand and squeezes it tight. "Well then, Lei. It sounds like you have two great guys on your hands. A little flawed? Yes. But all in all, two guys who care about you.

"So I can't help you with that part," she says. "This sounds like a decision that only your heart can answer." Mom pulls her spoon out of the ice cream tub. "Why don't you snuggle up in your covers, eat your ice cream, and really take the time to think about what you want."

Mom gets up from the couch. "And remember, Leila. If the right answer doesn't come to you, then that's fine, too. You are just starting your journey, my love . . . just stay true to yourself and the decisions you make will always be right."

At that moment, I think I hear a pair of socked feet walking away. But I don't have the energy to call Riley out—not tonight.

Mom stands up. "Now, if you'll excuse me, I'm going to go give Ben a call. Can you believe he left out of here without helping me with these dishes?"

Well, not that I'm defending Ben's actions, but . . . I mean, if I could skip out on dishes, I probably would, too.

Mom winks at me. "See what I mean? Great guy—but flawed . . ."

Hours later, I'm full of ice cream and exhausted from mulling over my situation. I'm leaning over my bathroom sink, wiping the makeup off my face, when Riley comes sneaking into my room well past her bedtime. She climbs into my bed and lies flat on her stomach, propping her chin up with her hands.

"I came in to give you your graduation gift," she tells me.

"You should probably save that for tomorrow afternoon," I tell her. But she shakes her head.

"I hate it when you're sad, Lei," she says. "And I think my gift could really help."

Riley looks so hopeful, holding her phone out toward me, that I quickly tie my night bonnet around my head to come join her on the bed. "Okay, show me what you've got," I tell her, forcing myself to perk up some.

Suddenly, Riley snatches her phone out of view. "Disclaimer. This is my first try at producing a documentary—so no judgment."

I raise my right hand. "No judgment here."

Riley smiles and brings the phone back out. "Here goes."

When Riley hits the play button, a montage of photos and videos appear on the screen. Photos of me from kindergarten until now. Video clips of me riding a bike for the first time, and graduating from preschool. Bree and me performing a dance routine at the community summer camp when we were twelve, and leaving with our bags packed on our way to sleepaway camp for the first time. My small role in the school's theater production last year. Dev and me off to prom last month.

"How did you get all of this footage?" I ask.

Riley smiles. "I just asked everybody to check their iClouds. There was plenty to work with."

I thump my sister on the head. "Smart girl . . ."

Riley smiles. "Pay attention, Leila. We're about to get to the grand finale."

The montage fades out and then Riley's on the screen. "Happy Graduation, Leila! I wanted to show you how much everyone loves you. You are the best big sister—even if you've neglected to subscribe to my podcast, after *numerous* reminders. Despite your flaws, I'm going to really miss you when you leave for college. And just in case you find yourself in your dorm room, crying your eyes out from missing us, here's something that might help."

The screen fades and then Dad appears next. He's sitting in his office at Houston Memorial. "Love is finding a way to show up for the ones that matter. Leila shows up every day for her mom, her little sister, and her friends—even me, when I call. Watching Leila show up for the people she cares about inspires me to be better. I love you, Leila!"

The video of Dad fades out and then Mom's on-screen, sitting on our couch in the living room.

I thump my sister again. "I see you, Riley. Your transition skills are on point."

With a tissue in her hand, Mom already looks overcome with emotion. "I've always said our Leila has been here before. She has an old soul and cares deeply about everyone around her. You don't meet too many people like that—with a pure heart, and a genuine spirit. Our Leila deserves as much love as she gives." As Mom's image fades, she wipes a stray tear.

Next up is Bree, hanging out with her feet kicked up on our deck. "Leila has this way of making everyone around her feel close. You feel like you could tell her anything: your biggest dreams, your deepest fears, your most terrible secrets.

You might have to remind her to keep them to herself every now and then, but overall, you know she's still going to be right there, by your side. Yep, our Leila is the one to love around here!"

Then Dev comes on the screen. It's footage of him from that day he was randomly at our house. Now his sudden appearance on my couch makes sense. "Love takes time to build," Dev says. "but once it's there, it's hard to replace. I've known Leila longer than anyone at Baldwin. She's every-thing a guy could ask for in a girl. I *know* she cares about me, and I trust her with my heart. I love Leila because I know now she's worth the commitment."

Then, a video of Tre', wearing his Last Chance Dance tux, pops up on the screen.

"When did you film Tre'?" I exclaim.

Riley gives me the sneakiest look. "When you went to the bathroom. I warned him we only had time for one take. He said one was all he needed."

I turn back to the screen, curious about what Tre' has to say. "I can choose a million words to describe what I love about Leila—but my words could never compare to what I feel in my heart. When you know—you just know." There's a brief pause, then Tre' goes, "Plus, I've never met a girl with a smarter mouth than mine. Trust me, Leila Bean is in her lane."

With fresh tears in my eyes, I give my little sister a big hug. Riley was right about giving me my gift early.

Despite all the heartache I experienced tonight, I'm *loved*.

I still don't have all the answers I need to figure out what I'm going to do about Dev and Tre'. But knowing I'm loved by the people that matter most in my life brings me enough peace to slowly drift off to sleep.

36

AT 1:57 A.M., my eyes pop open and I sit up straight in my bed.

"I need to talk to Dev," I say to the middle-of-the-night darkness. Somehow the little bit of rest has allowed me to clear my head—and know exactly what I have to do. I grab my phone off the charger in the wall, and send him a text.

You up?

Thirty seconds go by without so much as a dot-dot-dot. So I send another text.

I need to talk to you, Dev. It's important.

A minute later, still nothing. So I call, and he picks up on the second ring.

"Leila . . . ?"

"Come over," I tell him.

Dev yawns loudly, and then there's a slight pause. I already know he's checking the time on his phone screen. "Leila, it's two a.m. We have graduation in the morning."

I knew it. I've *always* known Dev so well.

"Please, Dev. I know it's not *logical* to get out of your bed in the middle of the night to come talk to me. But . . . I need to see you tonight."

Another loud yawn, and then I hear Dev's bed squeak in the background. A smile creeps across my face in the darkness. For once, Dev doesn't allow logic to direct his path. He hears the emotion in my voice and goes, "Okay, I'll be there in a few minutes."

I wait by my bedroom window until I hear the hum of Dev's car engine and see the flash of his headlights. I grab a cardigan, tiptoe down the stairs, and sneak out the front door.

"What are you doing, Leila?" Worried wrinkles line Dev's forehead. And I know I look a mess. Bonnet on. Makeup washed off. Bare feet and ashy ankles. But all the accessories that keep me looking so well put together aren't necessary tonight. Tonight, I'm coming to Dev as raw as I can be. He's getting the real Leila Bean, unfiltered.

"I love you, Dev." And the smile that appears on his face reminds me of the fourteen-year-old kid I met in that Target four years ago.

"I love you too, Leila."

I grab Dev's hand and stare into his eyes. "You were my first true love and you will always be an important part of my story. The love I have for you will never go away. What we had was real."

Dev gets a funny look on his face. "*Had?*"

"Fate may have brought us together in Target that day. Fate may have even brought us back together at the dance. But I can't let *fate* make my decisions for me anymore. It's time for me to trust myself, and stand by the decisions I make about my own life."

Dev doesn't look at me when he says, "If I could take back breaking up with you, I would."

I put my hand on top of his and shake my head. "No, Dev. You were right to end things. I just didn't see it at the time, because we were so great together. I would've been fine with the ways things were forever. And while it would've been nice, I would've missed out on the opportunity to meet new people—and to grow."

I squeeze his hand. "But our love still existed. And it will continue—just in a different way now."

I flash Dev an impish look. Then I reach inside my pajamas to retrieve the important item being held in place by the elastic waistband on my pants.

"Hey, cutie," I say to Dev. And I know I look crazy, with these polka-dot pajama pants that I cut into shorts two summers ago, and the mismatched pajama shirt with the hole in the armpit. And this old cardigan hanging off me like a shawl. But even in my busted state, I'm feeling confident that Dev can pick up on my flirty vibes. "Thanks for letting me borrow your calculator. It was effing awesome."

As I hand Dev the TI-84, I'm honored that such a great person allowed me to borrow his heart all these years.

Dev takes the calculator, with tears in his eyes. "Thanks for taking good care of it," he says, with a catch in his voice.

I'm just about to go in the house, when I hear:

"Leila, wait." When I turn back around, Dev is running back from his car with his yearbook in his hand. He opens it up and flips through the pages. He pulls a Sharpie from his back pocket and hands it to me. "Sign my yearbook?"

I make a face. "What?"

"Seriously, right here . . ."

I look down, and it's that picture again—our Cutest Couple photo. Except this one isn't cute anymore, or fun like the one of Tre' and Lou. It's just kind of sad.

I draw back my hand. "Seriously, Dev. Are you trying to hurt me?"

"Leila. No. Listen." Dev sighs. Then stares deep in my eyes. "I know I'm the one that broke things off. But, Leila, these four years meant everything to me—you have to know that. We won Cutest Couple because we deserved it." Dev wraps my fingers around the Sharpie. "I don't want you to think of these last few weeks when you remember us. I want you to remember us how we were in this photo. Smiling, happy, and loving each other more than anything in the world."

My heart flutters and then skips a beat.

"I don't care who we meet in the future, who we date, who we fall in love with—we will always be each other's first love, and that's something that no one can take away from us."

My heart swelling, I finally uncap the Sharpie and scrawl in big flowery letters at the bottom of our picture: *To Dev, Thank You 4 Four Years of True Love.*

37

DAD FLIES IN early the next morning—just in time for graduation. Mom, Ben, and Riley are already in the living room, dressed in their Sunday best.

I'm upstairs slipping into my formal dress—a white, short-sleeved, knee-length number—and the best accessory of all, my white graduation robe, topped off with my decorated cap and tassel. I'm slipping my club sashes over my head—a pink one for drama club and a baby blue one for chorus—when I hear the doorbell. The front door opens, and then I hear Riley scream, "Dad!"

I quickly run down the stairs—my white graduation robe flying out behind me—and jump into his arms, too.

"I missed my girls," Dad says, covering us with kisses. When we finally release him, he straightens himself back up and goes into Dr. Bean mode, extending a stiff hand in Ben's direction.

"Hi, I'm Rashad. I've heard great things about you,"

Mom clears her throat, and then walks over to give Dad a hug. "Cut the act, Rashad. We have never discussed Ben in detail."

Dad throws a fist bump Riley's way. "I have my ways of finding out everything I need to know."

Smiling, Ben walks over, shakes Dad's hand, and says, "Seems we work with the same informant. I've heard nothing but great things about you, too."

And just like that, any awkward energy that could've existed evaporates. Graduation is on everyone's brain now.

Graduation Day. Fifteen rows of seniors sit in folding chairs in the middle of the football field, facing the graduation stage. I look out into the bleachers and spot Mom and Riley sitting third row center. Dad sits on Riley's other side, while Ben sits next to Mom.

Ms. Mahoney has already gotten on the microphone twice to remind parents to hold their applause to the end as they begin to call names, but I hear three more air horn blasts anyway.

I take a look out over the rows of seniors sitting together in decorated graduation hats, realizing everybody's getting their happy ending. Halima, after the brief public humiliation of being dumped right before the dance, is on her own glow-up journey now. Coming to graduation in stilettos and a new hairstyle has half the senior class staring at *her*, instead of up at Leah Wilkins, giving the valedictorian speech at the podium. Bree and Eva keep making eyes at each other across the rows. And Mason has managed to squeeze in one last high school protest by decorating his hat with the phrase "Game of Loans. Interest Is Coming."

I catch Kai and Darby smiling from their seats, before my eyes settle in on Dev.

"Everything cool?" I mouth.

Dev smiles and unzips the front of his gown to reveal a red Cornell T-shirt. And I'm glad to know, even if our breakup will always sting a little, we'll both be okay.

But despite all that, I know for one last person, everything's not cool. And I want to make it right. I try to catch a glimpse of Tre' in the sea of black-and-white graduation gowns. But now that Leah's finished their speech, a sea of clapping hands makes him even more impossible to find.

Excitement builds as Ms. Mahoney returns to the podium, smiles, gives the first row a wink, and then raises her hand for us to rise.

Halima Abdul climbs the stairs first, her freshly dyed honey-blond highlights shining in the sun as she shakes first the superintendent's hand and then the principal's, pausing a moment to smile for the photographer snapping a picture at her feet.

Bree is next. Her usual bravado is gone. She simply takes

her diploma and heads for the exit stairs. But, right after, Kai Ballard hits the stage. He strikes a pose with his diploma and yells into the air. "New York, your newest supermodel is on the way!"

A few air horns blast. And some shouting comes from the bleachers.

And then it's my turn. And I swear, crossing that stage feels like I am traveling over burning sands. Thirteen years of hard work, determination, heartbreak, and then resolve follow me as I make my way from childhood into adulthood.

I barely remember shaking the superintendent's and the principal's hands, but my smile automatically appears on cue for the cameraman, from all the school picture day practice I've had over the years.

When I step down from the stage onto the grass, I'm filled with a sense of sadness. That, in an instant, it's all over. Spending thirteen years working hard to get to this moment, only for it to end as quickly as it began, feels surreal in a way.

But as I sit back down in my seat, a nagging in my heart tells me that this isn't it for me. I have unfinished business. And this could be my last chance to fix all the messiness.

The H row is lined up at the stairs by now, and suddenly, I'm up out of my seat too. I see a disapproving glance from Ms. Mahoney out the corner of my eye, but it's too late. I've already shimmied my way across the grass and over to the exit stairs on the other end of the graduation stage.

"Trevor Micah Hillman III," the principal announces. And there he is, bopping across the stage. He reaches for the superintendent's hand, pulls away, then shakes her hand for real. Then he shakes the principal's hand. Does a little twirl, spinning down into a double-peace-sign pose. He's so busy being an effing clown up there that he nearly bumps into me the second his feet touch back down on grass.

"What?!" Tre' looks like he's seen a ghost. And I get it, because I'm shocked I'm standing here, too. But my heart brought me this far, and I'm determined to finish what I started.

"I want a do-over," I tell Tre', grabbing his hand.

"Huh?"

I pull Tre' off to the side a little so that the twins, Diamond and Dallas Johnson, can exit the stage without bumping into either of us. "All four of my matches were doomed from the beginning. I only chose the first two to make my ex jealous. My best friend is dating my third pick. And my wild card match turned out to be a straight-up scam."

Tre' shudders a little at the word *scam*. But, I mean . . . ?

"So I want a do-over." I look Tre' in the eyes. "Because I only have one crush. And that's you."

Tre' smiles at me. "My first, second, and third picks are you, Leila Bean."

I flash him a smile. "I guess that's a match, then."

Tre' and I stare into each other's eyes for a moment. Then he smooths my hair back behind my shoulders, pulls me close, and it happens. Our lips come together, searching and getting to know each other at first before falling into perfect synchrony.

When I finally come up for air, I stare up into Tre's eyes with a heart full of hope—that joy can always be found when your heart is leading the way. And I know for sure I'm making the right choice.

This thing with us, it might be a summer fling. It might burn out by the end of fall semester, with all the back-and-forth trips we'll have to take to see each other. Maybe we'll last forever. Maybe we won't. But for right now, in this moment, I want to trust how I feel and what I want. Tre' is a new beginning.

Tre's arms are currently wrapped around me like he never wants to let me go. But we're forced to, because Ms. Mahoney is by our side before we realize it, and she's physically pulling us apart with a murderous look in her eye.

She grabs on to our arms and marches us back over to the seating section with me struggling to keep up and Tre' wriggling within her grasp, still determined to put on a show.

But this time, he's given the audience exactly what they came to see, because seconds after Marie Zane crosses the stage, the entire senior class is on their feet, clapping, stomping the grass, and cheering so loud you would think we'd skipped right to the cap-throwing part of the ceremony.

Ms. Mahoney drops me off in my seat and then sets out to park Tre' where he belongs. Tre' is blowing kisses to the crowd and I'm three seconds from believing we're about to get kicked out of our own graduation ceremony. And I don't even care. I have the guy I want, and I'm an official graduate of the Prince George's County public school system.

Ms. Mahoney makes a beeline for Mom as soon as family and friends are allowed to spill onto the football field to congratulate the graduates.

I catch the tail end of my ex-AP's complaint, which is something like, "This is a *classy* event and Ms. Bean should've known better."

But it's graduation day, and Mom basically waves her off with a *what's done is done* stance, which makes me happy.

Mom and Dad come over to take photos. And we do a mashup of me, Mom, and Dad. Me, Mom, Dad, and Riley. Me, Mom, and Ben. Me and Bree. Me and Tre' and Bree. And yes, even me, Dev, and Riley.

While Mom is trying to gather Dev's family together for a photo, I pull Bree to the side.

"Hey, I got you a graduation gift," I tell her.

Bree rubs her hands together. "*Yessss*. It's time for me to *secure the bag.* I accept Cash App, Venmo, and all other forms of electronic—"

"Bree, I just saw your grandma break you off with a nice check. This is something more personal." I hand her an old Christmas gift bag I found in the closet, last minute.

Bree reaches inside and pulls out a wrapped rectangular object. "What is it?" she asks.

"Just open it."

Bree tears off the paper, and when she opens it, she stares at it for a second before breaking out into a huge grin. She holds up the framed gift high in the air and calls out across the field. "History is being made today, y'all."

A bunch of newly graduated seniors look her way. Some come over for a closer look—including Eva. "What is this—a credit card in a frame?" Eva asks.

"Let me explain, let me explain." I tap my finger on the picture frame's glass. "This is Bree's player card—once used to achieve legendary levels of dating here at Baldwin High . . ."

Eva peers closer at a particular date I etched onto the card with a paint pen. "Is this the date Bree and I made things official?"

I smile. "All major player cards come with an expiration date!"

Bree holds her hand up and we high-five.

Then I point to the gift bag. "Now dig around in there for your last gift."

Bree reaches down under all the tissue paper I packed into the bag, and pulls out one more picture frame. This one displays a cute picture of me.

"To remind you," I tell Bree, with one eyebrow raised, "that girlfriends will come and go, but I'm your best friend. And I'm going to be around—" I do my best Cardi B look-back move. "*Forever . . .*"

Bree laughs and holds my picture up. "I think I can find a place to put this . . ."

"You can hang it up in a well-lit area of your dorm room."

And before I can get another word out, she swoops me up into the biggest hug ever. Riley spots us, and inserts herself all up in the mix. Then Eva joins the lovefest. So, of course, Tre' has to push his way through. Even Dev comes through, a little shy at first, but then with open arms. And all I can think about, with so many people I love wrapped around me, is if this is what true love feels like, I'm *never* letting it go.

Epilogue

LATER ON, AS the graduates and their families start trickling off the football field, heading to TGI Fridays or Applebee's for an after-graduation celebratory lunch, I'm alone for a minute.

Dad is chatting about sports with Dev, Tre', Ben, and Bree's mom. Mom is over there with Dev's mother, promising to stay in touch. Bree and Eva are kissing under that random tree. And Riley is running around getting Last Chance quotes from seniors.

"Come on. This is the last time you will ever be on Baldwin grounds as a student!" Riley says. "Give me something you've always wanted to get off your chest!"

And me? I'm walking across the field alone, headed for the end zone. Today marks the end of a huge chapter in my life. My childhood is finally tucked away. Some moments were phenomenal. Others? Not so great. But one thing's for sure, as I place one foot in front of the other and finally step into adulthood, I know that last chances are just a facade. That, as long as I believe in myself, there are always opportunities to discover joy.

And now, thanks to all the random heartaches—and moments of love and support, too—I've experienced over the years, I know now that whatever life sends my way, I can handle it. So, University of Rochester? Bring it on.

Acknowledgments

SOMETIMES YOU GET the opportunity to work with one great editor. I had the good fortune of working with two. Lanie Davis and Kelsey Murphy, thank you so much for all the time, energy, and wisdom you poured into this project. Josh Bank, I am looking forward to meeting you at the dry-erase wall again, someday!

Melanie Figueroa, when your number pops up, it still feels like Christmas! ☺ I'm so happy we found our way to each other, and I look forward to many more years, projects, and celebrating. When it comes to literary agents, you are top tier.

To my Alloy and Viking family, it doesn't go over my head that I am in business with two entities with names that represent strength. There is a lot to navigate in this publishing industry, and I am thankful to have your support.

Specifically, I want to thank Ken Wright, Tamar Brazis, Marinda Valenti, Leona Skene, Gaby Corzo, Ginny Dominguez, Alex Aleman, Gerard Mancini, Ellice Lee, Jim Hoover, Tony Sahara, Deborah Kaplan, Marcos Chin, Jen Loja, Jocelyn Schmidt, Robyn Bender, Pete Facente, Lathea Mondesir, Shanta Newlin, Elyse Marshall, Felicity Vallence, Shannon Spann, James Akinaka, Bezi Yohannes, Alex Garber, Christina Colangelo, Emily Romero, Bri Lockhart, Danielle Presley, Jessie Clark, Carmela Iaria, Trevor Ingerson, Summer Ogata, Rachel Wease, Judith Huerta, Venessa Carson, Felicia Frazier, Debra Polansky, Trevor Bundy, Talisa Ramos, Allan Winebarger, Todd Jones, Emily Bruce, Mary Raymond, Mary McGrath, Colleen Conway, Dandy Conway, Jill Bailey, Andrea Baird, Maggie Brennan, Nicole Davies, John Dennany, Doni Kay, Steve Kent, Carol Monteiro, Stacey Pyle, Kate Sullivan, Nicole White, Rachel Jacobs, Vanessa Robles, Nadine Britt, Amy White, Lisa Schwartz, Amanda Cranney, and Cherisse Landau. Thank you all for helping to bring this book into the world.

To my family and friends, thank you for making life meaningful and fun. To all my exes, thank you for teaching me the beauty in new beginnings. And most of all, Leilani and Alonzo, I love you.

Lakita Wilson is the author of several novels and nonfiction projects for children and young adults, including *What Is Black Lives Matter?* a part of the *New York Times* bestselling Who HQ Now series, and *Be Real, Macy Weaver.*

Lakita was born in Washington, DC, and grew up in Prince George's County, Maryland. A 2017 recipient of SCBWI's Emerging Voices Award, Lakita received her MFA in writing for children and young adults from Vermont College of Fine Arts. She is currently on faculty at Prince George's Community College in the education department. Lakita lives in Prince George's County, Maryland, with her two children and Lhasa apso. She can be found online at LakitaWilson.com.